NIGHT

Near the incline's base two white-furred creatures raised blind eyes to the light and slunk away squealing in fear. And Kane recognized them as rats the size of jackals.

Understanding came to him. Water, air – the caverns below held life. But an obscenely distorted form of life it was. Probably these outsized creatures had evolved from cave dwellers who somehow were trapped beneath the surface ages ago, or maybe retreated there from choice when the land became desert. In primeval night, without seasons, without light, they had mutated to grotesque, primitive forms adapted to the demented savagery of their environment. Falling stone had crushed bats as well as other nameless things, and now the scent of blood was luring the monstrous cave creatures to this area.

And what else dwells below, wondered Kane uneasily . . .

Also by the same author,
and available in Coronet Books:

Bloodstone
Darkness Weaves

Night Winds

Karl Edward Wagner

CORONET BOOKS
Hodder and Stoughton

First published in Great Britain 1979 by Coronet Books

The characters and situations in this book are entirely imaginary and bear no relationship to any real person or actual happening

Printed and bound in Great Britain for Hodder and Stoughton Paperbacks, a division of Hodder and Stoughton Ltd., Mill Road, Dunton Green, Sevenoaks, Kent (Editorial Office: 47 Bedford Square, London, WC1 3DP) by Hunt Barnard Printing Ltd., Aylesbury, Bucks.

ISBN 0 340 23472 5

Acknowledgments

Undertow, copyright © 1977, by Stuart David Schiff, for *Whispers* #10.

Two Suns Setting, copyright © 1975, by Ultimate Publishing Co., Inc., for *Fantastic*, May 1976.

The Dark Muse, copyright © 1975, by Karl Edward Wagner, for *Midnight Sun* #2.

Raven's Eyrie, copyright © 1977, by Daemon Graphics, for *Chacal* #2.

Lynortis Reprise, copyright © 1974, by Karl Edward Wagner, for *Midnight Sun* #1.

Sing a Last Song of Valdese, copyright © 1976, by the Nemedian Chronicles, for *Chacal* #1.

To Manly Wade Wellman—
Scholar and Gentleman,
Writer and man,
Friend—
It takes a giant to encompass all these qualities;
And we'll see no more of giants.

NIGHT WINDS

Contents

UNDERTOW

Prologue

"She was brought in not long past dark," wheezed the custodian, scuttling crab-like along the rows of silent, shrouded slabs. "The city guard found her, carried her in. Sounds like the one you're asking about."

He paused beside one of the waist-high stone tables and lifted its filthy sheet. A girl's contorted face turned sightlessly upward—painted and rouged, a ghastly strumpet's mask against the pallor of her skin. Clots of congealed blood hung like a necklace of dark rubies along the gash across her throat.

The cloaked man shook his head curtly within the shadow of his hood, and the moon-faced custodian let the sheet drop back.

"Not the one I was thinking of," he murmured apologetically. "It gets confusing sometimes, you know, what with so many, and them coming and going all the while." Sniffling in the cool air, he pushed his rotund bulk between the narrow aisles, careful to avoid the stained and filthy shrouds. Looming over his guide, the cloaked figure followed in silence.

Low-flamed lamps cast dismal light across the necrotorium of Carsultyal. Smouldering braziers spewed fitful, heavy fumed clouds of clinging incense that merged with the darkness and the stones and the decay—its cloying sweetness more nauseating than the stench of death it embraced. Through the thick gloom echoed the monotonous drip-drip-drip of melting ice, at times chorused suggestively by some heavier splash. The municipal morgue was crowded tonight—as always. Only a few of its hundred or more slate beds stood dark and bare; the others all displayed anonymous shapes bulging beneath blotched sheets—some protruding at curious angles, as if these restless dead struggled to burst free of the coarse folds. Night now hung over Carsultyal, but within this windowless subterranean chamber it was always night. In shadow pierced only by the sickly flame of funereal lamps, the nameless dead of Carsultyal lay unmourned—waited the required interval of time for someone to claim them, else to be carted off to some unmarked communal grave beyond the city walls.

"Here, I believe," announced the custodian. "Yes. I'll just get a lamp."

"Show me," demanded a voice from within the hood.

The portly official glanced at the other uneasily. There was an aura of power, of blighted majesty about the cloaked figure that boded ill in arrogant Carsultyal, whose clustered, star-reaching towers were whispered to be over-awed by cellars whose depths plunged farther still. "Light's poor back here," he protested, drawing back the tattered shroud.

The visitor cursed low in his throat—an inhuman sound touched less by grief than feral rage.

The face that stared at them with too wide eyes had been beautiful in life; in death it was purpled, bloated, contorted in pain. Dark blood stained the tip of her protruding tongue, and her neck seemed bent at an unnatural angle. A gown of light-colored silk was stained and disordered. She lay supine, hands clenched into tight fists at her side.

"The city guard found her?" repeated the visitor in a harsh voice.

"Yes, just after nightfall. In the park overlooking the harbor. She was hanging from a branch—there in the grove with all the white flowers every spring. Must have just happened—said her body was warm as life, though there's a chill to the sea breeze tonight. Looks like she done it herself—climbed out on the branch, tied the noose, and jumped off. Wonder why they do it—her as pretty a young thing as I've seen brought in, and took well care of, too."

The stranger stood in rigid silence, staring at the strangled girl.

"Will you come back in the morning to claim her, or do you want to wait upstairs?" suggested the custodian.

"I'll take her now."

The plump attendant fingered the gold coin his visitor had tossed him a short time before. His lips tightened in calculation. Often there appeared at the necrotorium those who wished to remove bodies clandestinely for strange and secret reasons—a circumstance which made lucrative this disagreeable office. "Can't allow that," he argued. "There's laws and forms—you shouldn't even be here at this hour. They'll be wanting their questions answered. And there's fees. . . ."

With a snarl of inexpressible fury, the stranger turned on him. The sudden movement flung back his hood.

The caretaker for the first time saw his visitor's eyes. He had breath for a short bleat of terror, before the dirk he did not see smashed through his heart.

Workers the next day, puzzling over the custodian's disappearance, were shocked to discover, on examining the night's new tenants for the necrotorium, that he had not disappeared after all.

I

Seekers in the Night

There—he heard the sound again.

Mavrsal left off his disgruntled contemplation of the near-empty wine bottle and stealthily came to his feet. The captain of the *Tuab* was alone in his cabin, and the hour was late. For hours the only sounds close at hand had been the slap of waves on the barnacled hull, the creak of cordage, and the dull thud of the caravel's aged timbers against the quay. Then had come a soft footfall, a muffled fumbling among the deck gear outside his half-open door. Too loud for rats—a thief, then?

Grimly Mavrsal unsheathed his heavy cutlass and caught up a lantern. He catfooted onto the deck, reflecting bitterly over his worthless crew. From cook to first mate, they had deserted his ship a few days before, angered over wages months unpaid. An unseasonable squall had forced them to jettison most of their cargo of copper ingots, and the *Tuab* had limped into the harbor of Carsultyal with shredded sails, a cracked mainmast, a dozen new leaks from wrenched timbers, and the rest of her worn fittings in no better shape. Instead of the expected wealth, the decimated cargo had brought in barely enough capital to cover the expense of refitting. Mavrsal argued that until refitted, the *Tuab* was unseaworthy, and that once repairs were complete, another cargo could be found (somehow), and *then* wages long in arrears could be paid—with a bonus for patient loyalty. The crew cared neither for his logic nor his promises and defected amidst stormy threats.

Had one of them returned to carry out . . . ? Mavrsal hunched his thick shoulders truculently and hefted the cutlass. The master of the *Tuab* had never run from a brawl, much less a sneak thief or slinking assassin.

Night skies of autumn were bright over Carsultyal, making the lantern almost unneeded. Mavrsal surveyed the soft shadows of the caravel's deck, his brown eyes narrowed and alert beneath shaggy brows. But he heard the low sobbing almost at once, so there was no need to prowl about the deck.

He strode quickly to the mound of torn sail and rigging at the far rail. "All right, come out of that!" he rumbled, beckoning with the tip of his blade to the half-seen figure crouched against the rail. The sobbing choked into silence. Mavrsal prodded the canvas with an impatient boot. "Out of there, damn it!" he repeated.

The canvas gave a wriggle and a pair of sandaled feet backed out, followed by bare legs and rounded hips that strained against the bunched fabric of her gown. Mavrsal pursed his lips thoughtfully as the girl emerged and stood before him. There were no tears in the eyes that met his gaze. The aristocratic face was defiant, although the flared nostrils and tightly pressed lips hinted that her defiance was a mask. Nervous fingers smoothed the silken gown and adjusted her cloak of dark brown wool.

"Inside." Mavrsal gestured with his cutlass to the lighted cabin.

"I wasn't doing anything," she protested.

"Looking for something to steal."

"I'm not a thief."

"We'll talk inside." He nudged her forward, and sullenly she complied.

Following her through the door, Mavrsal locked it behind him and replaced the lantern. Returning the cutlass to its scabbard, he dropped back into his chair and contemplated his discovery.

"I'm no thief," she repeated, fidgeting with the fastenings of her cloak.

No, he decided, she probably wasn't—not that there was much aboard a decrepit caravel like the *Tuab* to attract a thief. But why had she crept aboard? She was a harlot, he assumed—what other business drew a girl of her beauty alone into the night of Carsultyal's waterfront? And she *was* beautiful, he noted with growing surprise. A tangle of loosely bound red hair fell over her shoulders and framed a face whose pale-skinned classic beauty was enhanced rather than flawed by a dust of freckles across her thin-bridged nose. Eyes of startling green gazed at him with a defiance that seemed somehow haunted. She was tall, willowy. Before she settled the dark cloak about her shoulders, he had noted the high, conical breasts and softly rounded figure beneath the clinging gown of green silk. An emerald of good quality graced her hand, and about her neck she wore a wide collar of dark leather and red silk from which glinted a larger emerald.

No, thought Mavrsal—again revising his judgment—she was too lovely, her garments too costly, for the quality of street tart who plied these waters. His bewilderment deepened. "Why were you on board, then?" he demanded in a manner less abrupt.

Her eyes darted about the cabin. "I don't know," she returned.

Mavrsal grunted in vexation. "Were you trying to stow away?"

She responded with a small shrug. "I suppose so."

The sea captain gave a snort and drew his stocky frame erect. "Then you're a damn fool—or must think I'm one! Stow away on a battered old warrior like the *Tuab*, when there's plainly no cargo to put to sea, and any eye can see the damn ship's being refitted! Why, that ring you're wearing would book passage to any port you'd care to see, and on a first-class vessel! And to wander these streets at this hour! Well, maybe that's your business, and maybe you aren't careful of your trade, but there's scum along these waterfront dives that would slit a wench's throat as soon as pay her! Vaul! I've been in port three days and four nights, and already I've heard talk of enough depraved murders of pretty girls like you to—"

"Will you stop it!" she hissed in a tight voice. Slumping into the cabin's one other chair, she propped her elbows onto the rough table and jammed her fists against her forehead. Russet tresses tumbled over her face like a veil, so that Mavrsal could not read the emotions etched there. In the hollow of the cloak's parted folds, her breasts trembled with the quick pounding of her heart.

Sighing, he drained the last of the wine into his mug and pushed the pewter vessel toward the girl. There was another bottle in his cupboard; rising, he drew it out along with another cup. She was carefully sipping from the proffered mug when he resumed his place.

"Look, what's your name?" he asked her.

She paused so tensely before replying, "Dessylyn."

The name meant nothing to Mavrsal, although as the tension waxed and receded from her bearing, he understood that she had been concerned that her name would bring recognition.

Mavrsal smoothed his close-trimmed brown beard. There was a rough-and-ready toughness about his face that belied the fact that he had not quite reached thirty years, and women liked to tell him his rugged features were handsome. His left ear—badly scarred in a tavern brawl—gave him some concern, but it lay hidden beneath the unruly mass of his hair. "Well, Dessylyn," he grinned. "My name's Mavrsal, and this is my ship. And if you're worried about finding a place, you can spend the night here."

There was dread in her face. "I can't."

Mavrsal frowned, thinking he had been snubbed, and started to make an angry retort.

"I dare not . . . stay here too long," Dessylyn interposed, fear glowing in her eyes.

Mavrsal made an exasperated grimace. "Girl, you sneaked aboard my ship like a thief, but I'm inclined to forget your trespassing. Now, my cabin's cozy, girls tell me I'm a pleasant companion, and I'm generous with my coin. So why wander off into the night, where in the first filthy alley some pox-ridden drunk is going to take for free what I'm willing to pay for?"

"You don't understand!"

"Very plainly I don't." He watched her fidget with the pewter mug for a moment, then added pointedly, "Besides, you can hide here."

"By the gods! I wish I could!" she cried out. "If only I *could* hide from him!"

Brows knit in puzzlement, Mavrsal listened to the strangled sobs that rose muffled through the tousled auburn mane. He had not expected so unsettling a response to his probe. Thinking that every effort to penetrate the mystery surrounding Dessylyn only left him further in the dark, he measured out another portion of wine—and wondered if he should apologize for something.

"I suppose that's why I did it," she was mumbling. "I was able to slip away for a short while. So I walked along the shore, and I saw all the ships poised for flight along the harbor, and I thought how wonderful to be free like that! To step on board some strange ship, and to sail into the night to some unknown land—where *he* could never find me! *To be free!* Oh, I knew I could never escape him like that, but still when I walked by your ship, I wanted to try! I thought I could go through the motions—pretend I was escaping him!

"Only I know there's no escape from Kane!"

"Kane!" Mavrsal breathed a curse. Anger toward the girl's tormentor that had started to flare within him abruptly shuddered under the chill blast of fear.

Kane! Even to a stranger in Carsultyal, greatest city of mankind's dawn, that name evoked the spectre of terror. A thousand tales were whispered of Kane; even in this city of sorcery, where the lost knowledge of prehuman Earth had been recovered to forge man's stolen civilization, Kane was a figure of awe and mystery. Despite uncounted tales of strange and disturbing nature, almost nothing was known for certain of the man save that for generations his tower had brooded over Carsultyal. There he followed the secret paths along which his dark genius led him, and the hand of Kane was rarely seen (though it was often felt) in the affairs of Carsultyal. Brother sorcerers and masters of powers temporal alike spoke his name with dread, and those who dared to make him an enemy seldom were given long to repent their audacity.

"Are you Kane's woman?" he blurted out.

Her voice was bitter. "So Kane would have it. His mistress. His possession. Once, though, I was my own woman—before I was fool enough to let Kane draw me into his web!"

"Can't you leave him—leave this city?"

"You don't know the power Kane commands! Who would risk his anger to help me?"

Mavrsal squared his shoulders. "I owe no allegiance to Kane, nor to his minions in Carsultyal. This ship may be weathered and leaky, but she's mine, and I sail her where I please. If you're set on—"

Fear twisted her face. "Don't!" she gasped. "Don't even hint this to me! You can't realize what power Kane—

"What was that!"

Mavrsal tensed. From the night sounded the soft buffeting of great leathery wings. Claws scraped against the timbers of the deck outside. Suddenly the lantern flames seemed to shrink and waver; shadow fell deep within the cabin.

"He's missed me!" Dessylyn moaned. "He's sent it to bring me back!"

His belly cold, Mavrsal drew his cutlass and turned stiffly toward the door. The lamp flames were no more than a dying blue gleam. Beyond the door a shuffling weight caused a loosened plank to groan dully.

"No! Please!" she cried in desperation. "There's nothing you can do! Stay back from the door!"

Mavrsal snarled, his face reflecting the rage and terror that gripped him. Dessylyn pulled at his arm to draw him back.

He had locked the cabin door; a heavy iron bolt secured the stout timbers. Now an unseen hand was drawing the bolt aside. Silently, slowly, the iron bar turned and crept back along its mounting brackets. The lock snapped open. With nightmarish suddenness, the door swung wide.

Darkness hung in the passageway. Burning eyes regarded them. Advanced.

Dessylyn screamed hopelessly. Numb with terror, Mavrsal clumsily swung his blade toward the glowing eyes. Blackness reached out, hurled him with irresistible strength across the cabin. Pain burst across his consciousness, and then was only the darkness.

II

"Never, Dessylyn"

She shuddered and drew the fur cloak tighter about her thin shoulders. *Would there ever again be a time when she wouldn't feel this remorseless cold?*

Kane, his cruel face haggard in the glow of the brazier, stood hunched over the crimson alembic. *How red the coals made his hair and beard; how sinister was the blue flame of his eyes. . . .* He craned intently forward to trap the last few drops of the phosphorescent elixir in a chalice of ruby crystal.

He had labored sleepless hours over the glowing liquid, she knew. Hours precious to her because these were hours of freedom—a time when she might escape his loathed attention. Her lips pressed a tight, bloodless line. The abominable formulae from which he prepared the elixir! Dessylyn thought again of the mutilated corpse of the young girl Kane had directed his servant to carry off. Again a spasm slid across her lithe form.

"Why won't you let me go?" she heard herself ask dully for the . . . *how many times had she asked that?*

"I'll not let you go, Dessylyn," Kane replied in a tired voice. "You know that."

"Someday I'll leave you."

"No, Dessylyn. You'll never leave me."

"Someday."

"Never, Dessylyn."

"Why, Kane!"

With painful care, he allowed a few drops of an amber

liqueur to fall into the glowing chalice. Blue flame hovered over its surface.

"Why!"

"Because I love you, Dessylyn."

A bitter sob, parody of laughter, shook her throat. "You love me." She enclosed a hopeless scream in those slow, grinding syllables.

"Kane, can I ever make you understand how utterly I loathe you?"

"Perhaps. But I love you, Dessylyn."

The sobbing laugh returned.

Glancing at her in concern, Kane carefully extended the chalice toward her. "Drink this. Quickly—before the nimbus dies."

She looked at him through eyes dark with horror. "Another bitter draught of some foul drug to bind me to you?"

"Whatever you wish to call it."

"I won't drink it."

"Yes, Dessylyn, you will drink it."

His killer's eyes held her with bonds of eternal ice. Mechanically she accepted the crimson chalice, let its phosphorescent liqueur pass between her lips, seep down her throat.

Kane sighed and took the empty goblet from her listless grip. His massive frame seemed to shudder from fatigue, and he passed a broad hand across his eyes. Blood rimmed their dark hollows.

"I'll leave you, Kane."

The sea wind gusted through the tower window and swirled the long red hair about his haunted face.

"Never, Dessylyn."

III

At the Inn of the Blue Window

He called himself Dragar. . . .

Had the girl not walked past him seconds before, he probably would not have interfered when he heard her scream. Or perhaps he would have. A stranger to Carsultyal, nonetheless the barbarian youth had passed time enough in mankind's lesser cities to be wary of cries for help in the night and to think twice before plunging into dark alleys to join in an unseen struggle. But there was a certain pride in the chivalric ideals of his heritage, along with a confidence in the hard muscle of his sword arm and in the strange blade he carried.

Thinking of the lithe, white limbs he had glimpsed—the patrician beauty of the face that coolly returned his curious stare as she came toward him—Dragar unsheathed the heavy blade at his hip and dashed back along the street he had just entered.

There was moonlight enough to see, although the alley was well removed from the nearest flaring streetlamp. Cloak torn away, her gown ripped from her shoulders, the girl writhed in the grasp of two thugs. A third tough, warned by the rush of the barbarian's boots, angrily spun to face him, sword streaking for the youth's belly.

Dragar laughed and flung the lighter blade aside with a powerful blow of his sword. Scarcely seeming to pause in his attack, he gashed his assailant's arm with a upward swing, and as the other's blade faltered, he split the thug's skull. One of the two who held the girl lunged forward, but Dragar sidestepped his rush, and with a sudden thrust sent his sword ripping into the man's chest. The remaining assailant shoved the girl against the barbarian's legs, whirled, and fled down the alley.

Ignoring the fugitive, Dragar helped the stunned girl to her feet. Terror yet twisted her face, as she distractedly arranged the torn bodice of her silken gown. Livid scratches streaked the pale skin of her breasts, and a bruise was swelling out her lip. Dragar caught up her fallen cloak and draped it over her shoulders.

"Thank you," she breathed in a shaky whisper, speaking at last.

"My pleasure," he rumbled. "Killing rats is good exercise. Are you all right, though?"

She nodded, then clutched his arm for support.

"The hell you are! There's a tavern close by, girl. Come—I've silver enough for a brandy to put the fire back in your heart."

She looked as if she might refuse, were her knees steadier. In a daze, the girl let him half-carry her into the Inn of the Blue Window. There he led her to an unoccupied booth and called for brandy.

"What's your name?" he asked, after she had tasted the heady liquor.

"Dessylyn."

He framed her name with silent lips to feel its sound. "I'm called Dragar," he told her. "My home lies among the mountains far south of here, though it's been a few years since last I hunted with my clansmen. Wanderlust drew me away, and since then I've followed this banner or another's—sometimes just the shadow of my own flapping cloak. Then, after hearing tales enough to dull my ears, I decided to see for myself if Carsultyal is the wonder men boast her to be. You a stranger here as well?"

She shook her head. When the color returned to her cheeks, her face seemed less aloof.

"Thought you might be. Else you'd know better than to wander the streets of Carsultyal after nightfall. Must be something important for you to take the risk."

The lift of her shoulders was casual, though her face remained guarded. "No errand . . . but it was important to me."

Dragar's look was questioning.

"I wanted to . . . . oh, just to be alone, to get away for a while. Lose myself, maybe—I don't know. I didn't think anyone would dare touch me if they knew who I was."

"Your fame must be held somewhat less in awe among these gutter rats than you imagined," offered Dragar wryly.

"All men fear the name of Kane!" Dessylyn shot back bitterly.

"Kane!" The name exploded from his lips in amazement. *What had this girl to do . . . ?* But Dragar looked again at her sophisticated beauty, her luxurious attire, and understanding dawned. Angrily he became aware that the tavern uproar had become subdued on the echo of his outburst. Several faces had turned to him, their expressions uneasy, calculating.

The barbarian clapped a hand to his swordhilt. "Here's a man who doesn't fear a name!" he announced. "I've heard something of Carsultyal's most dreaded sorcerer, but his name means less than a fart to me! There's steel in this sword that can slice through the best your world-famed master smiths can forge, and it thrives on the gore of magicians. I call the blade Wizard's Bane, and there are souls in Hell who will swear that its naming is no boast!"

Dessylyn stared at him in sudden fascination.

And what came after, Dessylyn?

I . . . . I'm not sure. . . . My mind—I was in a state of shock, I suppose. I remember holding his head for what seemed like forever. And then I remember sponging off the blood with water from the wooden lavabo, and the water was so cold and so red, so red. I must have put on my clothes. . . . Yes, and I remember the city and walking and all those faces. . . . All those faces . . . they stared at me, some of them. Stared and looked away, stared and looked compassionate, stared and looked curious, stared and made awful suggestions. . . . And some just ignored me, didn't see me at all. I can't think which faces were the most cruel. . . . I walked, walked so long. . . . I remember the pain. . . . I remember my

tears, and the pain when there were no more tears. . . .
I remember. . . . My mind was dazed. . . . My memory . . .
I can't remember. . . .

IV

A Ship Will Sail. . . .

He looked up from his work and saw her standing there on the quay—watching him, her face a strange play of intensity and indecision. Mavrsal grunted in surprise and straightened from his carpentry. She might have been a phantom, so silently had she crept upon him.

"I had to see if . . . if you were all right," Dessylyn told him with an uncertain smile.

"I am—aside from a crack on my skull," Mavrsal answered, eyeing her dubiously.

By the dawnlight he had crawled from beneath the overturned furnishings of his cabin. Blood matted his thick hair at the back of his skull, and his head throbbed with a deafening ache, so that he had sat dumbly for a long while, trying to recollect the events of the night. *Something* had come through the door, had hurled him aside like a spurned doll. And the girl had vanished—carried off by the demon? Her warning had been for him; for herself she evidenced not fear, only resigned despair.

Or had some of his men returned to carry out their threats? Had too much wine, the blow on his head . . . ? But no, Mavrsal knew better. His assailants would have robbed him, made certain of his death—had any human agency attacked him. She had called herself a sorcerer's mistress, and it had been sorcery that spread its black wings over his caravel. Now the girl had returned, and Mavrsal's greeting was tempered by his awareness of the danger which shadowed her presence.

Dessylyn must have known his thoughts. She backed away, as if to turn and go.

"Wait!" he called suddenly.

"I don't want to endanger you any further."

Mavrsal's quick temper responded. "Danger! Kane can bugger with his demons in Hell, for all I care! My skull was too thick for his creature to split, and if he wants to try his hand in person, I'm here to offer him the chance!"

There was gladness in her wide eyes as Dessylyn stepped toward him. "His necromancies have exhausted him," she assured the other. "Kane will sleep for hours yet."

Mavrsal handed her over the rail with rough gallantry. "Then perhaps you'll join me in my cabin. It's grown too dark for carpentry, and I'd like to talk with you. After last night, I think I deserve to have some questions answered, anyway."

He struck fire to a lamp and turned to find her balanced at the edge of a chair, watching him nervously. "What sort of questions?" she asked in an uneasy tone.

"Why?"

"Why what?"

Mavrsal made a vague gesture. "Why everything. Why did you get involved with this sorcerer? Why does he hold to you, if you hate him so? Why can't you leave him?"

She gave him a sad smile that left him feeling naive. "Kane is . . . a fascinating man; there is a certain magnetism about him. And I won't deny the attraction his tremendous power and wealth held for me. Does it matter? It's enough to say that there was a time when we met and I fell under Kane's spell. It may be that I loved him once—but I've since hated too long and too deeply to remember.

"But Kane continues to love me in his way. *Love!* His is the love of a miser for his hoard, the love of a connoisseur for some exquisitely wrought carving, the love a spider feels for its imprisoned prey! I'm his treasure, his possession—and what concern are the feelings of a lifeless object to its owner? Would the curious circumstance that his prized statue might hate him lessen the pleasure its owner derives from its possession?

"And leave him?" Her voice broke. "By the gods, don't you think I've tried?"

His thoughts in a turmoil, Mavrsal studied the girl's haunted face. "But why accept defeat? Past failure doesn't mean you can't try again. If you're free to roam the streets of Carsultyal at night, your feet can take you farther still. I see no chain clamped to that collar you wear."

"Not all chains are visible."

"So I've heard, though I've never believed it. A weak will can imagine its own fetters."

"Kane won't let me leave him."

"Kane's power doesn't reach a tenth so far as he believes."

"There are men who would dispute that, if the dead cared to share the wisdom that came to them too late."

Challenge glinted in the girl's green eyes as they held his. Mavrsal felt the spell of her beauty, and his manhood answered. "A ship sails where its master wills it—may the winds and the tides and perils of the sea be damned!"

Her face craned closer. Tendrils of her auburn hair touched his arm. "There is courage in your words. But you know little of Kane's power."

He laughed recklessly. "Let's say I'm not cowed by his name."

From the belt of her gown, Dessylyn unfastened a small scrip. She tossed the leather pouch toward him.

Catching it, Mavrsal untied the braided thong and dumped its contents onto his palm. His hand shook. Gleaming gemstones tumbled a tiny rainbow, clattered onto the cabin table. In his hand lay a fortune in rough-cut diamonds, emeralds, other precious stones.

Through their multihued reflections his face framed a question.

"I think there is enough to repair your ship, to pay her crew. . . ." She paused; brighter flamed the challenge in her eyes. "Perhaps to buy my passage to a distant port—if you dare!"

The captain of the *Tuab* swore. "I meant what I said, girl! Give me another few days to refit her, and I'll sail you to lands where no man has ever heard the name of Kane!"

"Later you may change your mind," Dessylyn warned. She rose from her chair. Mavrsal thought she meant to leave, but then he saw that her fingers had loosened other fastenings at her belt. His breath caught as the silken gown began to slip from her shoulders.

"I won't change my mind," he promised, understanding why Kane might go to any extreme to keep Dessylyn with him.

V

Wizard's Bane

"Your skin is like the purest honey," proclaimed Dragar ardently. "By the gods, I swear you even taste like honey!"

Dessylyn squirmed in pleasure and hugged the barbarian's shaggy blond head to her breasts. After a moment she sighed and languorously pulled from his embrace. Sitting up, she brushed her slim fingers through the tousled auburn wave that cascaded over her bare shoulders and back, clung in damp curls to her flushed skin.

Dragar's calloused hand imprisoned her slender wrist as she sought to rise from the rumpled bed. "Don't prance away like a contrite virgin, girl. Your rider has dismounted but for a moment's rest—then he's ready to gallop through the palace gates another time or more, before the sun drops beneath the sea."

"Pretty, but I have to go," she protested. "Kane may grow suspicious. . . ."

"Bugger Kane!" cursed Dragar, pulling the girl back against him. His thick arms locked about her, and their lips crushed savagely. Cupped over a small breast, his hand felt the pounding of her heart, and the youth laughed and tilted back her feverish face. "Now tell me you prefer Kane's effete pawings to a man's embrace!"

A frown drifted like a sudden thunderhead. "You underestimate Kane. He's no soft-fleshed weakling."

The youth snarled in jealousy. "A foul sorcerer who's skulked in his tower no one knows how long! He'll have dust for blood, and dry rot in his bones! But go to him if you prefer his toothless kisses and withered loins!"

"No, dearest! Yours are the arms I love to lie within!" Dessylyn cried, entwining herself about him and soothing his anger with kisses. "It's just that I'm frightened for you. Kane isn't a withered greybeard. Except for the madness in his eyes, you would think Kane a hardened warrior in his prime. And you've more than his sorcery to fear. I've seen Kane kill with his sword—he's a deadly fighter!"

Dragar snorted and stretched his brawny frame. "No warrior hides behind a magician's robes. He's but a name—an ogre's name to frighten children into obedience. Well, I don't fear his name, nor do I fear his magic, and my blade has drunk the blood of better swordsmen than your black-hearted tyrant ever was!"

"By the gods!" whispered Dessylyn, burrowing against his thick shoulder. "Why did fate throw me into Kane's web instead of into your arms!"

"Fate is what man wills it. If you wish it, you are my woman now."

"But Kane . . . !"

The barbarian leaped to his feet and glowered down at her. "Enough snivelling about Kane, girl! Do you love me or not?"

"Dragar, beloved, you know I love you! Haven't these past days . . ."

"These past days have been filled with woeful whimperings about Kane, and my belly grows sick from hearing it! Forget Kane! I'm taking you from him, Dessylyn! For all her glorious legend and over-mighty towers, Carsultyal is a stinking pesthole like every other city I've known. Well, I'll waste no more days here.

"I'll ride from Carsultyal tomorrow, or take passage on a ship, perhaps. Go to some less stagnant land, where a bold man and a strong blade can win wealth and adventure! You're going with me."

"Can you mean it, Dragar?"

"If you think I lie, then stay behind."

"Kane will follow."

"Then he'll lose his life along with his love!" sneered Dragar.

With confident hands, he slid from its scabbard his great sword of silver-blue metal. "See this blade," he hissed, flourishing its massive length easily. "I call it Wizard's Bane, and there's reason to the name. Look at the blade. It's steel, but not steel such as your secretive smiths forge in their dragon-breath furnaces. See the symbols carved into the forte. This blade has power! It was forged long ago by a master smith who used the glowing heart of a fallen star for his ore, who set runes of protection into the finished sword. Who wields Wizard's Bane need not fear magic, for sorcery can have no power over him. My sword can cleave through the hellish flesh of demons. It can ward off a sorcerer's enchantments and skewer his evil heart!

"Let Kane send his demons to find us! My blade will shield us from his spells, and I'll send his minions howling in fear back to his dread tower! Let him creep from his lair if he dares! I'll feed him bits of his liver and laugh in his face while he dies!"

Dessylyn's eyes brimmed with adoration. "You can do it, Dragar! You're strong enough to take me from Kane! No man has your courage, beloved!"

The youth laughed and twisted her hair. "No man? What do you know of men? Did you think these spineless city-bred fops, who tremble at the shadow of a senile cuckold, were men? Think no more of slinking back to Kane's tower before your keeper misses you. Tonight, girl, I'm going to show you how a *man* loves his woman!"

But why will you insist it's impossible to leave Kane?
I know.
How can you know? You're too fearful of him to try.
I know.
But how can you say that?
Because I know.
Perhaps this bondage is only in your mind, Dessylyn.
But I know Kane won't let me leave him.
So certain—is it because you've tried to escape him?

Have you tried, Dessylyn?

Tried with another's help—and failed, Dessylyn?

Can't you be honest with me, Dessylyn?

And now you'll turn away from me in fear!

Then there was another man?

It's impossible to escape him—and now you'll abandon me!

Tell me, Dessylyn. How can I trust you if you won't trust me?

On your word, then. There was another man. . . .

VI

Night and Fog

Night returned to Carsultyal and spread its misty cloak over narrow alleys and brooding towers alike. The voice of the street broke from its strident daylight cacophony to a muted rumble of night. As the stars grew brighter through the sea mists, the streets grew silent, except for fitful snorts and growls like a hound uneasy in his sleep. Then the lights that glimmered through the shadow began to slip away, so stealthily that their departure went unnoticed. One only knew that the darkness, the fog, the silence now ruled the city unchallenged. And night, closer here than elsewhere in the cities of mankind, had returned to Carsultyal.

They lay close in each other's arms—sated, but too restless for sleep. Few were their words, so that they listened to the beating of their hearts, pressed so close together as to make one sound. Fog thrust tendrils through chinks in the bolted shutters, brought with it the chill breath of the sea, lost cries of ships anchored in the night.

Then Dessylyn hissed like a cat and dug her nails so deep into Dragar's arm that rivulets of crimson made an armlet about the corded muscle. Straining his senses against the night, the barbarian dropped his hand to the hilt of the unsheathed sword that lay beside their bed. The blade glinted blue—more so than the wan lamplight would seem to reflect.

From the night outside . . . Was it a sudden wind that rattled the window shutters, buffeted the streamers of fog into swirling eddies? A sound . . . Was that the flap of vast leathery wings?

Fear hung like a clinging web over the inn, and the silence about them was so desolate that theirs might have been the last two hearts to beat in all of haunted Carsultyal.

From the roof suddenly there came a slithering metallic scrape upon the slate tiles.

Wizard's Bane pulsed with a corposant of blue witchfire. Shadows stark and unreal cringed away from the lambent blade.

Against the thick shutters sounded a creaking groan of hideous pressure. Oaken planks sagged inward. Holding fast, the iron bolts trembled, then abruptly smouldered into sullen rubrous heat. Mist poured past the buckling timbers, bearing with it a smell not of any sea known to man.

Brighter pulsed the scintillant glare of the sword. A nimbus of blue flame rippled out from the blade and encircled the crouching youth and his terrified companion. Rippling blue radiance, spreading across the room, struck the groaning shutters.

A burst of incandescence spat from the glowing iron bolts. Through the night beyond tore a silent snarl—an unearthly shriek felt rather than heard—a spitting bestial cry of pain and baffled rage.

The shutters sprang back with a grunting sigh as the pressure against them suddenly relented. Again the night shuddered with the buffet of tremendous wings. The ghost of sound dwindled. The black tide of fear ebbed and shrank back from the inn.

Dragar laughed and brandished his sword. Eyes still dazzled, Dessylyn stared in fascination at the blade, now suffused with a sheen no more preternatural than any finely burnished steel. It might all have been a frightened dream, she thought, knowing well that it had not been.

"It looks like your keeper's sorcery is something less than all powerful!" scoffed the barbarian. "Now Kane will know that his spells and coward's tricks are powerless against Wizard's Bane. No doubt your ancient spellcaster is cowering under his cold bed, scared spitless that these gutless city folk will some day find courage enough to call his bluff! And against that, he's probably safe."

"You don't know Kane," moaned Dessylyn.

With gentle roughness, Dragar cuffed the grim-faced girl. "Still frightened by a legend? And after you've seen his magic defeated by the star-blade! You've lived within the shadow of this decadent city too long, girl. In a few hours we'll have light, and then I'll take you out into the real world—where men haven't sold their souls to the ghosts of elder races!"

But her fears did not dissolve under the barbarian's warm confidence. For a timeless period of darkness Dessylyn clung to him, her heart restlessly drumming, shuddering at each fragment of sound that pierced the night and fog.

And through the darkened streets echoed the clop-clop of hooves.

Far away, their sound so faint it might have been imagined. Closer now, the fog-muffled fall of ironshod hooves on paving bricks. Drawing ever closer, a hollow, rhythmic knell that grew deafening in the absolute stillness. Clop-Clop Clop-Clop Clop-Clop CLOP-CLOP CLOP-CLOP. Approaching the inn unhurriedly. Inexorably approaching the mist-shrouded inn.

"What is it?' he asked her, as she started upright in terror.

"I know that sound. It's a black, black stallion, with eyes that burn like living coals and hooves that ring like iron!"

Dragar snorted.

"Ah! And I know his rider!"

CLOP-CLOP CLOP-CLOP. Hoofbeats rolled and gobbled across the courtyard of the Inn of the Blue Window. Echoes rattled against the shutters. . . . *Could no one else hear their chill thunder?*

CLOP-CLOP *CLOP*. The unseen horse stamped and halted outside the inn's door. Harness jingled. *Why were there no voices?*

From deep within the chambers below echoed the dull chink of the bolt and bars falling away, clattering to the floor. A harsh creak as the outer door swung open. *Where was the innkeeper?*

Footfalls sounded on the stairs—the soft scuff of boot leather on worn planks. Someone entered the hallway beyond their door; strode confidently toward their room.

Dessylyn's face was a stark mask of terror. Knuckles jammed against her teeth to dam a rising scream were stained red with drawn blood. Dread-haunted eyes were fixed upon the door opposite.

Slipping into a fighting crouch, Dragar spared a glance for the bared blade in his taut grasp. No nimbus of flame hovered about the sword, only the deadly gleam of honed steel, reflected in the unnaturally subdued lamp-light.

Footsteps halted in front of their door. It seemed he could hear the sound of breathing from beyond the threshold.

A heavy first smote the door. Once. A single summons. A single challenge.

With an urgent gesture, Dessylyn signed Dragar to remain silent.

"Who dares . . . !" he growled in a ragged voice.

A powerful blow exploded against the stout timber. Latch and bolt erupted from their setting in a shower of splinters and wrenched metal. All but torn from its hinges, the door was hurled open, slammed resoundingly against the wall.

"Kane!" screamed Dessylyn.

The massive figure strode through the doorway, feral grace in the movements of his powerful, square-torsoed frame. A heavy sword was balanced with seeming negligence in his left hand, but there was no uncertainty in the lethal fury that blazed in his eyes.

"Good evening," sneered Kane through a mirthless smile.

Startled despite Dessylyn's warning, Dragar's practiced eye swiftly sized up his opponent. So the sorcerer's magic had preserved the prime of his years after all. . . . At about six feet Kane stood several inches shorter than the towering barbarian, but the enormous bands of muscle that surged beneath leather vest and trousers made his weight somewhat greater. Long arms and the powerful roll of his shoulders signalled a swordsman of considerable reach and strength, although the youth doubted if Kane could match his speed. A slim leather band with a black opal tied back his shoulder-length red hair, and the face beneath the close-trimmed beard was brutal, with a savagery that made his demeanor less lordly than arrogant. And his blue eyes burned with the brand of killer.

"Come looking for your woman, sorcerer?" grated Dragar, watching the other's blade. "We thought you'd stay hidden in your tower, after I frightened off your slinking servants!"

Kane's eyes narrowed. "So that's . . . Wizard's Bane, I believe you call it. I see the legends didn't lie when they spoke of the blade's protective powers. I shouldn't have spoken of it to Dessylyn, I suppose, when I learned that an enchanted sword had been brought into Carsultyal. But then, its possession will compensate in some part for the difficulties you've caused me."

"Kill him, Dragar, my love! Don't listen to his lies!" Dessylyn cried.

"What do you mean?" rumbled the youth, who had missed Kane's inference.

The warrior wizard chuckled drily. "Can't you guess, you romantic oaf? Don't you understand that a clever woman has used you? Of course not—the chivalrous barbarian thought he was defending a helpless girl. Pity I let Laroc die after persuading him to tell me of her game. He might have told you how innocent his mistress—"

"Dragar! Kill him! He only means to take you off guard!"

"To be sure! Kill me, Dragar—if you can! That was her plan, you know. Through my . . . sources . . . I learned of this formidable blade you carry and made mention of it to Dessylyn. But Dessylyn, it seems, has grown bored with my caresses. She paid a servant, the unlamented Laroc, to stage an apparent rape, trusting that a certain lout would rush in to save her. Well plotted, don't you think? Now poor Dessylyn has a bold defender whose magic blade can protect her against Kane's evil spells. I wonder, Dessylyn—did you only mean to go away with this thickheaded dolt, or did you plan to goad me into this personal combat, hoping I'd be slain and the wealth of my tower would be yours?"

"Dragar! He's lying to you!" moaned the girl despairingly.

"Because if it was the latter, then I'm afraid your plotting wasn't as intelligent as you believed," concluded Kane mockingly.

"Dragar!" came the tortured choke.

The barbarian, emotions a fiery chaos, risked an agonized glance at her contorted face.

Kane lunged.

Off guard, Dragar's lightning recovery deflected Kane's blade at the last possible instant, so that he took a shallow gash across his side instead of the steel through his ribs. "Damn you!" he cursed.

"But I am!" laughed Kane, parrying the youth's flashing counterattack with ease. His speed was uncanny, and the awesome power of his thick shoulders drove his blade with deadly force.

Lightning seemed to flash with the ringing thunder of their blades. Rune-stamped star-metal hammered against the finest steel of Carsultyal's far-famed forges, and their clangor seemed the cries of two warring demons—harsh, strident with pain and rage.

Sweat shone on Dragar's naked body, and his breath spat foam through his clenched teeth. A few times only had he crossed blades with an opponent his equal in strength, and then the youth's superior speed had carried the victory. Now, as in some impossible nightmare, he faced a skilled and cunning swordsman whose speed was at least his equal—and whose strength seemed somewhat greater. After his initial attack had been deftly turned away, Dragar's swordplay became less reckless, less confident. Grimly he set about wearing down his opponent's endurance, reasoning that the sorcerer's physical conditioning could not equal that of a hardened mercenary.

In all the world there was no sound but their ringing blades, the desperate rush of their bodies, the hoarse gusts of their breath. Everywhere time stood frozen, save for the deadly fury of their duel, as they leaped and lunged about the bare-timbered room.

Dragar caught a thin slash across his left arm from a blow he did not remember deflecting. Kane's lefthanded attack was dangerously unfamiliar to him, and only his desperate parries had saved him from worse. Uneasily he realized that Kane's sword arm did not falter as the minutes dragged past and that more and more he was being confined to the defensive. Wizard's Bane grew ragged with notches from the Carsultyal blade, and its hilt with slippery with sweat. Kane's heavier sword was similarly scarred from their relentless slash, parry, thrust.

Then as Kane deflected Dragar's powerful stroke, the youth made a quick thrust with the turning blade—enough so that its tip gashed diagonally across Kane's brow, severing his headband. A shallow cut, but blood flowed freely, matted the clinging strands of his unbound hair. Kane gave back, flung the blood and loose hair from his eyes.

And Dragar lunged. Too quick for Kane to parry fully, his blade gored a furrow the length of the sorcerer's left forearm. Kane's long sword faltered. Instantly the barbarian hammered at his guard.

The sword left Kane's grip as it clumsily threw back the star-blade. For a fraction of a second it turned free in midair. Dragar exulted that he had at last torn the blade from Kane's grasp—as he raised his arm for a killing stroke.

But Kane's right hand caught up the spinning blade with practiced surety. Wielding the sword with skill scarcely inferior to his natural sword arm, Kane parried Dragar's flashing blow. Then, before the startled barbarian could recover, Kane's sword smashed through Dragar's ribs.

The force of the blow hurled the stricken youth back against the bed. Wizard's Bane dropped from nerveless fingers and skidded across the wide oaken planks.

From Dessylyn's throat came a cry of inexpressible pain. She rushed to him and cradled Dragar's head against her lap. Desperately she pressed ineffectual fingers against the pulsing wound in his chest. "Please, Kane!" she sobbed. "Spare him!"

Kane glanced through burning eyes at the youth's ruined chest and laughed. "I give him to you, Dessylyn," he told her insolently. "And I'll await you in my tower —unless, of course, you young lovers still plan on running off together."

Blood trailing from his arm—and darker blood from his sword—he stalked from the room and into the night mists.

"Dragar! Dragar!" Dessylyn moaned, kissing his haggard face and blood-foamed lips. "Please don't die, beloved! Onthe, don't let him die!"

Tears fell from her eyes to his as she pressed her face against his pallid visage. "You didn't believe him, did you, Dragar? What if I did engineer our meeting, dearest! Still I love you! It's true that I love you! I'll always love you, Dragar!"

He looked at her through glazing eyes.

"Bitch!" he spat, and died.

How many times, Dessylyn?
How many times will you play this game?
(But this was the first!)
The first? Are you sure, Dessylyn?
(I swear it! . . . How can I be sure?)
And how many after? How many circles, Dessylyn?
(Circles? Why this darkness in my mind?)
How many times, Dessylyn, have you played at Lorelei?
How many are those who have known your summoning eye?
How many are those who have heard your siren cry, Dessylyn?
How many souls have swum out to you, Dessylyn?
And perished by the shadows that hide below,
And are drawn down to Hell by the undertow?
How many times, Dessylyn?
(I can't remember . . .)

VII

"He'll Have to Die . . ."

"You know he'll have to die."

Dessylyn shook her head. "It's too dangerous."

"Clearly it's far more dangerous to let him live," Mavrsal pointed out grimly. "From what you've told me, Kane will never permit you to leave him—and this isn't like trying to get away from some jealous lord. A sorcerer's tentacles reach farther than those of the fabled Oraycha. What good is it to escape Carsultyal, only to have Kane's magic strike at us later? Even on the high sea his shadow can follow us."

"But we might escape him," murmured Dessylyn. "The oceans are limitless, and the waves carry no trail."

"A wizard of Kane's power will have ways to follow us."

"It's still too dangerous. I'm not even sure Kane *can* be killed!" Dessylyn's fingers toyed anxiously with the emerald at her throat; her lips were tightly pressed.

Angrily Mavrsal watched her fingers twist the wide silk and leather collar. Fine ladies might consider the fashion stylish here in Carsultyal, but it annoyed him that she wore the ornament even in bed. "You'll never be free of Kane's slave collar," he growled, voicing his thought, "until that devil is dead."

"I know," breathed the girl softly, more than fear shining in her green eyes.

"Yours is the hand that can kill him," he continued.

Her lips moved, but no sound issued.

Soft harbor sounds whispered through the night as the

Tuab gently rocked with the waves. Against the quay, her timbers creaked and groaned, thudded against the buffers of waste hemp cordage. Distantly, her watch paced the deck; low conversation, dimly heard, marked the presence of other crewmen—not yet in their hammocks, despite a hard day's work. In the captain's cabin a lamp swung slowly with the vessel's roll, playing soft shadows back and forth against the objects within. Snug and sheltered from the sea mists, the atmosphere was almost cozy—could the cabin only have been secure against a darker phantom that haunted the night.

"Kane claims to love you," Mavrsal persisted shrewdly. "He won't accept your hatred of him. In other words, he'll unconsciously lower his guard with you. He'll let you stand at his back and never suspect that your hand might drive a dagger through his ribs."

"It's true," she acknowledged in a strange voice.

Marvsal held her shoulders and turned her face to his. "I can't see why you haven't tried this before. Was it fear?"

"Yes. I'm terrified of Kane."

"Or was it something else? Do you still feel some secret love for him, Dessylyn?"

She did not reply immediately. "I don't know."

He swore and took her chin in his hand. The collar, with its symbol of Kane's mastery, enraged him—so that he roughly tore it from her throat. Her fingers flew to the bared flesh.

Again he cursed. "Did Kane do that to you?"

She nodded, her eyes wide with intense emotion.

"He treats you as a slave, and you haven't the spirit to rebel—or even to hate him for what he does to you!"

"That's not true! I hate Kane!"

"Then show some courage! What can the devil do to you that's any worse than your present lot?"

"I just don't want you to die, too!"

The captain laughed grimly. "If you'd remain his slave to spare my life, then you're worth dying for! But the only death will be Kane's—if we lay our plans well. Will you try, Dessylyn? Will you rebel against this tyrant—win freedom for yourself, and love for us both?"

"I'll try, Mavrsal," she promised, unable to avoid his eyes. "But I can't do it alone."

"Nor would any man ask you to. Can I get into Kane's tower?"

"An army couldn't assail that tower if Kane wished to defend it."

"So I've heard. But can *I* get inside? Kane must have a secret entrance to his lair."

She bit her fist. "I know of one. Perhaps you could enter without his knowing it."

"I can if you can warn me of any hidden guardians or pitfalls," he told her with more confidence than he felt. "And I'll want to try this when he won't be as vigilant as normal. Since there seem to be regular periods when you can slip away from the tower, I see no reason why I can't steal inside under the same circumstances."

Dessylyn nodded, her face showing less fear now. "When he's deep into his necromancies, Kane is oblivious to all else. He's begun again with some of his black spells—he'll be so occupied until tomorrow night, when he'll force me to partake of his dark ritual."

Mavrsal flushed with outrage. "Then that will be his last journey into the demonlands—until we send him down to Hell forever! Repairs are all but complete. If I push the men and rush reprovisioning, the *Tuab* can sail with the tide of another dawn. Tomorrow night it will be, then, Dessylyn. While Kane is exhausted and preoccupied with his black sorcery, I'll slip into his tower.

"Be with him then. If he sees me before I can strike, wait until he turns to meet my attack—then strike with this!" And he drew a slender dirk from a sheath fixed beneath the head of his bunk.

As if hypnotized by his words, by the shining sliver of steel, Dessylyn turned the dagger about in her hands, again and again, staring at the flash of light on its keen edge. "I'll try. By Onthe, I'll try to do as you say!"

"He'll have to die," Mavrsal assured her. "You know he'll have to die."

VIII

Drink a Final Cup . . .

Spread out far below lay Carsultyal, fog swirling through her wide brick streets and crooked filthy alleys, hovering over squalid tenements and palatial manors—although her arrogant towers pierced its veil and reared toward the stars in lordly grandeur. Born of two elements, air and water, the mist swirled and drifted, sought to strangle a third element, fire, but could do no more than dim with tears its thousand glowing eyes. Patches of murky yellow in the roiling fog, the lights of Carsultyal gained the illusion of movement, so that one might be uncertain at any one moment whether he gazed down into the mist-hung city or upward toward the cloud-buried stars.

"Your mood is strange tonight, Dessylyn," Kane observed, meticulously adjusting the fire beneath the tertiary alembic.

She moved away from the tower window. "Is it strange to you, Kane? I marvel that you notice. I've told you countless times that this necromancy disgusts me, but always before have my sentiments meant nothing to you."

"Your sentiments mean a great deal to me, Dessylyn. But as for demanding your attendance here, I only do what I must."

"Like that!" she hissed in loathing, and pointed to the young girl's mutilated corpse.

Wearily Kane followed her gesture. Pain etching his brow, he made a sign and barked a stream of harsh syllables. A shadow crossed the open window and fell over the vivisected corpse. When it withdrew, the tortured form had vanished, and a muffled slap of wings faded into the darkness.

"Why do you think to hide your depraved crimes from my sight, Kane? Do you think I'll forget? Do you think I don't know the evil that goes into compounding this diabolical drug you force me to drink?"

Kane frowned and stared into the haze of phosphorescent vapor which swirled within the cucurbit. "Are you carrying iron, Dessylyn? There's assymetry to the nimbus. I've told you not to bring iron within the influence of this generation."

The dagger was an unearthly chill against the flesh of her thigh. "Your mind is going, Kane. I wear only these rings."

He ignored her to lift the cap and hurriedly pour in a measure of dark, semi-congealed fluid. The alembic hissed and shivered, seemed to burst with light within its crimson crystal walls. A drop of phosphorescence took substance near the receiver. Kane quickly shifted the chalice to catch the droplet as it plunged.

"Why do you force me to drink this, Kane? Aren't these chains of fear that hold me to you bondage enough?"

His uncanny stare fixed her, and while it might have been the alchemical flames that made it seem so, she was astonished to see the fatigue, the pain that lined his face. It was as if the untold centuries whose touch Kane had eluded had at last stolen upon him. His hair billowed wildly, his face was shadowed and sunken, and his skin seemed imparted with the sick hue of the phosphorescent vapors.

"Why must you play this game, Dessylyn? Does it please you to see to what limits I go to hold you to me?"

"All that would please me, Kane, is to be free of you."

"You loved me once. You will love me again."

"Because you command it? You're a fool if you believe so. I hate you, Kane. I'll hate you for the rest of my life. Kill me now, or keep me here till I'm ancient and withered. I'll still die hating you."

He sighed and turned from her. His words were breathed into the flame. "You'll stay with me because I love you, and your beauty will not fade, Dessylyn. In time you may understand. Did you ever wonder at the loneliness of immortality? Have you ever wondered what must be the thoughts of a man cursed to wander through the centuries? A man doomed to a desolate, unending existence—feared and hated wherever men speak his name. A man who can never know peace, whose shadow leaves ruin wherever he passes. A man who has learned that every triumph is fleeting, that every joy is transient. All that he seeks to possess is stolen away from him by the years. His empires will fall, his songs will be forgotten, his loves will turn to dust. Only the emptiness of eternity will remain with him, a laughing skeleton cloaked in memories to haunt his days and nights.

"For such a man as this, for such a curse as this—is it so terrible that he dares to use his dark wisdom to hold something which he loves? If a hundred bright flowers must wither and die in his hand, is it evil that he hopes to keep one, just *one*, blossom for longer than the brief instant that Time had intended? Even if the flower hated being torn from the soil, would it make him wish to preserve its beauty any less?"

But Dessylyn was not listening to Kane. The billow of a tapestry, where no wind had blown, caught her vision. Could Kane hear the almost silent rasp of hidden hinges? No, he was lost in one of his maddened fits of brooding.

She tried to force her pounding heart to pulse less thunderously, her quick breath to cease its frantic rush. She could see where Mavrsal stood, frozen in the shadow of the tapestry. It seemed impossible that he might creep closer without Kane's unnatural keenness sensing his presence. The hidden dirk burned her thigh as if it were sheathed in her flesh. Carefully she edged around to Kane's side, thinking to expose his back to Mavrsal.

"But I see the elixir is ready," announced Kane, breaking out of his mood. Administering a few amber drops to the fluid, he carefully lifted the chalice of glowing liquor.

"Here, drink this quickly," he ordered, extending the vessel.

"I won't drink your poisoned drugs again."

"Drink it, Dessylyn." His eyes held hers.

As in a recurrent nightmare—*and there were other*

nightmares—Dessylyn accepted the goblet. She raised it to her lips, felt the bitter liquor touch her tongue.

A knife whirled across the chamber. Struck from her languid fingers, the crystal goblet smashed into a thousand glowing shards against the stones.

"No!" shouted Kane in a demonic tone. "No! *No!*" He stared at the pool of dying phosphoresence in stunned horror.

Leaping from concealment, Mavrsal flung himself toward Kane—hoping to bury his cutlass in his enemy's heart before the sorcerer recovered. He had not reckoned on Kane's uncanny reflexes.

The anguished despair Kane displayed burst into inhuman rage at the instant he spun to meet his hidden assailant. Weaponless, he lunged for the sea captain. Mavrsal swung his blade in a natural downward slash, abandoning finesse in the face of an unarmed opponent.

With blurring speed, Kane stepped under the blow and caught the other's descending wrist with his left hand. Mavrsal heard a scream escape his lips as his arm was jammed to a halt in mid swing—as Kane's powerful left hand closed about his wrist and shattered the bones beneath the crushed flesh. The cutlass sailed unheeded across the stones.

His face twisted in bestial fury, Kane grappled with the sea captain. Mavrsal, an experienced fighter at rough and tumble, found himself tossed about like a frail child. Kane's other hand circled its long fingers about his throat, choking off his breath. Desperately he sought to break Kane's hold, beat at him with his mangled wrist, as Kane with savage laughter carried him back against the wall, holding him by his neck like a broken puppet.

Red fog wavered in his vision—pain was roaring in his ears . . . Kane was slowly strangling him, killing him deliberately, taunting him for his helplessness.

Then he was falling.

Kane gasped and arched his back inward as Dessylyn drove her dagger into his shoulder. Blood splashed her sweat-slippery fist. As Kane twisted away from her blow, the thin blade lodged in the scapula and snapped at the hilt.

Dessylyn screamed as his backhand blow hurled her to

the stones. Frantically she scrambled to Mavrsal's side, where he lay sprawled on the floor—stunned, but still conscious.

Kane cursed and fell back against his worktable, overturning an alembic that burst like a rotted gourd. *"Dessylyn!"* he groaned in disbelief. Blood welled from his shoulder, spread across his slumped figure. His left shoulder was crippled, but his deadliness was that of a wounded tiger. "Dessylyn!"

"What did you expect?" she snarled, trying to pull Mavrsal to his feet.

A heavy flapping sound flung foggy gusts through the window. Kane cried out something in an inhuman tongue.

"If you kill Mavrsal, better kill me this time as well!" cried Dessylyn, clinging to the sea captain as he dazedly rose to his knees.

He cast a calculating eye toward the fallen sword. Too far.

"Leave her alone, sorcerer!" rasped Mavrsal. "She's guilty of no crime but that of hating you and loving me! Kill me now and be done, but you'll never change her spirit!"

"And I suppose you love her, too," said Kane in a tortured voice. "You fool. Do you know how many others I've killed—other fools who thought they would save Dessylyn from the sorcerer's evil embrace? It's a game she often plays. Ever since the first fool . . . only a game. It amuses her to taunt me with her infidelities, with her schemes to leave with another man. Since it amuses her, I indulge her. But she doesn't love you."

"Then why did she bury my steel in your back?" Despair made Mavrsal reckless. "She hates you, sorcerer—and she loves me! Keep your lies to console you in your madness! Your sorcery can't alter Dessylyn's feelings toward you—nor can it alter the truth you're forced to see! So kill me and be damned—you can't escape the reality of your pitiful clutching for something you'll never hold!"

Kane's voice was strange, and his face was a mirror of tormented despair. "Get out of my sight!" he rasped. "Get out of here, both of you!

"Dessylyn, I give you your freedom. Mavrsal, I give

you Dessylyn's love. Take your bounty, and go from Carsultyal! I trust you'll have little cause to thank me!"

As they stumbled for the secret door, Mavrsal ripped the emerald-set collar from Dessylyn's neck and flung it at Kane's slumping figure. "Keep your slave collar!" he growled. "It's enough that you leave her with your scars about her throat!"

"You fool," said Kane in a low voice.

"How far are we from Carsultyal?" whispered Dessylyn.

"Several leagues—we've barely gotten underway," Mavrsal told the shivering girl beside him.

"I'm frightened."

"Hush. You're done with Kane and all his sorcery. Soon it will be dawn, and soon we'll be far beyond Carsultyal and all the evil you've known there."

"Hold me tighter then, my love. I feel so cold."

"The sea wind is cold, but it's clean," he told her. "It's carrying us together to a new life."

"I'm frightened."

"Hold me closer, then."

"I seem to remember now. . . ."

But the exhausted sea captain had fallen asleep. A deep sleep—the last unblighted slumber he would ever know.

For at dawn he awoke in the embrace of a corpse—the mouldering corpse of a long-dead girl, who had hanged herself in despair over the death of her barbarian lover.

TWO SUNS SETTING

I

Alone with the Night Winds

Sullen red disk, the sun was burying itself beneath a monotonous horizon of rolling gravel waste that stretched behind him miles uncounted—and possibly untrod save by his horse's hooves. Long before the sunlight failed, its warmth was snuffed out in the empty lifelessness of the desert, so that in its last hour the sun shone cheerless as the rising moon. Crimson as it climbed, the full moon seemed a false dawn to mock the dying sun, arriving prematurely, disrespectful as a greedy heir pacing in eager impatience before the master's deathbed. For a space the limitless skies of twilight displayed two rubrous globes low on either horizon, so that Kane mused as to whether his long journey across the desert might not have led him to some strange dusk world where two ancient suns smouldered in the heavens. The region seemed unearthly in its chill desolation, and certainly an aura of unguessable antiquity hung as a grey shadow over each tumbled bit of stone.

Kane had left Carsultyal with no particular destination or goal other than to ride far beyond that city's influence. There were those who said that Kane was driven from Carsultyal, his power there broken at last by fellow sorcerers jealous of his long-held prestige—and alarmed by the bizarrely alien direction his studies had taken in recent years. Kane himself considered his departure more or less voluntary, albeit precipitous, arguing privately that had he really wanted to, he could have fended off the attack of his former colleagues—even though he owed allegiance to neither god nor demon from whom he might have sought intercession. Rather, mankind's first great city had grown stagnant over the last century. The spirit of discovery, of renaissance that had drawn him to Carsultyal in its earliest years was burned out now, so that boredom, his nemesis, had overtaken Kane once more. To be sure, he had been restless, his thoughts drawn more and more to the world beyond Carsultyal—lands yet to know the presence of man. But that he returned to his pathless wandering without much forethought could be judged in that Kane had left the city with little more than a few supplies, a double handful of gold coins, a fast horse, and a sword of tempered Carsultyal steel. Those who sought to seize his relinquished power may have regretted their inheritance, but this minor vindication seemed pointless now.

With dusk, the wind began to rise, a whining chill breath from the mountains whose rusted peaks still burned with the final rays of the sun, now vanished beneath the opposite horizon. Kane shivered and drew his russet cloak closer about his massive shoulders, regretting the warm furs that scavengers now snarled over in Carsultyal. The Herratlonai was a cold, empty waste, where nights dropped to freezing. With the mountain wind, his outfit of green wool shirt, dark leather vest, and pants was less than adequate for the night.

The previous day he had eaten the last hoarded chips of dried fruit and jerky, after short rations for a week or more. Of water luckily there was yet half a bag; he had filled the skins to bursting before entering the desert, and a waterhole had providentially appeared along the ghost of a trail he followed. Or thought he followed. The gravel waste southeast of Carsultyal's domains was reputed to border on one of the prehuman realms of lost antiquity. There were tales of cities impossibly ancient buried beneath the gravel dunes. Kane had come upon what he hoped might be traces of a forgotten path across the desert to the fabled mountains of the eastern continent. He determined to follow this, and at times he discovered sentinel boulders whose all but effaced hieroglyphs might resemble those glimpsed in books of elder world lore—or might be the deluding artistry of wind and ice. Beyond this tantalization, Kane found nothing further to disrupt the monotonous desolation but stray patches of sparse scrub and gorgeous columns of agatized wood. The grass his mount cropped; for himself Kane had not seen even a lizard in days. Perhaps it had been rash to attempt traverse of a desert whose limits no man had knowledge of, at least without a packtrain of provisions. But Kane had not embarked under the brightest of circumstances, nor had the years dulled his reckless whim. Philosophically he congratulated himself on riding a course no enemy would care to follow.

Then the mountains had broken through the thin haze of the eastern horizon like a row of worn and discolored teeth. Their presence gave some cause for optimism—at least he was across the desert—but this hope was clouded when the late afternoon sun revealed the hills to be merely a more vertical variation on the present terrain. Dry slopes of gravel and crumbling bluffs appeared lifeless except for dark blotches of twisted underbrush. From the talus gleamed iridescent flashes of sunlight, colored then flung back by mammoth slabs of petrified wood, strewn about like a giant's plundered jewel hoard.

But with darkness had also come the startling smell of wood smoke in the mountain wind—a familiar scent uncanny in this stark desolation. Kane brushed smooth the grimy beard that hung like rust over coarse features, thumbed a few blowing strands of red hair back beneath a leather headband sewn with plaques of lapis lazuli, and sniffed the night wind in disbelief. His mount paced onward, the night deepened, and against the foot of the mountains ahead beckoned the light of a campfire. No, simply the light of a fire, he mused—there was no reason to be more specific. At this distance it must be a good-sized blaze.

He guided his horse closer, picking his way carefully over the gravel in the moonlight. With a twisting ache in his belly, Kane recognized the odor of roasting meat within the smoke, and there was no longer any doubt. Calculatingly he studied the still distant campfire. He had seen no evidence of habitation against the slope, and in this emptiness such would seem an impossibility. Not that it seemed any more probable, but indications were that he had chanced upon some other wanderer. As to who or what might be camped beside the ridge, or what circumstances had brought about his presence, Kane was at loss to conjecture. Nothing was known of those who might dwell beyond the settled northwestern crescent of the Great Southern Continent, and in the dawn world more races than mankind walked the Earth.

Whoever had built the fire, he ate his meat cooked and so could not be hopelessly alien. From the size of the campfire, Kane guessed it was a small party of nomads or savages—likely someone from whatever lay beyond the mountains. The significant point was the roasting meat. Licking dry lips, Kane unfastened his sword from the saddle and buckled it across his back, so that the familiar hilt protruded reassuringly over his right shoulder. The scabbard tip he left untied, so that it would pivot freely on its shoulder swivel when he grasped the hilt. Cautiously he approached the campfire.

II

Two Who Met by Firelight

His keen nostrils caught an animal smell, sour beneath the pungency of wood smoke and cooked flesh. At first the crackling firelight screened the shape crouched beyond, so that Kane warily nudged his steed toward another angle of vision to confirm his dawning suspicion. His face tightened at recognition. Only one man squatted beside the blaze—if a giant might be termed "man."

Kane had seen—had spoken with—giants in the course of his wanderings, although in recent decades they were seldom encountered. A proudly aloof, taciturn race he knew them to be. Few in number and scornful of mankind's emerging civilization, they lived a semi-barbaric existence in lands unfrequented by man. True, there abounded gruesome tales of individual giants who terrorized isolated human settlements, but these were outlaws to their own race—or more often the monstrous hybrid ogres.

This particular individual did not appear threatening. While he obviously had heard the clash of shod hooves on stone, his attitude seemed curious rather than hostile as Kane approached. Not that someone his stature need display an aggressive front at the appearance of a single horse and rider. In comfortable reach lay a hooked axe whose bronze head could serve as a ship's anchor. Kane realize that from the other's higher vantage point, his approach had been observed beyond the ring of firelight. Still the giant showed no sinister action. Spitted over sputtering flames turned an entire carcass of what looked to be goat. Hot, succulent meat . . .

Hunger overpowered caution. Poised to wheel and gallop away at the first sign of danger, Kane boldly rode up to the fringe of firelit circle and halted.

"Good evening," he greeted levelly, speaking the language of the giant's race with complete fluency. "Your campfire was visible at some distance. I wondered if I might join you."

The giant grunted and shielded his eyes with a hand larger than a spade. "Well, what's this here? A human who speaks the Old Tongue. Out of nowhere, too—and in a land that even ghosts have abandoned. This sort of novelty can't be ignored. Come on into the light, manling. We'll share hospitality of the trail." His voice, though loud as a man's shout, had an even bass timbre.

Kane muttered thanks and dismounted, deciding to gamble on the giant's apparent goodwill. As he stepped before the fire, he and his host exchanged curious inspection. At a bit over six feet and carrying past three hundred pounds of bone, sinew, and muscle, Kane was seldom physically overawed. This night he stood alone in the desert before one who could overpower him as if he were a weakling child.

He estimated the giant's height at somewhere around fifteen feet. It was difficult to tell, since he sat crouched on the ground, knees drawn up, enswathed in a cloak of bearskins like a misshapen hairy tent. Disregarding the matter of size, the giant's appearance was human enough—his proportions were those of a man in his prime, though he seemed somewhat lanky from a slightly disproportionate length of limb. Broadly muscled, his weight must be enormous. He wore rough boots the size of panniers, and under the cloak a crudely stitched tunic and leggings of hide. Calves and arms were matted with coarse bristles. Perhaps too bony to be called craggy, his features were not displeasing; his beard was shaggy, brown hair drawn back in a short braid at the nape. Brown also were his eyes, set wide beneath an intelligent brow.

Looking him over as a man might size up a stray dog, the giant glanced at Kane's face and gave an interested grunt. He gazed thoughtfully into Kane's cold blue eyes for a moment—something few cared to do. "You're Kane; aren't you?" he commented.

Kane started, then smiled bitterly. "A thousand miles. from the cities of man, and a giant calls me by name."

The giant seemed amused. "Oh, you'll have to wander far if you really seek anonymity. We giants have watched the frantic history of your race. We recall when mankind aborted from its womb, pretending to be adult instead of misbegotten fetus. To man these few centuries are time immemorial; to our race a nostalgic yesterday. We remember well the Curse of Kane and still recognize his mark."

"That history is already garbled and distorted," Kane murmured, eyes for a moment focused beyond. "Kane is becoming misty legend in the old homes of man—and lost in obscurity in the new lands. Already I've travelled through lands where men did not know me for who I am."

"And you kept wandering, too—because they soon learned to dread the name of Kane," concluded the giant. "Well, Kane, my name is Dwassllir, and I'm pleased to find a legend joining me at my lonely fire."

Kane shrugged an ironic acknowledgment. "What's that roasting in your lonely fire?" He looked hungrily at the grease-dripping carcass.

"A mountain goat I dropped this afternoon—good game is scarce around here, I've found. Hey, give that spit a nudge, will you?"

Kane heaved the spit to the rarest side. "You going to eat all of it?" he asked bluntly, too hungry for pride.

Dwassllir might well have done otherwise, but the giant seemed glad for the companionship and tore off a generous side of ribs that taxed even Kane's voracity. Again the image of stray dog occurred to Kane, but the growling in his belly claimed first place in his thoughts. The goat was tough, stringy, half raw and gamy in taste; it was ecstasy to devour. One eye still watching the giant warily, he gnawed on the ribs with gusto, washing down the greasy flesh with mouthfuls of stale water from Dwassllir's canteen.

With a belch that fanned the flames, Dwassllir stood and

stretched, licked his fingers, wiped face with hands, then scrubbed his hands with loose gravel. When the giant was erect, Kane realized that his height was closer to eighteen feet. Leisurely Dwasslir picked over the remains of the goat. "Want any more?" he inquired. Kane shook his head, still struggling with the ribs. A short tug wrenched loose the remaining hind leg, and the giant settled back with a contented sigh to gnaw the joint.

"Game is hard to run across in this range," he reflected, gesturing with the tattered femur. "Doubt if you'd find anything in that stretch of desert yonder. Likely that horse will be the only meat you'll find until you get into the plains east of here."

"I thought about eating him," Kane conceded. "But on foot I'd stand little chance of crossing this waste."

Dwasslir snorted disparagingly. Because of their enormous size, giants looked upon a horse as only another game animal. "The frailty of your race! Strip man of his crutches, and he's helpless to stand against his world."

"Don't oversimplify," Kane objected. "Mankind will be master of this world. In only a few centuries I've seen our civilization grow from a sterile paradise, from scattered barbaric tribes to a vast and expanding empire of cities, villages, and farms. Ours is the fastest rising civilization ever to burst upon this world."

"Only because man has stolen his civilization from the ruins of better races who preceded him. Human civilization is parasitic—a gaudy fungus that owes its vitality to the dead genius upon whose corpse it flourishes!"

"Wiser races, I'll grant you," Kane pointed out. "But it is mankind who has survived, not Earth's elder races. It is a measure of man's resourcefulness that he can salvage from prehuman civilizations knowledge that is invaluable to the advance of his own race. Carsultyal has risen thus from a fishing village to the greatest city in the known world. Her rediscovered knowledge has shaped the emergence of mankind to our present civilization."

Dwasslir snapped the femur explosively and sucked at its marrow. "Civilization! You boast that as man's major accomplishment! It is nothing—only an outgrowth of human weakness! Man is too frail, too unworthy a creature to live within his environment. He must instead prop himself up with his civilization, his learning. My race learned to live in the real world, to merge with our environment. We need no civilization. Man is a cripple who flaunts his infirmity, boasts of his crutches. You retreat into the walls of your civilization because you are too weak to stand before nature as part of the natural environment. Instead of living as partner to nature, man hides behind his civilization, curses and defies true life, distorts his environment to accommodate his own failings. Beware that your environment does not strike back from all your blasphemies, for that day mankind shall be snuffed out like the unnatural freak man is!

"Even you, Kane, you who are reviled as the most dangerous man of your race. Without your horse, your clothes, your weapons, could you have crossed that desert alive as you have just barely done? One of my race could!

"My race is older than yours. We had grown to maturity while a mad god was playing his idiot game of shaping mankind from the bestial filth that skulked where shadow lay deepest. Had man walked the Earth of my race's youth, his civilization would have protected him no better than an eggshell. That Earth was more feral than this world man knows. My ancestors defied storms, glaciers, catastrophes that would have swept away your cities like dry leaves before the wind! They stood naked before beasts more savage than any man has known—grappled and conquered the sabretooth, the great sloth, the cave bear, the woolly mammoth, and other creatures whose strength and ferocity are unknown in this tame age! Could man have survived in that heroic age? I doubt that all his cunning and trickery could have saved him!"

"Perhaps not, but then your race has considerable physical advantage," argued Kane, wondering how wise it might be to provoke the other. "If my stride were as long as yours, then I wouldn't need a horse to cross a desert—although I think your disdain might not exist, if there were a steed great enough for a giant to straddle. Nor would I need my sword if I were huge enough to crush a lion as if it were only a jackal. Your boast is founded on the fact that your size makes you physically superior to the dangers of your environment, which is a boast that any large and powerful animal could echo. Who is braver—one of your ancestors who barehanded throttled a cave bear close to him in size, or a man with a spear who kills a tiger many times his superior in physical power?"

He paused, waiting to see if the giant had taken offense. However, Dwassllir was not of volatile temper. Belly full and feet warm, he was in a pleasant mood for fireside debate with his diminutive companion.

"True, yours is an older race, and mankind an arrogant youth," Kane continued. "But what are the accomplishments of your race? If you scorn to build cities, to sail ships, to settle the wilderness, to master the secrets of prehuman knowledge, then what have you achieved? Art, poetry, philosophy, spiritualism —are these fields your race has mastered?"

"Our achievement has been to live at peace with our environment—to live as a part of the natural world, instead of waging war with nature," declared Dwassllir steadily.

"All right then, I'll accept that," Kane persisted. "Perhaps you have found fulfillment in your rather primitive life style. However, the measure of a race's attainments must finally be its ability to flourish within its chosen role. If your race has done this so well, why then do your numbers diminish, while mankind spreads over the Earth? Never has your race been a populous one, and today man encounters giants only rarely. Will your race then fade away with the passing years—until one day the giants will be known only in legend along with the fierce creatures your ancestors fought? What then will survive your passing? What will remain to tell of your vanished glory?"

Dwassllir became sadly pensive, so that Kane regretted having pursued the argument. "You humans seem too content to measure achievement in terms of numbers," he answered. "But I can't make full refutation of your logic. Our numbers have been declining for centuries, and I can't really tell you why. Our lives are long—I'm not as much your junior in years as you may suppose, Kane. We are slow to mate and raise children, but this was always so. Our natural enemies have all passed into extinction or retreated to the most obscure reaches.

Our simple medicines are sufficient to nurse us through whatever disease or injury might strike us. No, our deaths have not increased.

"I think our race has grown old, tired. Perhaps we should have followed the giant beasts of the savage past into the realm of shadow. At least our old enemies gave life adventure! It is as if my race has lived beyond its era, and now we perish from boredom. We're like one of your kings who has conquered all his enemies and now has only a dull old age to endure.

"My race rose in a heroic age, Kane! It was truly a day of giants in that era! But that age is dead. Gone are the great beasts. Vanished the elder races whose wars rocked the roots of mountains. Earth has been inherited by the insignificant scavenger. Man crawls about the ruins of the great age and proclaims himself to be Earth's new master! Perhaps man will survive to accomplish his insolent usurpation—more likely he will destroy himself in seeking to command mysteries the elder races found too awesome for even their powers to control!

"But when the day comes that man will be master of the Earth, my race will hopefully not be present to endure that humiliation! We are a race of heroes who have outlived the age of heroes! Can you blame us if we tire of existence in this age of boastful pygmies!"

Kane fell silent. "I understand your sentiments," he finally said. "But to abandon yourself to despair, to brood upon vanished glory, doesn't impress me as heroic."

He stopped, not wishing to deepen the shadow of melancholy that had gathered over their thoughts. "May I ask what brings you to this lost wilderness of dead rock?" he asked, thinking to change the subject. "Or do these nameless mountains border on the lands of your people?"

Dwassllir shook himself and tossed an uprooted shrub into the fire. The leaves hissed shrilly, then whipped loose from blackened stems to rise like red stars fading into the night. "What I seek is no secret," he replied, "although it may seem pointless to you as it has to some of my friends.

"Centuries ago, before this region was stripped barren of soil and hence of life, there were villages of my race along these mountains—which are not nameless, but are called the Antamareesi range. Under these hills lie immense caverns, which my ancestors used for shelter in days before they raised houses, then later mined for the veins of metal they discovered within. The climate was warmer, the land was green, game was plentiful—it was a good region to settle and to look upon in that age.

"Those were the great days! Life in that age was an ever challenging struggle between the savagery of the ancient Earth and the unyielding strength of my race! Can you imagaine the tremendous energy of those people? They stood chest to chest against a ferociously hostile world, and they conquered whatever enemy they faced! Their gods were Fire and Ice—the implacable opposites that were the ruling forces of their age! And their enemies were not only the forces of nature, or the great beasts—some of the elder races challenged the ascendency of my race as well!

"Perhaps it was their sorcery that left this region lifeless and barren. Our legends tell of battles with strange races and stranger weapons in the dawn world, and my ancestors were victorious over these enemies, too. The hero of one legendary battle, King Brotemllain, whose name you may know as the greatest king of my race, ruled over these mountains. His body was laid to rest within one of these caverns, and upon his brow remains the ancestral crown of my people—ancient even then, and given to him after death because of the undying greatness of his rule."

Dwassllir was afire now, his momentary depression seared away by intense fervour. He considered Kane thoughtfully, made a decision, and spoke earnestly, "I've been searching for Brotemllain's legendary burial place. And from certain signs, I think I'm about to discover it. I mean to recover his crown! King Brotemllain's crown is emblematic of my race's ancient glory. Although our wars and our kings are all past now, I believe that resurrection of this legendary symbol might unlock some of the old energy and vitality of my people. Perhaps the idea brands me a fool and dreamer, as many have scoffed, but I mean to do this thing! Surely this relic from an age of heroes could serve to spark some new flame of glory to my race even in these grey days!

"I wouldn't suggest this to another of your race, Kane, but because you are who you are, I'll offer both an invitation and a challenge. If you'd care to come along with me on this search, Kane, I'd welcome your company. It may be that you will understand my race better if you follow me into the shadow of that age of lost glory."

"Thank you for the invitation—and the challenge," declared Kane solemnly. The venture intrigued him, and the giant seemed to eat well. "I'll be proud to make that journey with you."

III

Dead Giant's Crown

The trees grew less far apart here, though still dwarfed and tortured by the chill breeze. Two days had Kane followed Dwassllir about the crumbling ridges, his horse matching the giant's restless stride. Now on the third day Dwassllir's whoop chorused by a hundred echoes announced the termination of his search.

The discovery seemed unimpressive. They had entered a deep valley and traced a course to its gorgelike head, where Kane glanced uneasily at the boulder-strewn slopes enclosing them overhead. At times Dwassllir had eagerly pointed out some rounded monument whose carvings the winds of time had all but obliterated. Again he would pause to examine some unprepossessing mound, where the drifting gravel nestled upon blocks of hewn stone and perhaps a shard of ceramic, a smear of charcoal fragments, or a lump of dried wood so ancient that it seemed more lifeless than the stones.

"There stands the entrance to the tomb of King Brotemllain," Dwassllir proclaimed, and he gestured to a rubble-choked patch of darkness that burrowed into the valley wall. The opening had been about twenty-five feet high and half as broad, although several feet were now filled in by debris. Evidence of masonry framed the entrance, along with great chunks of shredded wood, some of whose blackened splinters were conglomerate with verdigris—all that remained of portals at last fallen to time itself.

"I'm certain this is the valley described in our legends,"

the giant rumbled jubilantly. "The passage leads into a vast system of caverns. It was a natural opening my ancestors enlarged to enter a major side branch as it passes close to the surface. Beyond these ruins of the ancient monument should lie the domed natural chamber where Brotemllain's corpse was enthroned for the ages."

Kane frowned at the dark opening doubtfully, a whisper of unease drifting through his thoughts. "I wouldn't count on finding much in there but bats and dust. Time and decay generally devour the leavings of less hallowed thieves. Or does this tomb have its unseen guardians? It would seem unusual with so renowned a tenant and so legendary a treasure if this tomb were not guarded by some still vigilant spell."

With a shrug Dwassllir dismissed Kane's foreboding. "Unusual for your race, maybe. But this was a shrine most sacred to my race. Besides; who would dare pilfer the grave of a giant? Come on, we'll take torches and see if King Brotemllain still holds court."

While Kane struck fire, the giant scoured about for a supply of resiniferous wood. He returned with a dead tree as thick as Kane's thigh. Taking several shorn branches, Kane accompanied Dwassllir into the cave, the latter wielding a section of trunk.

Their progress was quickly interrupted. Blocking the passage but for a narrow crevice interposed a jumble of broken rock. A segment of the passage wall had collapsed.

Dwassllir examined the barrier thoughtfully. "It's going to take some time to dig through this," he concluded sourly.

"Assuming your efforts didn't bring down the rest of the mountain," was Kane's ominous comment. "There's a fault in the rock here, or this slide would not have broken through. If the caverns run as extensively as you say, there must be flaws undermining this entire range. The centuries have spread the cracks and further weakened the rock, so it's solid as a rotted tooth. It's a wonder these mountains haven't tumbled flat before now."

Jabbing out his torch, the giant craned his neck to peer along the crevice. "Passage opens up again, and just beyond, I think I can make out where it opens into the main cavern." He glowered at the obstruction helplessly for a moment, then gazed down at the man.

"You know, you could squeeze through that crack, Kane," he told him. "You could get past and see what's beyond. If there's nothing to be found, then there's nothing lost. But if this is King Brotemllain's tomb, then you can learn whether his crown still lies within."

Kane considered the crevice, his face noncommittal. "It can be done," he pronounced. Casually, not wishing to show his nerve less steady than the giant's: "I'll go look for your bones on my own, then."

The crack was inches too narrow for one of Kane's massive build, so that his clothing scuffed and flesh scraped as he wriggled through the tightest portion. But the wall had not collapsed in a solid thrust; rather, splintered chunks of stone had broken through in a disordered array, and the occlusion was spread like stubby fingers instead of a compact fist. Then his thrusting torch shone clear of the rubble, and Kane edged into an unobstructed passageway. Quickly he rebuckled his scabbard across his back, but the bare blade stayed in his left fist.

A short way beyond he found the cavern. A pair of steps too high for human stride completed the passage's gentle descent. Kane lifted the torch and looked about, his senses strained to catch any hint of danger. There was nothing to detect, but the obscure sense of menace persisted. Waving the brand to fan its light, he was unable to discern the cavern's boundaries, although this chamber seemed to extend for hundreds of feet. Stalactites hung from the ceiling far above, making a monstrous multifanged jaw with stalagmite tusks below. "I've just walked down the beast's tongue," mumbled Kane, clambering over the steps. Thin dust sifted over the stone; this cavern was long dead, too.

"What do you see, Kane?" roared Dwassllir from the crevice. High above the curtain of bats stirred fitfully.

Despite his familiarity with the giant's deafening tone, Kane started and nervously glanced toward the distant ceiling. The torch flared in his hand as he crossed the chamber, sword poised for whatever laired within the darkness.

Then he froze, a thrill tingling through his body as he gazed at what waited at the torchlight's perimeter.

"Dwassllir!" he shouted, in his excitement heedless of the booming echoes. "He's here! You've found the tomb! King Brotemllain's here on his throne, and his crown rests on his skull!"

Revealed in the torchlight jutted an immense throne of hewn stone, upon which its skeletal king still reposed in sepulchral majesty. In the cool aridity of the cavern, the lich had outlasted centuries. Tatters of desiccated flesh held the skeleton together in leathery articulation. Bare bone gleamed dully through chinks in the clinging mail of muscle and sinew, shrunken to ironlike texture. Throne arms were yet gripped by fingers like gnarled oak roots, while about the base was gathered a mouldering drift of disintegrating furs. The gaunt skull retained sufficient shreds of flesh to half mask its death's head grin with lines of sternness—forming a grimace suggesting laughter muffled by set lips. The eyes were sunken circles of darkness whose shadowy depths eluded Kane's torch. Not so the orbs that brooded from above the brow.

Red as setting suns in the torchlight, a pair of fist-sized rubies blazed from King Brotemllain's crown. Kane swore softly, impressed by the wealth he witnessed almost as deeply as he stood in awe of its grisly majesty. The circle of gold could belt a dancing girl's waist, and patterned about the two great stones were another ten or more rough-cut gems of walnut size. Ancient treasure from the giant's plutonian-harvested hoard.

Thinking of the kingdom encircled in the riches of King Brotemllain's crown, Kane bitterly regretted his shout of discovery. Had he reported the cavern empty, there might have been a chance to smuggle the crown past the giant—or return for it later. But now Dwassllir knew of the crown, and Dwassllir waited at the only exit to the tomb. To attempt to find egress through some hypothetical interpassage into the network of caverns said to run under the mountains would be suicidal—slightly less so than to challenge the giant for possession. Kane ruefully studied the treasure. Unless chance presented for stealthy murder . . .

"Kane!" The giant's bellow concluded his musing. "You

all right in there, Kane? Is it really King Brotemllain?"

"Can't be anything else, Dwassllir!" Kane yelled back, echoes garbling his words. "It's just like your legends told! There's a colossal throne of stone in the cavern's center! About twenty feet of mouldy skeleton's sitting on it, and on his skull there's a golden crown with two enormous rubies! Just a minute and I'll climb up and get it for you!"

"No! Leave it there!" Eagerness shook the giant's shout. "I want to see this for myself!" From the barrier sounded groan and rattle of shifting rubble.

"Wait, damn it all!" Kane howled, scrambling back to the passage. "You're going to bring the whole damn mountain down on us! I'll get your crown for you!"

"Leave it! This isn't just a treasure hunt! It's more than just recovering Brotemllain's crown!" puffed the giant, straining to roll back a boulder. "I've dreamed for more years than you can guess of standing before King Brotemllain's throne! Of standing where no giant has entered since the heroic age of my race! Of calling upon his shade for the strength to lead my race back to its lost glory! So I'll stand before King Brotemllain, and I'll lift his crown from his brow with my own hands! And when I return, my people will see and listen and know that the tales of our ancient greatness are history, not myth!

"Now come on and help me widen this crevice, will you? You can clear away this smaller stuff. This cavern's stood for millennia; We can risk another few minutes."

Kane cursed and joined him at the barrier, reflecting that it was useless arguing with a fanatical giant. Grimly he hauled back on a boulder jammed against the inner face of the blockage.

Sudden tearing groan and Dwassllir's gasp of dismay gave him barely enough warning. Kane catapulted backward just as the unbalanced rock slide protested their trespass. Like the irresistible fist of doom, the rock shelf burst from the wall and smashed against the opposite side.

Deafened by the concussion, pelted by splintered fragments, Kane twisted frantically to roll clear. He fell in a bruised huddle past the foot of the steps. For a moment of dazed confusion it seemed that the entire cavern rocked and bucked with a crescendo repercussion of the collapsed passageway.

When the last slamming echo had lost its note, the final chunk of cracked stone bounced past, Kane groggily sat up to lick his wounds. Sore, but no bones broken, a long gash down his left shoulder. His sword arm was numb where a rock splinter had struck, and it would need bandaging to staunch the trickle of blood. Relatively unscathed, he decided, considering he had nearly been crushed deader than King Brotemllain.

His sword was still sheathed, but the torch had been lost as he leaped away, and the chamber was as dark as a tomb could get. Kane did not need a torch to learn the worst; the absence of any ray of light told him that. King Brotemllain's tomb was also sealed as thoroughly as any tomb need be.

IV

A Final Coronation

Gloomily he felt his way back along the passage and pushed against the intervening wall of rock. There were boulders as wide as he was tall, and the spaces between were packed solid with lesser rubble. Given slaves and equipment enough, he might clear out another crevice. Dwassllir could perhaps burrow through, but the giant was probably a mangled keystone in the barrier right now.

Burnt pitch stung his groping fingers, and Kane tugged the extinguished torch out from under some debris. Since there seemed little else to do, he sat down and struck a fire. The torch alight once more, the rock slide appeared no less substantial. Angrily Kane kicked at a toppled boulder.

Air fanned the torch flame, however, pointing a yellow beckoning finger back into the burial cavern. Remembering this cave was a branch of a greater plexus, Kane eagerly sought to trace the faint stir of wind.

As he crossed the chamber, Kane saw the effects of the rock slide within the cavern. The sudden grinding force had sent a shudder through the tired stone, so that stalactites had plummeted like crystal lightning bolts from their eternally dark heaven. One had missed spearing Brotemllain by scant yards.

A sighing wind breathed corpse breath through a gaping pit many yards across at the cavern's one end. The explosive concussions that rocked the stone had not been the fantasy of a head blow then. Evidently in the chain reaction shock wave which the slide had drummed the brittle stone, a large section of rock from the high ceiling had struck here. Its impact had driven through the chamber floor to reveal another cavern beneath this one. The network of caves must bore through the mountains like the tortuous course of a feasting worm, thought Kane, peering into the pit.

Wind gusted faintly through the hole, bringing a sick smell of dampness—a stale, unclean animal smell that intrigued Kane. It seemed he could hear the rush of unseen waters. An underground river probably—deep underground it must be, too. The wind stole in through rotted chinks in the mountains' shell most likely. At least Kane hoped his deductions were correct.

The floor of this new cavern appeared to be about seventy-five feet below him. The collapsing stone had made a chaotic incline down which progress seemed possible. "I've found another road to Hell," Kane muttered aloud.

A rustle beyond him made him look to its source; then he knew he was on the threshold of Hell. At the edge of light danced a cockroach—incredibly, a bone white cockroach nearly a yard in length. With chitinous concentration, it was nuzzling a dead bat, and it waved its antennae querulously at the offending light. In disbelief Kane tossed a rock in its direction, and the roach scuttled off chuckling into the darkness.

Fascinated, Kane returned to the pit and thrust his torch out over the aperture. Near the incline's base two white-furred creatures raised blind eyes to the light and slunk away squealing in fear. And Kane recognized them as rats the size of jackals.

Understanding came to him. Water, air—the caverns below held life. But an obscenely distorted form of life it was. Probably these outsized creatures had evolved from cave dwellers who somehow were trapped beneath the surface ages ago, or maybe retreated there from choice when the land became desert. In primeval night, without seasons, without light, they had mutated to grotesque, primitive forms adapted to the demented savagery of their environment. Falling stone had crushed bats as well as other nameless things, and now the scent of blood was luring the monstrous cave creatures to this area.

And what else dwells below, wondered Kane uneasily. He drew away from the pit, deciding that so certain a path to Hell could rest untrod until all other chances of escape were eliminated. Even digging out through the passage seemed a brighter prospect.

As he returned to the rock fall, he caught the sound of stone grating on stone. For a moment he feared the slide was shifting, but as he watched tensely he saw this was not so. Excitement cutting through despondency, Kane quickly stepped to the barrier and rhythmically pounded against a boulder with a chunk of rock.

After a pause, his tapping was dimly echoed from the opposite side. So the giant had escaped the avalanche. His strength could clear the passage if it were at all possible.

Eagerly Kane began to dig into his side of the barrier. Not daring to contemplate another slide, he strained his powerful back to roll away small boulders, tore his fingers scrabbling doglike through the chipped stone. Luckily it was a bed of broken rock that had slid into the passage, rather than a solid stone shelf.

Time crawled immeasurably, marked only by the dwindling torch and the deepening excavation. Kane's hands were raw and blistered when a sudden wrenching of stone tore open a patch of daylight. Filtered by distance and dust, the ray of sunlight seemed of blinding brilliance to his eyes.

"Dwassllir!" shouted Kane, peering through the chink in the barrier. A shaft perhaps the size of a man's head had been formed between the angle of two boulders, although several feet of debris yet blocked the passage.

A huge brown eye squinted back at him. "Kane?" The giant sounded pleasantly surprised. "So you dodged the slide, manling! You're as hard to kill as legend tells!"

"Can you get me out of here?"

"Can if I'm going to get myself in!" Dwassllir returned stubbornly. "I think I can prop up these boulders so we can dig out space enough for me to crawl through."

"One of the characteristics of higher life forms is the ability to learn by experience," grumbled Kane, bending his back to dislodge a portion of rubble. But the giant's determination was as unyielding as the rock about them.

Slowly the crevice began to reappear, and with freedom outlined in an ever broadening patch of light, the grueling work seemed less fatiguing. Only a precariously balanced jumble of boulders remained.

But this time warning came too late.

A sudden shriek of rasping stone as Dwassllir recklessly hauled back on one of the piled boulders. Released from pressure, a second slab of rock plunged forward like a catapult missile. Kane yelled and tried to dodge. He had been unbalanced with effort, and even his blurring speed was too slow to evade the tumbling projectile.

Thundering as it struck, the slab caromed crazily upon the piled boulders, spun about and smashed against the wall where Kane stood. Kane hissed in pain. At the last instant he had twisted behind a sheltering boulder. This had absorbed the impact of the falling slab, but the explosive force had jammed the intervening rock against his thighs, pinning him to the wall.

Blood oozed from torn skin, trickled into his boots. Grimacing in pain as he tried to wriggle free, Kane discovered he had escaped crushed bones by the smallest fraction.

Miraculously, the rest of the pile had held stable. Dwassllir was cautiously poking at the opening. "Kane? Damn! You're harder to kill than a snake! Can you squeeze out of there?"

"I can't!" grunted Kane, straining to slide the rock. "Lot of rock fragments all jammed together, holding it in place! My feet are pinned in!" He cursed and writhed against his pillory, scraping off more skin as the only evident result.

"Well, I'll pull you out as I dig through," boomed Dwassllir reassuringly, and he once more attacked the rockslide.

But Kane heard sounds of grating rock not turned by Dwassllir's hand. From within the burial cavern he could hear a heavy body climbing over loose stone.

Teeth bared in defiant snarl, Kane stared wild-eyed into the funeral chamber.

At first he thought the corpse of King Brotemllain had risen on skeletal limbs, for wavering in the darkness he could discern two ruby coals throwing back the torchlight. But the crown had not moved and still made a sullen glow above the throne.

These were truly eyes he saw—eyes that held him in a baleful glare. Climbing from the aperture in the cavern floor came a creature from beneath the abyss of night.

Sabretooth! Or nightmare spawn of sabretooth tiger and stygian darkness. The gargantuan creature that shambled forth from the timeless caverns of night was as demented a progeny of its natural forebears as were the other grotesque cave beasts Kane had seen. Rock crunched beneath taloned tread as it stalked from the gaping pit, an albino behemoth more than double the stature of its fearsome ancestor. Dripping jaws yawned hungrily in a cough of challenge—sabre-toothed jaws that could close upon Kane as a cat snaps up a rat.

Lord Tloluvin alone might know what fantastic demons stalked the unlighted caverns that crawled down into his hellish realm, what depraved savagery in their nighted netherworld bred the cave beasts to grotesque giantism. Drawn by the noise and the scent of blood, this monster had left its sunless lair to hunt on the threshold of a land barred to its demonic kin for uncounted centuries.

It sensed its prey.

Unable to squirm free, Kane drew his sword for a hopeless defense. The cave creature had located him—in the darkness its hunting senses must be preternaturally keen—but it hesitated to spring. Seemingly it was confused by the wan rays of sunlight trespassing upon its realm.

The torch lay thrust between rocks almost within Kane's reach. By a series of desperate lunges he succeeded in spearing it on his sword tip and drawing it to him. Answering the sabretooth's growl, he swung the brand to flaring brilliance. The cat retreated somewhat, still intent on its trapped prey, but uncertain how to cope with this blazing light that seared its all but sightless eyes.

"Dwassllir! Can you break through?" The torch had burned through much of its length, so that the dwindling flame stung Kane's fingers.

The giant groaned with frantic effort. "There's a slab of rock midway I can't shift without bringing down the whole slide! If I had a beam I could use for bracing,

I could grub out the boulders holding it up and crawl through! Not enough room through there otherwise!"

The sabretooth coughed angrily and advanced a step, stubby tail twitching. Its hunger would soon overwhelm its caution, Kane realized in sick dread, as the cat drew its mammoth bulk into a crouch. In a minute its spring would crush him against the stone.

Eyes blazing feral hatred, Kane steadied his sword. There would be time for only one hopeless thrust as the cat's irresistible spring splintered his chest to pulpy ruin, but Kane meant for his slayer to feel his steel.

"I'll try for his throat when he leaps!" Kane shouted grimly. "Wound him bad as I'm able! Go back and hunt up a log to brace with, Dwassllir. If my sword thrusts deep enough to cripple, there's a chance you can kill this beast with your axe. Brotemllain's crown waits there for you, and when you return to your people you can tell them the price of its winning!"

Dwassllir was tearing away rubble furiously, though Kane did not risk a glance to note its progress. "Keep the cat back as long as you can, Kane!" His voice became muffled. "It was my doing got you into this, and I'll not abandon you like a slinking coward!"

The torch was sputtering; moments of life remained for both flame and wielder. Came a low rumble of shifting stone, but Kane glared unwaveringly into the cat's wrathful eyes. The tiger started, spat in sudden bafflement. Kane braced himself to meet its deadly lunge, then saw in amazement that the sabretooth was edging away.

A flaming length of trunkwood slithered across the stones, propelled by a bass roar from down low. Turning in disbelief, Kane saw Dwassllir's grimy face grinning triumphantly up at him from beneath a jutting shelf of rock.

"Made it, by damn!" the giant bellowed. He grunted breathlessly as he wriggled his colossal frame through the burrow he had dug. "Used my axe to shore up that main slab! She creaked some, but her haft's seasoned hickory, and she'll likely hold till we're out of here!"

At the sudden appearance of a creature rivalling its own awesome bulk, the sabretooth had retreated into the darkness of the cavern. Dwassllir shoved his torch farther down the passage, then bent to Kane. A heave of his mighty shoulders drew back the imprisoning stone.

Kane pitched forward. Biting his lips against the agony, he slithered out of the crevice to freedom.

"Can you walk, manling?"

Wincing, Kane took a few unsteady strides. "Yes, though I'd rather ride."

The giant hefted the torch. "I'll see King Brotemllain now," he declared.

"Don't be a fool, Dwassllir!" Kane protested. "Without your axe you're no match for that monster! You haven't driven it off—it's still prowling in the cavern! We'll be lucky to crawl out before it decides to attack!" The giant brushed him aside.

"Look, at least let's draw back and give that cat a chance to leave! We can find timber to shore up the ledge and free your axe! Then we'll try for the crown!"

"Not enough time!" Dwassllir's face was resolute. "I never really expected that axe to hold. It'll give way any second, and this shaft will be sealed forever! Can't even risk trying to wrench it free! The torch will keep the beast at bay long enough to get the crown. Besides, he won't be the only demon to crawl up from the pit. You don't need to stay, though."

Kane swore and limped after him.

"Ha! Sabretooth!" roared Dwassllir, scooping up a broken section of stalactite. A growl answered him from the cavern's echoing recesses. "Sabretooth! Do you know me? My ancestors were your enemy! We fought your forebears in ages past and made necklaces for our women from your pretty fangs! Hear me, sabretooth! Though you're three times the size of your tawny ancestor, I've no fear of you! I am Dwassllir, last true son of the old kings! I've come for my crown! Hide in your hole, sabretooth—or I'll have a white fur cloak to wear with my royal crown!"

The giant's challenge echoed through the cavern, rolled back by the sabretooth's angry snarl. Somewhere in the shadows the cat paced stiff-legged, but the canophony of echoes made its position uncertain. Bats swooped in panic; dust and bits of stone trickled over them. Kane shifted his sword uneasily, not caring to think what silent blow might strike back.

"King Brotemllain! The legends of my race do not lie!" breathed Dwassllir in awe. Reverently he stood before the throne of the ages-dead hero, his face aglow with visions of ancient glory. Reflected in his eyes was crimson brightness from the ruby crown.

The giant discarded his stalactite club, and stretched to touch the dead king's crown. With gentle strength he broke it free from its encrusted setting. "Grandsire, your children have need of this. . . ."

An avalanche of ivory-fanged terror, the sabretooth bolted from the darkness. Shattering silence with its killing scream, it leaped for the giant's unprotected back. Off guard, Dwassllir pivoted at the final instant to half evade the cat's full rush. Its crushing impact hurled giant and cave beast against the throne and onto the cavern floor.

Jaws locked in Dwassllir's shoulder, the tiger raked furiously against his back, talons tearing deep gashes. Kane limped in, sword flashing. But his movements were clumsy, and at first slash a blow of the creature's paw spun him away. He fell heavily at the foot of the throne and shook his head dully to clear his vision.

Dwassllir howled and lurched to his knees, huge hands clawing desperately to dislodge the murderous fangs. His flailing arm touched the fallen torch and he seized it instantly, smashing its blazing end into the monster's face. Seared by the blinding heat, the sabretooth released its death grip with an enraged shriek, and the giant's punishing kick flung them apart.

Smoke hung over the cat's gory maw. Gouts of scarlet spurted from the giant's deeply gouged shoulder. "Face to face, sabretooth!" roared Dwassllir wildly. "Skulker in shadow! Slinking coward! Dare now to attack your master face to face!"

Even as the tiger crouched to spring, Dwassllir leaped upon it, crippled left arm brandishing the torch. They grappled in midair, and the cavern seemed to quake at their collision. Over and over they rolled, torch flung wide, while Kane groggily tried to regain his feet. The giant struggled grimly to stave off those awful fangs, to writhe atop the sabretooth's greater bulk. Fearsome jaws champed on emptiness as they fought, but its slashing claws were goring horrible wounds through the giant's flesh.

Stoically enduring the agony, Dwassllir threw all his leviathan strength into tightening his grip on the cat's head. He bellowed insanely—curses of pain, of fury—locked his teeth in the beast's ear and ripped away its stump with taunting laughter. Life blood poured over his limbs, made a slippery mat of scarlet-sodden white fur. Still he howled and jeered, chanted snatches of ancient verse—sagas of his race—and pounded the sabretooth's skull against stone.

With a sudden wrench, Dwassllir hauled himself astride the cat's back. "Now die, sabretooth!" he roared. "Die knowing defeat as did your scrawny grandsires!"

He dug his knees into the creature's ribs and clamped heels together beneath its belly. The cat tried to roll, to dislodge him, but it could not. Great fists knotted over frothed fangs, arms locked champing jaws apart; Dwassllir bunched his shoulders and heaved backward. Gasping, coughing breath snorted from the cat's nostrils; its struggle was no longer to attack. For the first time in centuries, a sabretooth knew fear.

Blood gleamed a rippling pattern across the straining muscles of the giant's broad back. Irresistibly his hold tightened. Inexorably the tiger's spine bowed backward. An abrupt, explosive snap as vertebrae and sinew surrendered.

Laughing, Dwassllir twisted the sabretooth's head completely around. He spat into its dying eyes.

"Now then, King Brotemllain's crown!" he gasped, and staggered away from the twitching body. The giant reeled, but stood erect. His fur garments were shredded, dark and sticky. Blood flowed so freely as to shroud the depth and extent of his wounds; flaps of flesh hung ragged, and bone glistened yellow as he moved.

He groaned as he reached the throne and slumped down with his back braced against it. Kane found his senses clear enough to stand and knelt beside the stricken giant. Deftly his hands explored the other's wounds, sought vainly to stanch the bright spurting blood from the sabre gouges. But Kane was veteran of too many battles not to know his wounds were mortal.

Dwasslir grinned gamely, his face pale beneath splashed gore. "That, Kane, is how my ancestors overcame the great beasts of Earth's dawn."

"No giant ever fought a creature like this," Kane swore, "nor killed it bare-handed!"

The giant shrugged weakly. "You think not, manling? But you don't know the legends of our race, Kane. And the legends are truth, I know that now! Fire and Ice! Those were heroic days!"

Kane looked about the cavern, then bent to retrieve a fallen circle of gold. The rubies gleamed like Dwasslir's life blood; the crown was heavy in his hands. And though there was a fortune in his grasp, Kane no longer wanted King Brotemllain's crown.

"This is yours now," he muttered, and placed the crown upon Dwasslir's nodding brow.

The giant's head came erect again, and there was fierce pride in his face—and sadness. "I might have led them back to those lost days of glory!" he whispered. Then: "But there'll be another of my race, perhaps—another who will share my vision of the great age!"

He signed for Kane to leave him. Already his eyes looked upon things beyond this lonely cavern in a desolate waste. "That was an age to live in!" he breathed hoarsely. "An age of heroes!"

Kane somberly rose to his feet. "A great race, a heroic age—it's true," he acknowledged softly. "But I think the last of its heroes has passed."

THE DARK MUSE

Prologue

Lightning colors, whining, whirling dirge of sonic pain, coalesced to ecstasy. More dimly now, the tones muted, submerged. Form returned, images of imprisoned light. Scintillant shapes that shimmered with the siren melody, colors of piercing brilliance, sparkles of sound shivering through his senses. Lancinations of unendurable ecstasy ravened through his consciousness, starbursts of warring sensory impulses that slipped once more to coherent phenomena, an instant before his mind shattered to follow into final chaos.

Lustrous figures of nude beauty formed pirouetting patterns of dazzling perfection. For a timeless space he marvelled upon their kaleidoscopic resplendency, his consciousness merged within the coruscant mosaic of their dance. Their dance, the beauty of their dance . . . soul-wrenching wonder that staved off the shrill voices of pain, of terror that yammered upon the fringes of his awareness. An infinity of goddesses—or numberless images of a goddess—weaving through the glacial mists of throbbing color.

Now he understood that they were but infinite reflections of the one goddess—the goddess of beauty, shimmering upon all the mirrors of the cosmos. He desired to behold the true image of this beauty, and his spirit soared through the swirling patterns, in search of the one true image. Time elapsed. Like a mote of interstellar debris drawn by the compellent attraction of a dark star, he fell unerringly toward the central focus of the ceaseless shifting labyrinth.

At the heart of the vortex of pulsing color his quest was ended. Over the true image of beauty his awareness descended. He gazed upon the glowing porcelain of the goddess's perfect flesh, creamy majesty of unblemished form that radiated a warm luster of indescribable color. Her breasts were cones of floral delicacy, her hips dark with mystery, her limbs soft witchery as she pirouetted through the whirling dance. She saw him. The fierce welcome of her scarlet smile, the burning summons of her violet eyes invited him to share her dance.

The chords of needle-pain color roiled about them as they spun, wove shards of light into feather-mounds of song. She fell back upon the waving softness of fern patterns, opened to him her arms and red lips. As he drifted to her embrace, he marvelled endlessly over the radiant perfection of line, the living fire of her flesh, sorcerous porcelain of warmth and velvet.

Her smile changed, shadowed in pain . . . or cruelty. Her breasts heaved with the pulse of her heart, her chest shuddered from the exertion of her breath. Her creamy torso split apart along midline; the ribs sprang outward, like spreading carpels of a blossom, beckoned in the breeze of sound. Explosive color washed over her altered form; her slender, unjointed arms waved for him like filaments of some obscenely tempting orchid. The smile broadened, and an impossible length of curling scarlet tongue licked toward his throat. Vibrations of perfumed anguish engulfed him. In sudden terror he struggled against her embrace, buffeted the enfolding, smothering petals. Her claws tore at his face, the needle tongue stabbed for his throat as he seized her boneless neck in a stranglehold, fought desperately to keep from merging with the vampirish ecstasy of death . . .

The dream abruptly dissolved.

Blood trickling from the gouges of her nails, Opyros stared numbly at the limp form whose throat he gripped. Dully he released his fingers, one by one. Ceteol's mottled face flushed as breath whistled past her bruised lips. Her heart was strong beneath Opyros's palm, although she showed no sign yet of recovering consciousness. Vaguely relieved that he had not killed the girl, Opyros carelessly draped the bed robes over her still form and rose to find his clothing. The room shimmered through drug-mists of ghost image—from each whorl of the dark oak paneling leered a face—so that he rested a moment on the edge of the bed until his head cleared and his long legs felt stronger.

The temper of his present mistress was difficult to foresee. Best to leave before she awoke, the young nobleman reflected. The touch of his garments was strange to his fingers; after drawing pants and loose shirt over his bony frame, he despaired of his sandals and left the chamber barefoot. The evening was warm, though he was uncertain which evening it was. This new drug had left his mouth dry and foul, his mind a burned-over forest of half-consumed and heat-corroded shapes. For this, ale and diversion . . .

The rambling townhouse lay silent and empty as he padded through it. His servants—had he given them the night off? Too many gaps in his memory—perhaps he would remember later. Retrieving a folder of unbound parchment from the litter of his study, Opyros the poet stumbled from his manor and drifted through the shadows of Enseljos in search of Kane.

I

Poet in the Night

Greasy light oozed onto the damp pavement from the doorway of Stanchek's Tavern and cast puddles of smoky yellow through the tattered leather curtain. The colors still danced before his eyes, as Opyros stepped over dark pockmarks in the broken paving, uncertain about the faces which peered back at him from the pools of black water. It had rained sometime not long before, though the night above Enseljos's sprawling skyline was clear, as had been the autumn morning when he and Ceteol had dissolved a few grains of the new drug in a flagon of wine. Presumably this was the same day, since there was only a vague hint of hunger.

A snarl of challenge came from the black alley adjoining the tavern, and he heard the rasp of unseen steel. Swinging the folio up like a shield, Opyros groped for the knife at his belt. But a second shape stirred in the darkness and growled, "Forget him, Hef! Don't you recognize the mad poet?"

Opyros sidled past the alleyway, wondering whether he had been accosted by thieves or guards. Evidently this Hef was a stranger, since the poet made frequent visits to Stanchek's Tavern. No sign marked the murky doorway, nor had the place any name other than Stanchek's, after the limping ex-mercenary who owned it. But the tavern was well known to the sort who gathered there, for Stanchek's was a dive of evil reputation even in the brawling turmoil of Enseljos. The city guard did not patrol this, the oldest section of Enseljos; a monthly donation to its commander convinced him that it was an unwarranted risk of his men to send them into this iniquitous slum where truly no man of honest intentions would venture. Law-abiding folk had their inns and taverns, and the growing ranks of Halbros-Serrantho's soldiery—even his hot-tempered mercenaries—tended to frequent the less forbidding places of amusement: the Red Bear, the Hanging Bandit, the Hound and Leopard, the Bad Dog, or even the Yardarm. To Stanchek's gathered the night creatures of Enseljos's underworld, and others whose role in life was less evident but of similarly dubious achievement.

The folio snared a tattered fold as Opyros pushed through the grimy curtain, and he maintained his hold clumsily. Threescore pairs of eyes looked toward his rattling entry, considered him briefly, and returned to other matters. The poet padded down the low flight of worn stone steps that lapped like waves of poured honey in a crescent past the doorway to the room below. Once the townhouse of a wealthy merchant, Stanchek's displayed the sunken central room with high vaulted ceiling and horseshoe gallery of another age's architecture. Only in places across the floor could the original tiles be glimpsed, effaced and filthy, and ungainly pillars of mismatched construction shored up the sagging galleries. Doorways opened onto rooms from off the gallery, or led into cellars that ran like interconnected burrows beneath the tavern and surrounding buildings, blocked (supposedly) by rubble in back, where the main living quarters lay in toppled ruin. Business of a less open nature was conducted in these dim chambers, and although he believed he had visited them all, Opyros was not sorry to know that his search would not lead him into these warrens tonight.

Seated at a corner table opposite the entrance—but close by the gaping darkness of the downward-leading stairs—Opyros caught sight of Kane. Even to his mazed vision and in the uncertain light, there was no mistaking the massive, square-torsoed figure, or the coppery glimmer of Kane's hair and short beard. He was not alone. Beside him at the table lounged a thuggish trio of indeterminate origins. Two of them, whose hulking stature and dark features bore the similarity of kinship, were coaxing a private show from a tavern dancer; the third, whose thin frame seemed to carry only gristle and tight-stretched muscle, was intent upon the fifth man at the table. This latter, a sharp-faced outlander whose clothes bore the dust of long miles, was arguing earnestly with Kane.

Some sort of agreement was concluded as Opyros threaded his way to the back corner. Kane nodded to his lean companion, who produced a heavy purse and pushed it toward the traveller. The other loosened its drawstrings, released the furtive gleam of gold; then Kane's broad hand closed over the almoner, and with a cold smile he drew it back across the table. The outlander appeared satisfied and rose to his feet. Kane remained seated, gave terse instructions to his three companions. The lean man retrieved the purse and, flanked by the brawny pair, followed the outlander from the room.

Opyros exchanged nodded greetings as they passed, then dropped into the chair beside Kane. Abandoned by her patrons, the dancing girl glanced at the poet uneasily, seemed relieved that the newcomer returned her stare without interest, and departed in a brassy rustle of bell-hung silks. At Kane's wave, a husky serving girl trotted over. Thudding her crockery pitcher upon the table, she began to reach for the empty mugs. Kane shook his head as she stretched for those beside him and pointed to the mug used by the outlander. Leaving the others, she recovered this one, wiped the mouth of the stein on her greasy leather apron, filled it with dark ale from her pitcher, and pushed it toward the poet. Opyros gulped down the mug's bitter contents in the time it took for her to fill Kane's stein and had the girl pour another before she left them.

Kane's cold blue eyes studied the poet's scratched face, a sardonic grin breaking over his brutal features. "I rather expected you last night," he commented.

What happened to last night? "I've been trying the new drug," Opyros answered.

"And returned to tell the tale," observed Kane. "No mean feat, if Damatjyst blended the powder faithful to the formula I gave you." He lifted the folio onto the table; Opyros had carelessly leaned it against Kane's unbuckled sword. "Did you find the experience worth-while?"

"I think so," concluded Opyros. The ale seemed to hush the whining yammer at the threshold of his consciousness. "There was a great deal of powerful visual imagery to it; some flashes of inspiration that I jotted down. Some of it I think I can use, though I still find myself blocked on *Night Winds*." He fumbled through the loose sheets of the folio. "Have you . . . are you going to be too busy tonight?"

Kane absently scraped his nail across a flaking smear of brown which clung to the carven silver death's head of his sword pommel. "Nothing that my men can't attend to. It promises to be a dull night, unless you're interested in watching Eberhos gamble away ten lifetimes' earnings at dice. Damatjyst will find he has a pauper for First Assistant come morning."

"Then I'll read you some of this," invited Opyros. He frowned over a loose page, turning the parchment sheet to the best exposure in the murky light. "Oh, here's some more work on that *Gods in Darkness* fragment you tossed me:

In their castle beyond the night,
In their dungeon's evil light,
Gather the Gods while even fades,
And Darkness weaves with many shades . . ."

"I never wrote that," protested Kane.

"Ceteol did that," Opyros explained. "She has a keen mind for rhyme and meter."

"It rolls across the tongue well enough, but the rhyme has made it inaccurate to the substance of the poem. I thought we were agreed to strive for coherent imagery, without the interference of rhyme. Meter will be intrusive enough, if you translate. . . ."

"Just thought you'd be interested to hear how it could be done," Opyros broke in defensively. "I still maintain that a poem well sung is far more effective than a poem well read—and infinitely superior to merely reading the words to yourself. Poetry is an expression of beauty, and beauty is an emotional awareness which for total appreciation demands a total sensual participation and response from its audience. You're asocial, Kane; you treat imagery on an individual intellectual level—perhaps because your personal autism believes intellectual and emotional stimulation are inseparable. . . ."

"Vaul! You're in a profound mood tonight," Kane cut in sarcastically. "Are you certain of your insight, though? Drugs and ale will foster more prophecies and philosophies than a sober mind can hold together."

"That may be," Opyros countered, "but they sometimes open doorways to truths obscured by the clutter of ordered thought." He started to replace the parchment sheet, his expression injured.

Kane made an apologetic grimace. "Let's hear the rest of what you've done," he requested, and signed to a passing serving girl. His long fingers plucked the heavy pitcher from her cradling hip and placed it before the poet.

Opyros carefully refilled his stein before returning to the closely written lines. His voice calmer now, he began to read, moistening his throat now and again. Occasionally Kane interrupted to quarrel upon a point of syntax or such—until Opyros, wondering at the other's command of a language not his own, made marginal notations with a metal pen, which he dipped in slopped ale and rubbed against a chunk of ink.

The poet had long ago given up any effort to penetrate the shroud of mystery that enswathed Kane. Even so simple a matter as Kane's age defied certainty—physically he appeared not far past Opyros's thirty years, but this was deceptive, since Kane's experience ranged somewhat beyond this. The stranger was an enigma, and Opyros valued his friendship too highly to make indiscreet inquiries. He accepted the mystery, musing only privately over certain dark hints that whispered from the shadow of Kane's past.

Well over a year had passed since Opyros had first met him, wandering pensively through the forest-buried ruins of the Old City at dusk. Sensing a kindred spirit despite the other's forbidding appearance, Opyros had called out to him from his favorite perch alongside a crumbling fountain. The stranger returned his greeting in cultured tones of indefinable accent, and for the first time Opyros felt the murderous chill of Kane's blue eyes. Casual remarks had revealed as astonishing knowledge of the Old City on the stranger's part, and Opyros was surprised when this man nonchalantly spoke upon various points of mystery and arcane lore surrounding the ruins of which the poet was only vaguely aware, although his study of such things was an avid one. Opyros made some speculative observations on the reasons for the abandonment of the Old City over two centuries ago, and Kane had laughed strangely. Less piqued than curious, the poet sought to draw the other out, but Kane had made only evasive replies to his questions until Opyros introduced himself.

Kane immediately expressed interest in the poet's work and, losing some of his brooding reserve, invited him to further their acquaintance across a tavern table. Chance meeting developed into friendship, and Opyros soon became even more familiar with the dark alleys and hidden ways of Enseljos as he regularly sought out Kane's company. The exact nature of Kane's business in the northern city Opyros cared not to discover, although he sensed it was a more subtle game than the various underworld activities he knew Kane to have assumed control over. It was only another mystery surrounding the stranger—like his unexpected depth of learning, his easy familiarity with the writings of poets and sages of strange lands and other ages. Kane's critical abilities Opyros found to be sound and perceptive, so that he frequently brought fragments of his own work to read to the other, finding worthwhile the arguments and tangled, far-reaching discussions that usually lasted from darkness to light.

It was a rare friendship for Opyros, and he guessed such was the case with Kane as well. The poet was an outcast among the aristocracy of Enseljos to which he was born, nor did he care for their shallow company. Although his work was becoming widely known across the Northern Continent, and the genius of his verses was unquestioned, the macabre direction of his interests had earned Opyros a shadowed reputation among the intellectuals and dilettantes of his audience. Thus literary acclaim escaped him—although notoriety did not—and Opyros was loved no better by those with pretensions of culture than by those whose pride was their lineage and wealth. He knew no kinship with the lower classes of society, and they in turn believed him mad. Society's rejection of the poet and his work, while it left him bitter, did not raise a barrier to his writing. As final heir to his family's estates and fortune, he was able to ignore this alienation and to pursue the untravelled paths along which his genius led him. It often occurred to Opyros that he was as much an outlaw as Kane and the hard-eyed creatures who passed about them.

"Anything new on *Night Winds*?" asked Kane, once Opyros had finished reading from the parchment.

His companioin frowned. "Oh, I've written a few more lines—written and rewritten a dozen times. Still can't bring it around to what I want."

Kane grunted sympathetically. Opyros had been struggling with *Night Winds* for months now, overtaxing himself to create what he intended to be his masterpiece, a perfect statement of his conception of art. As usually happens with any attempt toward a consciously conceived masterwork, the zeal for perfection overwhelmed the artist's ability to create. Opyros had made countless false starts, had worked himself into nervous exhaustion, spent days obsessed with the preciseness, the imagery of a single line of verse, and *Night Winds* had advanced little beyond the initial torrent of inspiration which had burst from a fevered dream. Thinking some diversion might relax the poet after this intense concentration, Kane suggested some fragments of another poem for him to develop. Opyros dutifully worked on *Gods in Darkness* for Kane, along with a number of his own projects, but *Night Winds* continued to loom over his imagination.

"Well, let's hear some of it," Kane prompted.

Opyros ran a nervous hand through his sandy hair and down his face, absently noted the stubble starting from his jaw where the goatee did not extend. *What day was this?* Again he filled his stein; the ale was soothing the shrieking afterimages in his mind. Without preamble —somewhat defiantly—he seized another smudged and scribbled sheet and read:

At night when sleep will not come—
And darkness hangs in thick, smothering folds,
To throttle my breath, crush the heart in my breast,
And squats on my belly like a hot, bloated succubus;
When I lie burning in restless, sick pain,
Listening to the rush of my pulse, the hammer of my
  heart,
And sense without caring that this is the last hour—
Night winds come.

Then let the night winds come to me—
Pass through a clear window, blow out the sick flame,
Touch cold breath to this fever-burnt flesh,
Caress with chill kisses this fever-seared mind,
Take up my poisoned soul in your restoring embrace,
Bear me off to strange lands, show me those unseen
  sights
Along untrod paths—you and the stars know their
  secrets—
Though death be your destination, I'll not beg to
  linger—
When night winds come.

Then let the night winds take me—
Lift my crippled spirit on your vast black wings,
And I'll soar with you through the shadow;
Whisper softly in my desolate thoughts,
And I'll learn the wisdom of the dark;
Brush your fingers across my blinded eyes,
And I'll see the secret world of night;
And with you I'll explore those lost and hidden
  places—
Where only night winds come.

(Opyros read on haltingly, as the poem became more fragmented—little more than disjointed passages of description. His half-formed verses told of sand drifting over a desert tomb and why it lay empty, of wind in a forest where a goddess lay dying, of broken battlements and the pale beauty who walked them, of black surf on fanged cliffs and the shadows that lurked there, of mountains of eternal ice where an elder race dreamed . . .)

He finished with a pained grimace. Angrily he slapped the folio together, swept up his mug and drained it in a huge gulp that shuddered down his long throat. "Well."

Kane's expression was noncommittal. "I think you're getting it together—what there is of it, I like. The images you propose are more compelling this time—the atmosphere is beginning to project, almost without awareness of the mounting tension. Structually it seems rough yet, though the mood begins to impress me as . . ."

"Forced!" Opyros snorted. "Artificial and forced! It's still a first draft, though I've lain sleepless over it for months now. My imagery is either overpowering or too vague. I can't seem to project the vitality, the *reality*, of the mood!"

"It's starting to come across," Kane protested. "The atmosphere will improve as the work progresses, I think. Hell, put some of these fragments together for once, and give it some sort of conclusion, however indecisive it sounds at first. Work off the rough edges, and then judge what needs to be done with it—at least you'll have something concrete to grapple with. I think you're already close to writing as brilliant a work as any you've completed."

Opyros made a scornful noise in his mug. "Yeah, as brilliant as anything I've done—as imperfect, you mean! Damn it, Kane, for once I'd like to feel I'd written something that was *perfect!* No, don't start on one of those creaky philosophical discussions upon the nonexistence of true perfection. I mean, I'd hope at least once to be able to create a poem that I myself could call perfect—to hell with any other point of reference! There isn't a single thing I've done that I'm totally satisfied with. All of it represents a compromise between what I'm able to create and what I want to create. I know when a verse isn't exactly right, but, damn it, I can't understand how to improve it beyond a certain point!"

"And what is perfection to your mind?" queried Kane sardonically, thinking that this conversation in one form or another had dried their throats on more nights than this.

"A perfect poem," declared the other without faltering, "is one which completely involves its audience in the totality of the poem. It should be a total sensory and emotional projection of the artist's mind into the mind of the listener. He should identify fully with the perspective, the reality of the poem—share the thoughts, sense the atmosphere, see the visions, unite with the mood. Any fool clever with words can create a poem that any fool can listen to; a good poet can create a poem so that a sensitive mind can share and be stirred by his thoughts. . . . But to create a poem that can totally draw any dull imagination into its spell—that, Kane, is perfect art, and *that* is the creation of true genius!"

"An intriguing theory of art," Kane commented after a slight pause. "But I think you'll destroy yourself emotionally if you keep up this quest for an unobtainable perfection. I have a high regard for your talents, Opyros, but it seems to me the genius you've proposed transcends human limitations."

"Don't tell me Kane is suddenly preaching that pious doctrine of man's inevitable failure whenever he dares challenge those heights to which only gods may aspire!" sneered Opyros—and immediately regretted his words.

Kane's baleful eyes held him in cold speculation for a moment, wondering how much of this was a chance taunt. "That wasn't what I said, or what I meant, as you must know," he returned with icy calm. "More bluntly, can you realistically consider your own 'genius' equal to this goal?"

Opyros stared at his clenched hands. "I don't know," he confessed, wishing to escape Kane's gaze. "That's what tortures me! Technically I know how to do it—rhyme, meter, the words, the notes. I understand how the material should be woven . . . only I still can't grasp the substance! I need inspiration—a flash of insight—something that will lift my imagination from where it's mired down in commonplace ideas. What use to waste my creativity in turning out another poem like all the rest—the same tired images, the same dull emotions. There has to be some new vitality to my poem—I must create it from ideas and images that are unique, not simply the rewritten thoughts of past artists."

He muttered fitfully under his breath and reached again for the pitcher. Surprisingly, someone had emptied it already.

II

The Muse of Dream

Thoughtfully Kane considered the slouched figure of his friend. Unbidden, a serving girl replaced the pitcher with a brimming one. Deciding to leave Opyros with his mood for the moment, Kane was reaching to refill his half-emptied mug when he noticed someone moving toward them.

The thickset figure of Eberhos, First Assistant to Damatjyst the alchemist, drew to a nervous halt across the table from him. His sweaty face showed lines of strain, and his deep-set eyes darted about uneasily, sensing that others across the crowded room were watching his course with interest. Though the other was not a frequent visitor to Stanchek's, Kane knew Eberhos through his dealings with Damatjyst. Leaning back in his chair, Kane waited for the man to speak.

"I've come to ask a favor of you, Kane," Eberhos began, licking his pale lips. "A favor that will be repaid in double this same night!"

"I think you want to borrow money," Kane returned dryly.

The alchemist's assistant wiped his hands across his beefy thighs. The wool of his trousers was adorned with bits of strange powders and stains from his work at his master's forges. "I do," he admitted, "but you might think of it more as an investment. The dice go against me for a moment, and I've temporarily lost all my holdings. A few more tosses, and my luck will change. However, these bastards will give me no credit."

"Nor do I blame them. You've lost ten times the year's earnings of a merchant prince. Why accept a note from a pauper—an unlucky one, at that? Instead of throwing away more good coin, why not consider how to explain matters to the rightful owner of this gold you've gambled away—since I doubt it came from your savings."

Eberhos blanched. "I'm no thief," he growled.

"Well, you're certainly no gambler."

Ignoring Kane's obvious dismissal, Eberhos dropped into the seat opposite him and leaned forward confidentially. "Listen, Kane! I'm only telling you this because there's no one else I can look to to back me in a game at these stakes. I've planned for tonight—this isn't a sudden spree. I've read the stars carefully for weeks, ever since I foresaw this conjunction—yes, and I've made augury by all the signs Damatjyst has taught me. The answer is always the same—tonight is the night that fortune obeys me! In any game of chance, I cannot lose!"

"And now we know you're no astrologer," Kane commented cruelly. He had never cared for Damatjyst's assistant. The man was obsequious and fawning with his master, a sullen bully toward his inferiors; Kane discerned the grasping, malignant spirit that lay beneath his ingratiating facade.

Desperation squeezed the anger from the other's face. "Scoff all you want—I admit fortune hasn't seemed to favor me since coming into Stanchek's. But this isn't my first stop tonight. You think I begged or stole the money I lost here? Well, that's only one of your mistakes. I entered the Hound and Leopard this evening with ten gold sarmkes and some silver, hoarded from the pittance Damatjyst pays me. Once I was down to just the silver, but I stayed with it, and when I left, the others were broke and I had nearly a hundred sarmkes in gold. At the Yardarm it was the same; they thought to clean me out at one point, but soon no one would play against me, and I had over half a thousand in gold and silver. So I came to where I might play for higher stakes, and once more I seem to be finished. But lend me what I need now, Kane, and I'll need two slaves to carry away my winnings. Let me have fifty sarmkes now, and I'll return a hundred this same night."

Kane laughed scornfully in reply.

Desperately Eberhos looked toward Opyros, who stared hypnotically at something in his stein. The poet had wealth, but he never carried more than a few coins on his person. Seeing only dismissal, the alchemist's assistant made a final play. "What if I offer collateral?"

"What do you have against fifty sarmkes?" asked Kane without interest.

With unsteady fingers Eberhos removed a packet from a scrip at his belt. Wordlessly he passed it to Kane.

His manner one of skeptical curiosity, Kane unwrapped the soft leather. A gleaming flash of light rolled darkly upon his broad palm. Kane's eyes narrowed for an instant, then widened.

"The dark muse," he breathed in surprise.

"What?" asked Opyros, coming awake. He craned his neck.

Held in Kane's hand lay the figurine of a nude girl, carven of black onyx and in length about five inches. The stone was flawless, the artistry exquisite. She lay supine, in an attitude of repose, though awake. Her head rested upon her left hand and a mass of flowing tresses; the other arm was lifted in a beckoning gesture; the legs were flexed and slightly apart. The eyes were compelling, and her lips were open in a secret smile—a suggestion of mystery to the obvious invitation. For there was a note of cruelty about the face that underlay the smiling promise, so that another might wonder to what pleasures she summoned him. The shifting light licked soft caresses upon the aristocratic features, rounded breasts, slim hips, and long limbs. She looked to be a goddess, frozen in ebon miniature.

"You know it, then," grinned Eberhos nervously.

"It's Klinure, the muse of dream, whom some call the dark muse," Kane stated. "More specifically, the simulacrum of Klinure, from a set of the sixteen muses sculpted centuries ago by the mage Amderin. His workmanship is unmistakable, and the carvings are legendary, although most of them are believed lost. I had heard rumor that one or more were held by Damatjyst . . . but then you're no thief."

Eberhos bit his lip. "Its absence won't be noticed at

once. I only slipped it from its case because I thought this situation might arise. The figurine is priceless, you know that. Will you lend me one hundred sarmkes against it? I'll return you twice that in an hour."

Kane shrugged his heavy shoulders. "I have no reason to cross the threshold of dream, nor do I care to pile up stolen *objets d'art* at the moment."

"Advance him the money, Kane," interceded Opyros with sudden interest. "I'll cover it if he loses."

"Make it fifty, then," said Kane, after a surprised glance at the poet. "That way you'll feel only half the regret when you come to your senses."

Eberhos squirmed in protest, but kept silent fearing that his patron would change his mind. Ten heavy gold coins slid across the table, streaking through the spilled ale. The alchemist scooped them up and hastened back to his game.

"Tell me about her, Kane," demanded Opyros. "When you said, 'cross the threshold of dream,' I seemed to remember something. What is the figurine's history?"

Kane passed the onyx carving to the poet and adjusted the fastenings of his almoner. "Well, Amderin was one of the more brilliant sorcerers of Carsultyal's declining years, and a sculptor of tremendous talent as well. He wished to excel in every aspect of human potentiality, so he created simulacra of the sixteen muses. With them he could evoke the muse appropriate to any endeavor his interests might direct. He might well have become the first truly universal genius."

"Why didn't he?"

"He died not long after the project was completed."

"Suicide?"

Kane glanced at him sharply. "Strange guess. No, though his death was an inexplicable one. His body was found across his bed—crushed and broken as if he had fallen from a very great height. Afterward the set of carvings passed through many hands, became scattered, so that today only a few are known to exist."

"And this is Klinure," murmured Opyros, turning the statuette all about with reverent touch. "The muse of dream."

"The dark muse," Kane went on. "Carved from

onyx, black as the starless night of sleep, the night she dwells within, the night from which she calls. She lives in the shadow of unfinished dreams—the dreams from which we awaken and never return to. Their ghosts wait forever in limbo, incomplete visions that man will never realize."

"Her attitude is one of beckoning."

"She invites you to cross the portals of dream."

"Her face has a strange smile."

"She suggests the secret wisdom that lies hidden within the veil of dream."

"I see mockery, too."

"For the false wisdom and inchoate images that delude the dreamer as truth."

"There is cruelty in her eyes."

Kane laughed bitterly. "Cruelty? Yes—for much of dream is nightmare. Join her in her embrace, and instead of the wonders she seems to promise, the dark muse may draw you into some fathomless vortex of black terror."

He glanced toward the doorway. Slipping past the smoky entrance came the three men who had been with him earlier. Of the outlander there was no sign. Casually they crossed the crowded floor to the corner table, where they dropped into chairs and became busy with the ale pitcher. Opyros, who had met them often before, exchanged mumbled greetings.

"Any problems, Levardos?" asked Kane.

His cadaverous lieutenant shook his head. "No trouble. Want to see it?"

"Not right now. Stanchek know it's here?"

"Yeah. Brought it through the back. He looked it over. Seems satisfied with the deal."

Kane nodded and left the subject.

His face pensive, Opyros continued to examine the onyx figurine. Webbre and Haigan, half-brothers from some anonymous mountain settlement, leaned forward curiously to see the object. It struck a chord in their memories, and Webbre, the younger of the two, wandered off down the stairs to reclaim the dancing girl.

Presently he reappeared with the girl in tow, her face flushed and costume disarrayed. The knuckles of his right hand were raw, and when he displayed his fist to Haigan, they broke into laughter. Uneasily the girl protested she could not dance without music,. at which the grinning brothers produced panpipes and began to blow a discordant melody. Sighing helplessly, the dark-haired girl danced to the near tuneless notes.

Opyros tried to speak through the discord, and Kane gestured for the two to move away. Without pausing in there tune, Webbre and Haigan arose and stomped into the corner, where they stood about the entrapped dancing girl and continued their fierce piping. Levardos shook his head and remained seated, his expression as usual one of aloof watchfulness.

Opyros hunched forward. "I said, did Amderin's secret die with him?"

"Secret?"

"The evocation of the muses through their simulacra."

"Oh, that. No, it didn't. Actually the evocation is a simple enough spell. Amderin's genius lay in the creation of the simulacra; with them any competent student of the occult can perform the evocation."

"Do you know the spell?" asked the poet in a strained voice.

Pressing his lips together thoughtfully, Kane stared at his friend, wondering how much he had guessed. "I do," he stated.

Opyros remained silent for a long pause. The cacophonic piping wailed on, punctuated by chattering bells and the girl's hoarse breathing. The noise of the tavern seemed driven back by an unseen wall; the sharp exclamations from the dice table were drowned and distant.

"If I could cross the threshold of dream," intoned Opyros in a low voice, "if I could witness the birth of a dream, follow the ghosts of dreams from whose spell the awakened mind of the dreamer was torn . . . By the Seven Eyes of Lord Thro'ellet, Kane! Can you imagine the torrent of inspiration that would engulf my soul!"

"And likely annihilate your soul!" warned Kane grimly. "Assuming your spirit wasn't blasted instantly by its plunge into a world of free-form thought and prechaotic images, what if Klinure should lead you into the realm of nightmare? What if instead of some long-dead artist's never-finished vision of unearthly beauty, you found yourself trapped in an unhallowed nightmare from which some fever-poisoned madman awoke shrieking? The dark muse cares not whether her dreams portray ethereal beauty or mindless horror."

The poet formed an easy smile. "If I wanted to write poems on sunshine and flowers and love, this might worry me. But you know my thoughts well enough. I'll weave my verses for the night, sing of the dark things that soar through nameless abysses—unfold the poetry of the macabre, while others prattle about little things. Hell, Kane, we've talked many a night away on these matters, and found our minds too close together even to argue, only to second the words of one another. True beauty lies in the dark side of life—in death, in the uncanny—in the grandeur of the unknown. The pure awareness of beauty is as overwhelming an emotion as blind fear; to feel inexpressible love is as soul-wrenching a sensation as to know relentless terror. When fired to the ultimate blaze, the finest emotions become one intolerable flame, and ecstasy and agony are inseparable.

"I'm blocked on *Night Winds* because I can't enter this dark world, can't get close enough to this point of fusion to understand the emotions I'm trying to recreate. I've looked everywhere for inspiration—read through dull volumes, chased after tepid vices, haunted the desolate places, dabbled in strange drugs. . . . And I've learned nothing. If I can induce Klinure to give me the inspiration of lost dreams, I'll risk any nightmare—no, I'll welcome them—if I find the creative energy I need to create a perfect poem!"

Kane frowned, too similar of spirit to the other to dissuade him further, but uneasy nonetheless. "It's your decision, of course. But make certain you understand the risks which await you beyond the threshold of dream. You'll not be asleep, but in Klinure's embrace, so that you'll not awaken from those nightmares which drove their dreamers into screaming wakefulness. There are many dreams of falling, for example, from which one awakens before ending his plummet. . . ."

Opyros thought for a moment. "Vaul!" he swore in understanding. "Then you think Amderin . . . ?"

"It's a risk—only one among uncounted others whose nature we can't begin to conceive."

A clamour had arisen across the tavern, and the huddle about the dice table suddenly began to break up. Many voices were raised at once—cries of anger, protest, disbelief, congratulations. As the milling figures drifted away, the thickset figure of Eberhos could be seen. He was followed across the floor by a blond Waldann mercenary, whose broad shoulder sagged under the burden of the bulging saddlebags slung across it.

Eberhos's flushed face made his grin seem all the broader. "I've won it all!" he announced. "No man has gold or spirit enough to play against me further!" With an arrogant gesture he poured a handful of gold coins upon the table. "There's a hundred in payment as I promised. You'd have a hundred more, had you been less quick to judge another man a fool. The carving now, please."

The piping stopped. Kane's cold eyes met Eberhos's gaze, and his jubilant sneer retreated. Not looking at the gold, Kane slid it back to the alchemist's assistant.

"You owe me no debt," he explained casually. "I've decided to keep the figurine. Its price of fifty sarmkes has been paid."

A shadow of worry crept over Eberhos's victory-lit face. "I didn't sell it, Kane—it was collateral. Now I've met my side of the bargain as stated. There's a hundred sarmkes, and now I need that carving." He made a motion to reach for the onyx figurine where it lay before Opyros.

"I wouldn't," advised Kane.

Eberhos flexed his fingers in nervous anger. He did not reach out, however. "I have to get it back before Damatjyst notices that it's been taken," he explained.

"Well, just tell your master what you would have had to tell him if you'd lost the money I gave you," Kane offered without sympathy. "Or now that you're wealthy, why not see if one of the southern cities needs another alchemist."

"All right, I'll give you two hundred for it."

Kane shook his head, a mirthless smile starting on his lips.

"Two hundred fifty—no more!"

"But earlier tonight you admitted the carving was priceless."

"Name your price, damn you! I don't dare risk Damatjyst's anger."

"You'll find my anger no better risk," retorted Kane.

Rage made the veins bulge along his thick neck, and Eberhos moved his hand closer to his sword hilt. Behind him, his Waldann bodyguard shifted the gold-laden saddlebags uneasily.

Webbre and Haigan had nonchalantly strolled over to either side of Kane; their brutal faces sneered at the alchemist. His expression one of detached interest, Levardos had, unnoticed, drawn back his chair. A quick glance around the tavern disclosed others of Kane's men had laid hands on their weapons and were slowly approaching. The squat figure of Stanchek could be seen muttering instructions to his henchmen, who moved unhurriedly to cover the door.

Kane took the onyx carving from the table and began to roll it on his palm; there was mockery in his smile, and death grinned from his eyes.

And Eberhos knew that death hovered close.

"Hell, what do I care about Damatjyst's wrath," he laughed suddenly. It sounded like a death rattle. "I've learned all that old miser can teach me, and I've gold enough to make my life what I will. Keep the damned carving if it pleases you, Kane—if Damatjyst wants it, he can go look for it. I'm going to find another tavern and some rich fools to play against me."

With slippery fingers he retrieved the gold coins, smiled servilely, and made for the door. His worried bodyguard clung to his back like a shadow, and the pair disappeared through the tattered curtain.

Webbre and Haigan laughed and hooted, and hugged the frightened dancing girl between them. Opyros took the carving from Kane and gazed upon it with worshipful eyes. Levardos permitted himself a thin smile.

Kane caught Stanchek's quizzical gestures and shook his head with a frown. "His luck held out," he remarked at Levardos's unspoken question. "Several thousand in gold, one man to guard him, and the bastard left here alive—Stanchek thought I was going to take care of it."

"We can still find him," offered his lieutenant, starting to rise.

"Don't count on it," Kane advised. "Still, I've made a deadly enemy, and when I had the chance, I let him live. Levardos, have you ever known me to be that careless?"

"No," admitted the other, and slipped his dirk back into the sheath hidden beneath a bloused sleeve.

III

In the Hour Before Dawn

Kane continued to stare moodily toward the curtained doorway. It occurred to Opyros that his fascination for the black figurine might have thrown Kane into unforeseen difficulty. After all, Kane did have frequent dealings with the alchemist, and Damatjyst was almost certain to learn into whose hands his carving had fallen.

"Don't worry about Eberhos," Kane scoffed, when the poet voiced his concern. "Unless he has even less brains than I give him, he'll be far from Enseljos before another night. His master will surely blame him for the theft, and Damatjyst is most exacting in the matter of debts.

"More to the point, now that it's yours, what do you mean to do with the simulacrum?"

But the poet had already made his decision. "As I've said, I hope to summon Klinure—to follow her into the secret realm of dream. I'd be grateful if you'll show me the spell, since your knowledge of these things seems to lie far deeper than you choose to reveal. But if you're opposed, then I'll look elsewhere for the spell of evocation."

"It would take little enough effort to discover," said Kane. "No, if you're certain in your mind, I'll do what you want. But there *is* an unknown degree of danger, and I think you may want to wait until your thoughts are somewhat clearer than tonight before you get into this too deep."

"Well, I'm going to try it," Opyros asserted. He refilled his stein with painstaking attention. "Though I think I will wait for my head to clear; I'll want my thoughts unclouded for this venture. Shall we try it tomorrow?"

"Tomorrow night, if you wish," Kane agreed. "Night is the realm of Klinure. I'll see to the arrangements."

"Where? Will my study do?"

Kane shook his head. "I think another place would be better. Atmosphere is extremely important, and we need solitude—someplace free of distractions and conflicting aurae. Dreams are influenced by the dreamer's surroundings, and the *genius loci* of Enseljos is not conducive to the tone of dream you seek. I think the Old City is evocative of the mood you desire, and one of its abandoned temples should retain sufficient occult magnetism to facilitate communion with the dark muse."

"The temple of Vaul yet stands," Opyros suggested.

"A warrior god of somewhat cold and prosaic nature," argued Kane. "I was thinking of the temple of Shenan. The moon goddess should favor this venture."

"I didn't know her cult ever reached this far north. Where is her temple?" *How can he say these things so casually!*

"I'll show you," the other promised, and went on to speak guardedly of Shenan's worship in the days of the Old City.

They talked on into the night, Levardos leaving them at one point to attend to some errand. When he returned to draw Kane aside for low conversation, Opyros discovered himself yawning. Innumerable mugs of ale had at last dulled his drug-tortured nerves, driven the ghost voices and afterimages from his mind, As a matter of fact, Opyros decided, it was quite probable he was drunk.

"Well, I think I'll wander back and get some rest," he announced, smothering a belch. "Or is that backwards—should I concentrate on staying awake maybe, so I can sleep tomorrow night?"

"No, get some rest," Kane told him. "If we succeed with the evocation, there'll be no need to lie asleep. Klinure herself will lead you beyond the gates of dream."

"Well then, till tomorrow evening," drawled the poet, fumbling to fasten the folio. The onxy figurine he had already restored to its wrappings and secured at his belt.

"Wait. I'll accompany you," Kane offered. He signed

for his men to follow. "Should by chance you run into Eberhos, you might find the greasy tub of guts ungrateful for the stake you gave him tonight."

It could not be far from dawn, Kane noted as they left Stanchek's. The skies had not grayed perceptibly, but the stars were beginning to dim. It was cold, very quiet. Crisp night air was stunning to inhale after the close, smoky atmosphere of the tavern. Few were abroad; it was an hour of the night when even those who disdained sleep went about their business within doors.

Certainly it was not the time of day Kane might expect a beggar to accost him. They heard her sobbing, wail through the darkness, and shortly came the shuffling sound of her step. Then through the island of a rare streetlight they saw her approach, drawn by the flame of the torch Haigan carried.

"Please, kind gentlemen, please, can you spare a coin for a poor mother? A coin for a poor mother and her child!" She was not old, though her sordid rags and haggard face made her appear twice her years. A baby, so enswathed in rags as to seem no more than a shapeless bundle, nursed at her breast, his face buried by her shawl.

Haigan moved to shove her away, but not liking the mad glare of her eyes, he turned to let her pass.

"Kane! Is it truly Milord Kane!" she moaned, pressing nearer to him. "Ah, Kane, you'll spare a coin to help this poor mother and her sickly babe? He has food, but I've none, and soon my babe must seek his food elsewhere, unless this poor mother has coin to buy bread and meat."

Kane thought her face familiar, though too pale and drawn to place the memory. "Why do you beg at the most desolate hour of night?" he murmured, digging his fingers into his almoner.

"I cannot mingle with the crowds by day. They drive me from the streets when honest folk see me," she whined. "The guard takes no pity on a poor mother and her son." There was a heavy stench about her, a foulness less squalid than charnel.

Though his fingers touched smaller coins, a whim moved Kane to place a gold sarmkas in the woman's emaciated hand. It would buy food and shelter for several months.

"May Lord Thro'ellet spread his wings to guard you, Kane!" she blessed him, clutching the coin as if to crush it. She pressed closer; Kane saw the baby's face and knew the reason for her pallor.

Her voice lowered. "As you pass the corner, there are eight men who wait in an alley. Two have crossbows. They speak of Kane."

Swiftly she slipped past them, crooning to her babe. She must have shifted him to her other breast, for he gave a brief cry—more a snarl than whimper. Kane heard a troubled fluttering noise, suggestive of the flap of leathery wings. Then the only sound was the mother's crooning, fading into the night.

"Strange," remarked Opyros. "She blessed you in the name of a demon."

"She spoke of an ambush!" said Levardos, who had stood close enough to overhear. "Should we get more men, or take another street? Thoem's horns! It's that bastard Eberhos—he'd know to waylay us on the street that leads to Opyros's manor!"

"So I was thinking," growled Kane. "But if it isn't Eberhos, I want to know who it is that dares this! No, we won't waste time returning for more men—if they've seen our torch, they'll grow suspicious and change position. Since we know where they're waiting, the trap can be reversed."

"They outnumber us, and they've got crossbows," pointed out Webbre.

"I don't pay you just to hear you blow on those pipes," Kane returned.

Haigan threw an arm over his brother's shoulders. "Now, don't you worry, little brother. I'll save a little one for you."

Webbre grinned and pushed him away. "Careful with that damn torch."

"Keep your voices down!" Kane snarled. "Let's not pause any longer, or they might start wondering. I'll circle around and take care of the crossbows. Meanwhile, walk slowly toward the corner with the torch, so they can see the light coming. Stop before you get there—Opyros, give a yell that you dropped the carving, and the rest go back with the light and make a show of looking for it. That should give me time to reach the alley from the far side. Come fast when I yell."

Seeing they understood, Kane slipped away into the night, loping as fast as he dared without making noise.

"He sees in the dark like a cat," muttered Levardos as he vanished into the deep shadow.

Enseljos was not laid out according to any orderly pattern, but its winding avenues did intersect with equally haphazard cross streets, and islands of property lay between. This particular segment was given over to shops and small dwellings—often combined—with a center courtyard. The alley where the attackers lurked gave access to this courtyard—a squalid wilderness of refuse heaps, small vegetable plots, and animal pens.

Rapidly Kane picked his way around the block of buildings. His course seemed reckless, but his senses were keenly alert for any sign of danger. He kept to the obscurity of the outward-projecting walls, where not even the dim luminance of the stars could reach, moving swiftly with no more sound than a shadow. His was the greatest risk, but Kane cared not to trust this job to any of his men. The silent snarl of a stalking predator touched Kane's lips, and anger stirred a blue flame in his killer's eyes.

Abruptly he halted before a locked door. This building, he recalled, had stood vacant for some months. A heavy padlock secured the door, placed there more to keep out squatters than thieves, since the building contained little of value. For one of Kane's massive strength, it would take little effort to force the door—tear the lock from its brackets—but there would be noise, and the city lay in silence. From his boot Kane produced a thin metal pick; in a moment the lock fell open. Cautiously he pushed open the door and let himself into the empty shop. Silence and dust and soft scurryings were all that greeted him.

With stealthy stride, Kane passed through the empty rooms and into the storeroom at the rear. Another door opened onto the courtyard. A heavy wooden bar was jammed in place, so that he had to twist it free before drawing it clear. Its creaking complaint sounded like an explosion in the predawn stillness, but Kane doubted if it carried to those in the alley. Thinking about the crossbows, he wiped spit over the hinges, then inched the door open—soundlessly—far enough to glide through.

No unseen shafts streaked toward him. Thankful for the jumbled litter of the courtyard, Kane stole past the doorway and dropped low against the ground. So far as he could discern, no enemy lurked within the square. Taking advantage of the spotty cover, he crossed the intervening ground, moving with unerring speed despite the darkness and the obstacle-strewn yard.

At the mouth of the alley his caution doubled. Dimly he could see the figures crouched at the far end, not more than sixty feet from him. At least a couple were turned in his direction, but they had not observed his stealthy approach. Kane's unnatural night vision enabled him to make out the two men who waited with crossbows cocked. Their attention was fixed on the approach of his men, whose voices came through the night—else they might have sensed the death that stole upon them from behind.

Kane stepped into the alley. From either boot he drew a knife—two flat blades, balanced for throwing. His left arm moved with the blurring speed of a striking cobra; in almost the same instant his right arm uncoiled with the same lethal precision.

To the lurking assailants, it was as if a murderous phantom had risen in their midst. Dull impacts and frightened death howls marked the flight of the knives as the two crossbowmen staggered under the agony that pierced their backs, stumbled into the street to die. Released by the spasm of their fingers, the iron-fanged bolts skittered a trail of sparks across the darkened pavement.

With a feral yell, Kane tore out his sword with his left hand and leaped into the alley. His opponents had waited in darkness; only dimly could they glimpse the looming death that burst upon them. Steel flashed and clangoured. Another of the lurkers was hurled aside with a mangled chest, never knowing his killer's face.

Then someone flung open a dark lantern, hidden behind some rubble. In the thick darkness, its glare was dazzling. In that instant the five startled assassins saw that only one man stood against them—and in the heartbeat it took for them to realize who their enemy was, Kane's blade snaked toward the throat of another opponent, and then there were only four.

Bringing up their blades, the four rushed upon him. The first to meet him lost his sword and his arm with it; he fled screaming into the night, a spattered trail marking his flight. Then Kane's blade was engaged by a more skillful swordsman than his fellows, so that Kane fought with furious speed to keep the other two from striking past his guard. Only the long knife he wielded with his right arm turned back their desperate thrusts.

But in a matter of seconds, his men had gained the alley. A lethal tide of steel, they surged into the melee. Levardos quickly dispatched one of the would-be ambushers as Kane beat aside the swordsman's stubborn guard to thrust his heavy blade through the man's heart. The remaining assailant fled into the courtyard, Webbre and Haigan close behind. A clamour of overturned litter, howl of agony, and the brothers returned looking satisfied.

"I don't suppose you took him alive so I could question him," panted Kane.

The brothers each one pointed to the other, claiming he had struck the death blow, then fell into a fit of laughter.

"Never mind, Kane," announced Levardos, holding the torch over an upturned face. It was the last man Kane had killed. "This was that Waldann bodyguard Eberhos had with him at Stanchek's."

Kane grunted. "The puke-blooded whoreson used some of his gold to hire these sewer rats to waylay us. Must have guessed Opyros wouldn't go back alone. By Thoem, this won't be the last of our quarrel!"

IV

Across the Threshold of Dream

Dusk was overtaking them as they neared the Old City.

Next to Opyros rode Ceteol; a high collar masked her bruised throat. Why she came, Opyros was at a loss to decide. She had leaped at him with harsh curses on his return to the manor, clawed and fought until he pinned her in a drunken embrace and unfolded the night's story, after which he could not dissuade her from accompanying them to the Old City. He suggested—at least hoped—that her professed desire to see him destroyed by his unnatural delvings was not her true motive.

Kane was in a black mood; he had driven his men in search of Eberhos since before dawn, but no trace of the alchemist had been found. In addition to Levardos, Webbre, and Haigan, Kane had brought with him the new man, Hef, and a hawk-nosed thug named Boulus. Whether Eberhos would make another attempt to recover the carving—and it seemed likely he had fled the city—Kane could not guess. He rather hoped the alchemist would be so rash.

Fired with the spirit of the venture, Opyros was in a voluble mood, and eventually he succeeded in stirring Kane from his choler. Kane declined from further argument over the poet's design, and as the other spoke of his hopes for the evocation, of his eagerness to explore the unknown wonders of dream, he found himself sharing Opyros's enthusiasm. *To unlock the gates of dream . . .* Kane, too, sensed deep fascination for such an exploration. True, there were risks,. unknown risks—but what great adventure had ever been free of danger? In fact, by definition, how could there be adventure without danger? Security equals boredom equals stagnation equals death. Kane listened and nodded, added thoughts of his own, so that by the time they entered the forest-buried walls of the Old City, Kane was contemplating the onyx figurine with a thoughtful brow.

"There's that damn shadow again," remarked Ceteol suddenly.

"Shadow?" asked Opyros.

"It's gone again," she said with a frown. The girl pointed. "See how our shadows are all strung out in a line?" The declining sun cast light enough yet to throw the riders' spindly, misshapen shadows against the trees which crowded the unfrequented road wherever there was sufficient clearing to let them pass from under the shadow of the trees opposite.

"I've seen it a couple of times," Ceteol continued, "just out of the corner of my eye. When we come to a sunny spot, I've noticed how all our shadows writhe alongside us. But a couple of times I thought it was strange, because I can tell my shadow, and there's two men riding behind me—except I saw *three* shadows following my own."

"What sort of shadow?" Kane wanted to know. "Like another horse and rider?"

"No, not like that." She jammed the heels of her palms together and wriggled her fingers. "It was sort of . . . *crawly*."

Opyros laughed and looked at her eyes. "Your eyes are still bedazzled from the drug, love. It'll clear away before long."

Tossing back her brown hair, Ceteol made a tight face. "I may see shadows, but I don't half kill a girl and then go off and get drunk with thieves and killers. So don't laugh at me, damn it."

"Tell me next time you see it," suggested Kane. Then to Opyros: "You did say nothing untoward took place after I left you."

The poet shook his head, trying to tell how much of Ceteol's sullenness was only affected. "No, nothing happened. After I . . . ah . . . told Ceteol of our plans, I slept until not long before you called. I remember that damned pack of dogs started yelling—woke me up."

"Didn't see them when we rode up," mused Kane.

"Somebody else chased them off, I gathered. But where in all this ruin is the temple of Shenan?"

"Not far, though it's a little past the main body of the ruins."

The Old City had a certain ghostly beauty in the twilight, the melancholic serenity of ancient walls returning to dust with their secret memories of another age. Compared to its sprawling offspring Enseljos, the Old City had been but a town. Most of its buildings had been of timber, and these were long since weed-shrouded mounds of earth—forgotten graves in the forest. Here and there a low stone wall or heap of broken masonry indicated the site of some antique structure, but more often there was only an overgrown depression along the fading streets to mark the foundation of a long-toppled dwelling. Still, there were places where the walls of one of the Old City's more impressive buildings yet rose in tired defiance of time. As the dusk deepened, the darkness within these mouldering skulls seemed to flow from staring windows and yawning doorways and mingle with the gathering shadows of the forest.

"Here," announced Kane, and he urged his horse between the closely hemmed brushy barriers. A late morning rain had drenched the forest, so that progress through the brush left their legs sodden against their mounts' flanks.

The waning light fell upon a grey stone structure standing in gloomy solitude among the shouldering trees. Its walls rose to almost clear of the encroaching branches; buttressed and vaulted after the southern fashion, portions of the temple yet retained an arched ceiling. The deeper shadow within had spared its interior the rank undergrowth which strangled much of the Old City's ruins, although age had stripped the walls to bare stone and littered the floor with crumbling debris. As twilight closed upon the ruined temple, the velvet-leather curtains which festooned its high-vaulted ceiling spread a thousand wings and flapped chittering through the broken apertures.

Kane dismounted and directed his men to clear away some of the rubble which barricaded the entrance. The poet pressed forward in excitement; Ceteol, aloofly curious, followed him, her calf-length pleated skirt slapping against high riding boots. As soon as he had kindled a pair of links, Kane joined them, and while his men shoved away the rotting tangles of anonymous debris, he spoke further on the temple's history, raising his torch to point out some item of architectural interest. Opyros again sensed an uneasy wonder at Kane's nonchalant familiarity with the ruins.

Moonlight poured molten silver over the brooding grey stones by the time Kane judged their work sufficient. Showers of silver light fell through the high, narrow windows and jagged rifts in the walls, gathered in a deep pool about the altar, where a vast circular skylight showed the same night skies to which priestesses centuries dead had raised their chants. In a few areas where the litter had been cleared away, the damp stone tiles yet bore traces of strange mosaic patterns.

At Kane's orders, Levardos saw to posting the men outside. They were well paid, and if their leader chose to waste the night pursuing a mad poet's unhallowed whim, that was Kane's affair. Theirs was to watch for Eberhos, in case the alchemist had followed them with another band of hirelings. That he had fled Kane's anger was their consensus, but if not . . . their blades were ready.

Kane turned to his friend. "Well," he said, half in question.

The poet's eagerness was undiminished. "I'm ready if you are, Kane. This place is perfect—really it is! The atmosphere—it's . . . hell, I've tried to capture it again and again in my verses! What dreams hover about us here! Kane, if the muse will only come to me tonight . . . I feel I can . . . can . . . I feel I can grasp the inspiration I've searched for so long! *Night Winds* and a hundred more could soar from my soul tonight!"

A bitter smile twisted his face. "As you wish, then," assented Kane. He extended his hand. "The simulacrum."

Opyros thrust the carving into Kane's hand. "No musty tomes? No evil-fumed braziers and elder-glyphed pentacles?" But his levity was more bravado than banter.

"As I've said, a simple spell," returned Kane levelly. "I'll need a drop of your blood."

And while Ceteol watched with unfathomable eyes, Kane led the poet into the pool of moonlight; there by the forgotten altar of dark, flawless stone he performed those things which the ritual required.

Now it seemed to the poet that Kane's rhythmic chant of evocation had become a fading echo, hypnotic ebb and flow of rippling sound. The ruined walls seemed to recede; moonlight and shadow merged into a vortex of formless image. Even the cold hardness of stone pressing against his back, where he lay beside the onyx carving, grew distant—physical sensation drifting apart from his psychic awareness. . . .

And no longer did he lie beside a figurine of carven onyx. The carving blurred, rushed upward in size—or did he diminish? There was a sense of motion, of vertigo. . . . Lying next to him now was a figure of black—not a figure *in* black, but *of* black. A shadow in three dimensions of a nude girl. Of the dark muse.

She moved. Klinure turned toward him languidly. She saw him; the profile of darkness smiled an invitation. . . . *The cruel indifference of her smile* . . . She beckoned. Opyros moved against her; his arms closed about her ebony figure . . . His arms, too, were fashioned of darkness—as was his entire body. Then their bodies entwined in a lovers' embrace. There came wrenching ecstasy, intolerable vertigo. . . .

Then no darkness. His body had returned to substance. In his arms was a pale-skinned girl of exquisite beauty, with smiling lips, eyes of ageless wisdom. She broke from his embrace, still holding his hands . . . raised the poet to his feet (now he saw on what they had lain) . . . led him irresistibly, unresistingly forward. . . .

And now he understood the cold cruelty of her face. . . .

Ceteol gasped. The shimmering mists that for a moment had obscured the streamers of moonlight about the altar suddenly broke apart, drifted like phantom shapes into the night. Where Opyros and the black statuette had lain there was now only bare stone.

"What did you—where is he?" she exclaimed.

"He's crossed the threshold of dream," murmured Kane, a shadow of wonder touching his face.

"When will he return?" Ceteol persisted. "Hell, *how* will he return?"

Kane ran a hand over his beard. "That, of course, is the risk we spoke of. He'll return once the dream into which Klinure thrusts him is ended. When—I don't know. It depends on how long they wander through her realm before Opyros is caught up in the flow of a single dream, and then on how long that dream takes to reach its end. Only, how closely does time in a dream world follow the span of time as we know it? There time moves in obedience to the dream, not to natural law—an hour may pass like a second, or the reverse. Hell, for that matter, how does a dream actually end? Is there ever a certain terminus to a single dream, or does one segment merge into another, endlessly, until the dreamer awakens and shatters the stream of image?"

"You don't know!" Ceteol's aristocratic face twisted with emotion. "Damn you, Kane! You've killed him!"

"Perhaps," he shrugged. "But it was Opyros's decision to try this, and I explained that there were unknown risks."

"Weird," she murmured, her face again expressionless. "You're both weird. I don't know which of you is stranger." She fell to watching the moonlit circle of the altar, hunched together with knees drawn up, chin on fists, arms compressed between body and thighs.

"This may take most of the night," Kane said with a vague gesture. "My men have a small fire going to keep off the damp. Why not wait out there?"

Ceteol shook her head and muttered something indistinct. Her wide eyes seemed to stare without blinking into the moonlight.

Thus she remained when Kane returned from a hurried check of his men, who had nothing to report. The alchemist had to all appearances abandoned his efforts to recover the simulacrum. Since the night was not cold, Kane told Levardos to let the fire burn out. If enemies still sought them in the darkness, it seemed pointless to illuminate their position with a campfire. The moon—just past full—gave light enough for eyes accustomed to the night. A pair of torches inside the temple afforded all the light Kane might need, and in the darkness without, his men could stand guard unseen by an approaching enemy.

Plainly, there was nothing to do but wait. After Ceteol had declined, Kane drank a little wine from the skin they had brought and settled against a slab of rock to keep watch. After a while, the silence of the ruined temple broken only by the girl's regular breathing, he decided she slept.

But Ceteol was awake. "Kane, there's that shadow again."

Kane spun to look where she pointed—too late to see any definite shape. In time to catch a flicker of movement as something passed through the path of moonlight where its beams pierced the darkness. There was no sound.

"A bat," he told her. "Some night bird."

"That size?"

Only Kane had sensed the chill presence of fear, the sudden aura of danger that whispered through the brooding melancholy of the ruins. And he knew that death stalked the night.

"Stay here," he ordered. "Make no sound unless . . . you need to." His sword hissed from his scabbard, and Kane vanished into the darkness beyond.

Levardos glanced up from his post near the entrance. "What is it?" he whispered, noting Kane's expression.

"I don't know. Did you see, hear anything?"

The lean-faced man shook his head. "What is it?" he repeated.

Without answer, Kane brushed by him, stepping over the dead ashes of their fire. There was danger in the night, of this he felt certain. *But what danger lurked among these ebon-shrouded ruins . . . ?*

He began a circuit of the temple. Neither Webbre nor Haigan, posted close by, had noticed anything out of the ordinary; they expressed wonder at their leader's sudden unease. Thinking on the direction from which the shadowy movement had seemed to come, Kane redoubled his caution as he slipped farther away from the walls.

The moon overhead cast thick and misshapen shadows through the tangled trees, shone bright on jutting fragments of stonework that were strewn about like piles of discarded bone. Sodden underbrush clung to the mounds of decayed timber, cloaked the shadowed depressions of rubble-laden cellars. Through this maze of pitfalls and thorny barricades, Kane stalked in silence, sword poised to strike at the nameless menace which he knew to be creeping through the night with him. Yes, there was danger close by—danger that hinted of inhuman evil—for too often had Kane quested along paths of hidden knowledge to doubt this subconscious warning. Perhaps the ghost of unease he had felt earlier this evening had not arisen, as he supposed, from the matter of the dark muse. . . .

He had swung out far enough, he decided, still without finding any reason for his concern. Maybe then it was just nerves; he had started at the shadow of a low-flying owl. Only he could not convince himself of this. Turning toward the silent temple, Kane slipped around to check with his other two men.

A short time later he halted. Unless he had lost his bearing, Boulus should be posted here. There was no sign of the man. Kane bit his lip and looked more closely. No, he was not mistaken. Here was the lightning-spiraled oak in whose shadow Boulus had waited. By the blotches of moonlight, the ground showed no evidence of a struggle. The man should not have left his post. . . . unless he had something to report.

Cursing himself for ignoring the obvious, Kane quickly threaded his way back to the temple. With such stealth did he move that he was standing next to Hef before the other man called a challenge. Hef's sword wavered for an instant, but he recognized Kane's hulking figure.

"Nothing," he whispered, grinning ruefully that his leader had come upon him unseen.

"Boulus hasn't come by." As he asked it, it was no longer a question.

Hef made a negative grunt. "Unless he slipped by me as quiet as you just done."

"Something's wrong then," gritted Kane. "He's not at his post." The sense of danger tightened. Boulus should have checked with Hef if he had noticed anything in their area. But there was only silence about them.

"Maybe he shifted over a ways," Hef suggested. "Quiet

as you move, if you didn't see him, he wouldn't of seen you."

"Maybe. I'll check again. Watch it." Kane stole away in the direction he had just come.

But of Boulus there was still no trace. Softly Kane called his name—alarmed to the point of taking this risk. Not even an echo. Not even the call of a night bird. *Had something frightened the forest to silence?*

The aura of menace was very near.

Thinking furiously, Kane returned to where he had left Hef. Stronger than ever came the sense of lurking terror. *Was there something stalking him?*

Again there sounded no challenge. Hef was not at his post.

Feeling the muscles of his neck draw tight, Kane searched about him. There was nothing to be seen; no sign of disturbance here; nothing. He was starting for the temple, when his foot struck something. A boot. Hef's boot. Bewildered, Kane caught it up.

Something warm and damp ran across his wrist as he lifted it. Hef's foot remained in the boot. His calf had been sheared off so cleanly as to clip through the top of the leather.

There had been no sound.

Levardos sensed his leader's alarm as Kane plunged from the nighted forest. He met the urgent question in Kane's look and shook his head, his parchment-fleshed face alert.

In a harsh whisper Kane called for Webbre and Haigan to pull back instantly. Muffled thrashing in the brush indicated they had heard. Something evil, something deadly, hovered near, very near.

"Kane! What *is* it!" hissed Levardos.

"I'm not sure," he grated. "Boulus is gone. Hef, too. In the space of a few minutes, something *took* Hef—not a few score yards from me, though I heard nothing! There was just his foot, lying there on the ground like a cast-off boot!"

"Why no sound of attack? You should have heard the rush of steel. A man would scream as a blade sundered his leg!"

Kane's face was worried. "No blade did that—there was

no more blood than from a slopped wine cup. Something snatched him up; something with jaws like a dragon—jaws that could close upon a man in an instant, and never notice if a tiny morsel of flesh dropped away from its scissored fangs!"

"But a beast that huge!" his lieutenant protested. "We'd see it—hear it!"

"But we didn't."

The two brothers burst from the undergrowth. "Quick! Inside the temple!" Kane ordered, snapping out a terse explanation. "Whatever's out there, these walls may give us some defense!"

From their tethers, the horses began to stamp and nicker. For a second Kane debated leaving them to their fate, then decided not to risk being left on foot. "Bring in the mounts!" he ordered Webbre and Haigan.

Then as he dashed through the temple entrance, he knew something was wrong here as well. He had left a torch burning near the altar; it lay dark against the tiles, extinguished. Ceteol had vanished.

Kane snatched up the remaining torch from its crevice within the entrance. The link was nearly burned out; perhaps the other had fallen and gone out. Ceteol?

No time for conjecture. From outside came a shrill scream. A second voice—Webbre's bass roar—cursed and howled. Then the screams of the horses drowned out everything. With a thunder of panic-spurred hooves, their mounts pounded off into the night.

Kane whipped the torch to flaring life. Their blades wavered yellow as he and Levardos leaped from the deserted temple. Branches shook; the last of the horses could just be glimpsed as darkness engulfed them. The two brothers had disappeared. Kane called only once, for he did not expect an answer.

"That shadow!" breathed Levardos, pointing.

"Ah!" hissed Kane, and thrust out his torch.

No shape. Only a looming shadow that writhed against the trees, swept across the fallen stones. Retreating too quickly for the eye to judge its form.

"What is it? *Where* is it!" gasped Levardos. For the torchlight disclosed nothing that might cast such a shadow

—nor was there any sound or show of movement to mark its passage.

"Something overhead?" guessed Kane, though the angle of the creeping shadows denied this.

The link flickered and smoked. Its pitch was almost exhausted, so that the tow was beginning to smoulder.

As its light failed, the misshapen shadow surged across the moonlight toward them. Terror brushed chill talons toward their throats. With a curse, Kane whirled the torch about; bits of the tow spun loose and dashed like tiny stars across the night. Flame leaped up once more. The onrushing shadow fell back. Still there was no sign of what cast it.

"Back into the temple!" Kane ordered. "I think it hates the light!"

Breathlessly they stumbled past the rubble of the portal. The thick walls afforded some sense of protection from the unknown horror that lurked beyond the light.

The link snapped and fumed. "The other torches?" asked Kane anxiously.

"They were with the horses and gear!" groaned Levardos.

"Then we'd better find something to burn!" Kane scrambled through the litter of the temple. His boot kicked through the mounds of rotted timber; the material sprayed from his thrusting foot, damp and crumbling loam. Only bare stone and mould-eaten decay. The enclosing roof had held out the undergrowth, fallen branches that cluttered the ground outside.

The sputtering flame threatened to leap and die. "Isn't there any dry wood in here?" cursed Kane.

"Outside . . ." began Levardos, glancing toward the doorway. He did not finish. Shadow blocked the entrance.

Kane lunged with the dwindling torch. Moonlight again fell through the opening.

"Here's something!" Levardos crushed together an armload of dead wood—a few branches that had fallen through the broken roof. With frantic care, Kane thrust the link into the heap of brush. It was damp, rotten. The flame dwindled, refused to catch. Desperate breaths fanned the smouldering tow. From the corner of his eye, Kane saw the shadow spread across the doorway.

Then the branches caught. Painfully, unsteadily, the flickering heat crept through the broken tinder. Ignoring blistered hands, the two men nudged embers together and fed the trembling flames—cursed as the damp wood smoked and steamed without igniting.

Somehow they got the fire burning. Moonlight spilled past the portal once again. But the smothering cloud of deadly fear did not leave them. Beyond the walls, an unseen stalker paced in silent hunger, blotted out the shafts of moonbeam as it crept about the ruin.

"We'll need more wood than this," judged Kane. In the dancing firelight he could see other branches and scraps of crumbling timber—pitifully few. *When these were gone?*

"Maybe with a torch we could bring wood in from outside," he considered. Levardos nodded uneasily, not wanting to think of the death that waited beyond the light.

With this in mind, Kane left the fire to retrieve the fallen torch by the altar. As he bent, his brow furrowed. The link had not burned out; someone's foot had crushed it against the tiles. Wondering, Kane picked it up. In the horror of the moment, he had spared little thought for Ceteol. Her disappearance now took on another aspect.

"Kane! Above you!"

Kane hurtled back from the altar. The pool of moonlight no longer poured down. Its circle was broken as a writhing shadow crept across the opening in the roof. Risking a glance upward, Kane saw only darkness, flowing darkness that blotted out the stars. A crawling, obscene shadow wriggled across the altar—slithered too rapidly to suggest more than vaguely its true shape. If indeed it had true shape. The aura of alien evil bore down upon them in crushing waves.

"It makes no sound!" cried Levardos as Kane retreated to the fire. "And its size! How can these mouldering stones bear its weight?"

"It has no weight—no substance as we understand!" Kane snarled, recognizing the creature at last. "It's a sort of demon—an elemental from the subworld of chaos, an elemental fashioned of darkness! Darkness lends it substance, but light strips away its borrowed flesh—shows only the shadow of its malevolent spirit. Moonlight doesn't affect it, since the moon casts no true light. The demon must have followed us here; waited for nightfall, for our fires to die. If we can keep a fire going until dawn, we can escape it."

A laugh answered him from beyond the altar. "Will you burn stone, then?" asked a mocking voice. "Your fire already flames less brightly. Soon you'll have to venture out into the damp forest—and what if your torch goes out? Will you find some rotten branch to light your way? And the stars say it will rain again before dawn!"

Eberhos's burly figure slunk through a rift in the temple's far wall. He carried a burden. Ceteol. The girl hung limp in his arms; her hands were tied, and a gag was fixed between her jaws.

Kane's eyes blazed. He took a step toward the alchemist.

A dagger flashed in Eberhos's hand. "Stay where you are!" he ordered. "Or I'll slit her pretty throat and be gone before you get halfway here! Want to chase me into the night?"

Seeing that Kane subsided, he sneered, "So you know what demon stalks you, Kane. You're most erudite, aren't you? Did you guess who summoned it, who commanded it to pursue, to slay? Surely not uncouth Eberhos, Damatjyst's flunky and errand boy!"

His voice grew shrill. "Did you think I had kissed ass for that miserly tyrant all these years and never learned to count past my fingers? Well, my days of taking that piss-blooded bastard's orders are just about over! I've planned my move for years, waited patiently while I did apprentice's chores for the fool! I'll not let the theft of that carving destroy his trust in his loyal First Assistant just when all I've planned for is in reach!"

He chuckled and shifted the girl's drooping form. Kane saw the smear of crimson dark against her hair. Ceteol began to regain consciousness, moaned through her gag.

"Followed you here," Eberhos grinned. "Followed my

little pet. While you were out playing with it in the dark, I slipped inside to get my carving. Your man didn't seem to be on guard any more, did he? But when I didn't find the figurine, I thought the little lady might want to tell me where you hid it—I know you and that crazy poet were going to try something with it here tonight.

"Tell you what, Kane. Give me the carving—if you aren't carrying it, tell me where it's hidden—and I'll take it and go. Once I'm clear, I'll send the demon back to the realm of chaos from which I summoned it."

"What chance is there you'll keep your part of the bargain?" growled Kane, weighing the chances of a knife throw. The distance was great, and Eberhos held the girl like a shield. And the fire was dropping low already.

"Well, now, I guess you'll just have to trust my word of honor," the alchemist chuckled. "Is that rain I hear off in the trees?"

The wind was starting up in listless gusts. Kane answered Eberhos with a curse and edged a step closer.

Eberhos touched his dagger to Ceteol's straining throat. "One more step, and she gets a new mouth! Give me the carving, Kane. Maybe you and Opyros want to watch the girl die?"

Kane realized that in the poor light Eberhos had mistaken Levardos for the poet. Crouched beyond the flickering fire, his lieutenant could only be glimpsed as a gaunt figure with blond hair—like Opyros. "Why should I care what you do with the girl?" scoffed Kane. "She means nothing to either of us."

Eberhos's beefy face grew crafty. "No? Well, maybe your verse-singing friend will change his mind when he sees I don't bluff. It won't be a quick death. . . ."

The fire was dying down. Levardos shoved in the last of the fuel they had gathered. The damp, pulpy wood all but smothered the flames.

"Take the girl as hostage, go back and call off your demon," offered Kane. "I'll return the carving to you tomorrow—and give you my word not to take vengeance for this."

Laughter taunted him. "Getting edgy, Kane? And you didn't even see what happened to your friends—but I did! No, you aren't the one who makes the bargain tonight, Kane. You'll take my offer, or die!"

"I see no reason to trust you," Kane snarled. The fire was not igniting the rotted fragments of timber.

"Then I'll show you that you can trust me to carry out a threat! The carving, quick now, or the girl gets the knife! Slow. I'll let you watch to see how she likes it."

Eberhos shoved the still dazed girl into a shaft of moonlight that lanced through one of the high, narrow windows. The window was not much wider than a balistraria, but the ray of light clearly showed Ceteol's white face. Should they rush him, the alchemist could easily slash her throat and dart through the broken wall, a few steps away.

"Watch!" he jeered. Pinning her against his chest, he hooked his arm around and drew the dagger point through the fabric of her beaded blouse. The cloth parted to expose her straining breasts. Grinning, Eberhos carved a thin crescent below each pale cone of flesh. Blood traced patterns down her ribs and belly.

Ceteol whimpered through the gag. The pain had returned her to full consciousness. As the alchemist shifted his blade for another cut, she smashed the heel of her riding boot into his shin.

Her boots were spurred. Fashionable spurs for a lady, but sharp nonetheless. Their rowels gored a furrow down to Eberhos's sandaled foot.

Cursing in pain, the alchemist hurled her against the wall. Ceteol's head cracked aganst the window's edge, and she slumped down. Blood flowed from Eberhos's leg as he leaped upon her and raised his dagger for a killing stroke.

Shadow flickered across the moonlight. A loop of *something* dark and half-seen snaked through the window; Kane thought of a great black cat darting its paw into a rat hole after catching a glimpse of its prey within. Eberhos shrieked—one terrible shriek—as something that *might* have been a tentacle lashed about his chest, tore him from the floor and through the window into the night.

Presumably the demon would not have harmed its master. Likely the scent of blood, the proximity of the girl, Eberhos's sudden lunge confused the enraged leviathan that waited in the darkness outside. The creature instantly released the alchemist.

As much of him as had passed through the narrow window.

Ceteol made a choking sound in her throat and stumbled groggily away from the dripping aperture. Kane caught her up, removed her bonds, and the girl huddled next to the fire, cursing dispassionately between shuddering gasps. Blood continued to seep along her ribs, but the gashes were shallow, so that she was barely aware of their pain in the presence of far greater horror.

But the clinging atmosphere of terror which had closed about them had lifted—vanished with the alchemist's death.

"What . . . happened?" puffed Levardos, daring to pause in his frenzied efforts with the fire. The flames quivered and sputtered, but burned more strongly now.

"I think it's gone," Kane hazarded. "Eberhos summoned the demon, commanded it to stalk us; his death should have released it from its bond—allowed the creature to return to the nameless realm of chaos."

"Gone, do you think?" asked Levardos, eyeing the darkness with suspicion.

"So it would appear. Do you see its crawling shadow? Can you sense that smothering cloud of unearthly fear the demon seemed to exhale?"

His lieutenant shook his head slowly, then glanced toward the steaming fire. The chunks of rotted timber would soon be consumed. "We'll know for sure before long," he commented laconically.

Kane gingerly retrieved the remaining link from the cheerless flames. Pitch still boiled from its tow—fuel which had kept the fire going after Levardos had shoved it into the dying embers. "I'll find out now," he growled, carrying the torch toward the door.

Despite his assurance that the demon had left them, Kane's broad muscles bunched in tight cords as he stepped into the darkness of the ruin-haunted forest. Drops of rain splashed invisibly through the trees, spat at the flaring torch. But no unseen demon reached out for him; no writhing shadow lurked beyond the nimbus of light. Forcing unpleasant thoughts from his mind, Kane cast about for dead limbs and eventually returned through the enveloping drizzle with a small tree scraping behind him.

"The demon," he announced, "is gone." Kane flung down his load of wood, then released the disintegrating torch; he had to use his free hand to pry away his locked fingers from their grip on its shaft.

They kept the fire going. It was a worn, grim trio huddled within the ruined temple. More mist than droplets, the rain wrapped itself about them, plopped from countless crevices in the smoke-hung roof. They waited for daylight, waited for the poet to return to them; the shadow of terror which had fallen over this night made the evocation of the dark muse seem distant, unreal. Touched by the spirit of gloom that haunted the ruins, they waited through the night, each silent in his thoughts.

They grey light of dawn was touching the altar when Kane muttered an exclamation that woke the others from their doze. "Look!" he cried, pointing toward the circle of dawnlight.

Streamers of opalescent mist, not of the rain nor of the morning, gathered upon the bare stone, splashed clean by the raindrops. The swirling mists slowed, hovered closer. Coalesced. Vanished.

On the rain-polished stone lay a man, a man who looked to be asleep. Beside him rested a nude figurine of black onyx, a figurine whose carven face smiled an invitation to unknown wonders, whose eyes shone with mysterious cruelty. . . .

"Opyros!" called Ceteol, running to him. She touched his arm.

The poet's eyes flashed open. He drew away, fear distorting his face. His eyes were unfocused, vacuous.

"Opyros?" Kane's voice was shaken.

The poet's empty eyes looked past Kane. He worked his throat as if to scream, but only a hiss of insurmountable terror escaped his contorted lips. He hissed again and again, then began to sob mindlessly.

When they sought to lift him, Opyros broke away and fled with frightened mewing into a shadowed corner of the ruin. They had difficulty pulling him from under the debris, as he moved with surprising speed for a man wriggling on his belly.

V

Cruel Mystery of Her Smile

They carried Opyros back to Enseljos.

For weeks he lay in a locked room of his manor, attended only by Ceteol after his howling drove away most of his servants. A sense of fulfillment seemed to settle over Ceteol, who would explain with a soft smile just exactly who was to blame. Only through the drugs Kane left for him could the poet take sleep, and for days he remained huddled in a nest of soiled bedding, shivering and mewling. At times he muttered snatches of speech, guttural syllables in a strange language—if language it was—that no one could recognize, although Kane once listened carefully as if he understood, and left the chamber shuddering.

Almost certainly any other man would have gone to the end of his days in this gibbering state of frightened madness. Perhaps Opyros's was an exceptionally resilient consciousness, or possibly the repeated flights of his imagination into the shadow lands of the macabre had to some extent inured him to those greater horrors which would have utterly shattered another's soul. Some core of ego yet burned beneath the choking mists of insanity.

Little by little he seemed to come to himself. Though the nightmares still haunted his drugged sleep, he became able to sit composedly while awake, to feed and care for himself. After some months he began to prowl quietly about his manor, examining his books and effects as if submerged memories were rising from far depths of his consciousness—like a traveller who returns from a distant journey of many years, to find the vaguely remembered home of his childhood awaiting him untouched by the age which has passed since last he held his toys. Eventually he began to talk, fumbling with the words as if the language were unfamiliar from disuse, but as the weeks passed, his stammering phrases grew to careful sentences and then to normal conversation. He ventured out on the streets of Enseljos once more and greeted his old acquaintances, who were privately alarmed as to how greatly his recent nervous collapse had aged the poet. And thus, after many months of convalescence, Opyros reassumed management of his affairs much as before.

But long before this time he had begun to write.

Kane greeted Opyros one night as the poet made a surprise visit to his new quarters. Only rarely did he see his friend since Opyros's recovery, for the poet stayed locked in his study for long hours these days, working in secret at his writing. No longer did he come to Kane with fragments of verse and half-formed ideas; all his writing he now did alone. Kane hoped the poet did not feel some unspoken ill will against him for his part in the evocation of the dark muse. On the contrary, Opyros expressed no regret for his experience, though he never told of it. Nonetheless, Kane could read nothing in his eyes of the poet's secret thoughts.

"*Night Winds* is finished," he declared with a tired smile.

Warmly Kane congratulated his friend. "Are you at last satisfied with it, then?"

Opyros looked introspective as he accepted a crystal chalice of brandy. "I think so. My journey with the dark muse was worth it, Kane, for I found the inspiration I sought—though there was a price for it."

"And is *Night Winds* the perfect poem you spoke of once to me?"

Opyros savoured the liquor before tasting it. "I think so."

"Then I should very much like to read it. Have you brought it?"

Opyros shook his head. "No, it's locked safely away. Forgive my conceit, Kane, but this is the masterwork I have devoted my life, my soul, to creating. I want its unveiling to be an affair of some . . . ah . . . magnitude —do you understand?"

Kane nodded, studying the other's face intently.

"There will be a formal reading in a week or so, as soon as I can circulate invitations to those who should have them, arrange a hall, and the like. I don't want this another uncouth public reading, with slobs tramping in and out through it all, peddlers hawking food and drink. This will be a private affair—closed door, you know—a few hundred guests, literary colleagues and critics, the nobility who attend this sort of socal function. There'll be enough trouble with these dilettantes' gossiping and backbiting . . . but then I've said a perfect poem should hold the minds of its audience."

"I'll look forward to attending."

"I'm tempted to let you see this first, anyway," Opyros grinned nervously. "It's somewhat different from my earlier work—I've done a lot of things that no writer has thought to. . . . Well, it's finished, and I'll wait for the formal reading, to stand acclaimed as genius or be laughed at as pretentious fool, when the world first hears it."

"To *Night Winds* and its author," toasted Kane, touching goblets.

"To the dark muse," answered Opyros.

But Kane did not attend the first reading of *Night Winds*, although the poet's announced presentation of his first work in over a year had attracted great interest and comment from across the land. Halbros-Serrantho had required Kane's presence in secret on the night of the reading. Kane could not deny this summons from the ambitious ruler of Enseljos, whose dreams included building an empire from the tiny states of the Northern Continent. Such plans were of no little interest to Kane as well.

So Kane was forced to miss the first reading of *Night Winds*.

It often moved him to wondering regret. For although he was never to hear the masterwork of Opyros, the mad poet, Kane knew that his friend had in truth found inspiration in the embrace of the dark muse. Opyros had in truth created the perfect poem of his dark genius.

For as he left the palace of Halbros-Serrantho, the first horrified tales were spreading across the city—tales of what had awaited the frightened guards when they at last broke down the locked doors of that now silent audience hall.

RAVEN'S EYRIE

Prologue

The child awoke at the sound of her own scream. A thin scream, imbued with the fever that parched her throat. And still a scream tight with the terror of her dream. Its echo hung on the bare-timbered walls of her narrow room as she bolted from her damp pillow.

Her fever-bright eyes stared wide with fear as they darted about the room's shadowy corners. But the phantoms of her nightmare, if nightmare it was, had receded. Klesst brushed the clinging tendrils of red hair from her moist forehead and sat up.

Through the greenish bull's-eye glass of her lattice window she could see the declining sun, impaled upon the reddened fangs of the mountains. The late autumn night would close quickly, and the darkness of her nightmare would surround her. And this was the night when the Demonlord walked the earth. . . .

Shivering despite her heightened temperature, Klesst dropped back against the straw mattress. "Mother!" she called plaintively, wondering why her outcry had not brought someone to her side.

"Mother!" she called again. She longed to call Greshha's name, but remembered that the stout serving woman had been sent away from the inn for the night. Greshha had not wanted to leave her. Not when she was sick, not on the night of her birthday. Not on *this* night. It was cruel of her mother to send her away, Greshha whom she looked upon as her nurse. Smiling Greshha, Greshha of warm hands and soft bosom. Not hard and cold like Mother.

Greshha would have answered her cry. It was cruel of Mother to ignore her like this.

"What is it, Klesst?" Mother's frown regarded her warily from the doorway. She had heard no footsteps on the thick boards of the long hallway. Mother moved so silently always.

"I'm thirsty, Mother. My throat feels so hot. Please bring me some water."

How pretty Mother was. . . . Her long black hair brushed down the sides of her face, clasped at her nape, and let fall over her shoulder and down her left breast. Under her shawl, her straight shoulders rose bare from her wide-necked blouse of bleached muslin, full-sleeved and gathered at her wrists. Her narrow waist was cinched by a wide belt of dark leather, crisscrossed with scarlet cord. Her skirt of brown wool fell in wide pleats to low on her calves, and her small feet were shod in buskins of soft leather. Klesst wore gold circlets pierced through each earlobe—just like Mother—but Greshha had helped her sew bits of embroidery on her garments, while Mother's were unadorned.

Her mother crossed the tiny room with her quick stride. She caught up the crockery pitcher from the stand beside Klesst's bed, then frowned as it sloshed. "There's water here, Klesst. Why can't you get your own drink?"

Klesst hoped she had not triggered her mother's cold anger. Not when loneliness shadowed her room, and the night was closing over the inn. "The pitcher is so heavy, and my arms feel so weak and shaky. Please, Mother. Give me some water."

Silently her mother poured water into Klesst's cup and placed the blue glazed mug in her hands. Greshha would have held it to her lips, supported her head with her strong arm. . . .

Klesst drank thirstily, gripping the cup with both her hands—surprisingly long-fingered for a child's hands. Her great blue eyes watched her mother over the brim, searching her face for anger, impatience. Mother's face was impassive.

The child's febrile lips sucked noisily at the last swallow

of water, and her mother took the empty cup from her fingers. She returned it to its place beside the pitcher, then turned to go.

"Please, Mother!" Klesst spoke quickly. "My head—it burns so. Could you place something cool on my head?"

Her mother laid her thin hand over the girl's brow. *Yes, that was so cold. . . .*

"I had the bad dreams again, Mother," whispered Klesst, hoping her mother would not leave.

"You have a fever still. Fever brings bad dreams."

"It was that same nightmare."

Mother's eyes were wary. "What nightmare, Klesst?"

Would she get angry? Might she stay beside her if she knew her fear? Klesst dreaded the thought of being alone in the darkness.

"It was the dog again, Mother. The great black hound."

Her mother drew back and folded her long arms under her high breasts. "A great black hound?" she said. "Do you mean a wolf?"

"A giant hound, Mother. Bigger than the bear hounds, bigger than a wolf. I think he's even bigger than a bear. And he's black, all black, even his chops and his tongue. Just his fangs are white. And his eyes—they burn like fire. He wants me, Mother. In my dream I see him hunting along the ridges in the mist, sniffing the night winds for my scent. And I can't run, but he keeps hunting closer—until he's snuffling up to the inn. Then he sees me, and his eyes glow red and freeze me so I can't scream, and his jaws yawn open and I see smoke curling from his fangs. . . ."

"Hush! It's only a bad dream!" Her mother's voice was strained.

Klesst shuddered as the memory of her fear crept back again, and she wished Greshha were here to hold her. "And I can see something else walking the ridges. There's a man, all in black with a great black cloak that flaps behind him. A man who hunts with the black hound. I can't see him clear because the night hides him—but I know I mustn't look at his face!"

"Stop it!"

The child gasped and looked wonderingly at her mother.

"Talking about it will only make you have the bad dream again," her mother explained tensely.

Klesst decided not to mention the other strange man who walked through her nightmare. "Why are they hunting for me?" she asked in a frightened whisper. *Dared she ask Mother to stay with her?* She again glanced to see if she were angry.

Her mother's face was shadowed, her lips tight and pale. She spoke in a whisper, as if thinking aloud. "Sometimes when your soul is so torn with pain and hatred . . . it can burn you out inside, so your spirit can never feel anything else. . . . and you can think thoughts that are different, turn to paths that you wouldn't . . . before.. And later maybe your soul is burned out and cold. . . . But the fire of your hatred smoulders and waits . . . And you know there's a bad moon rising—but there's no way to hold it back."

A gust of wind rattled dry leaves against the panes. Outside the lattice window, night was striding over the autumnal ridges.

I

Ridges of Autumn

"How is he?"

Braddeyas shrugged. "Alive, I think, but that's about all. He'll be dead by morning if we don't stop soon."

Weed spat sourly and nudged his horse alongside the wounded man's mount. The man slumped over his horse's neck was huge, but his thick muscled frame was now nerveless, and only the ropes which held him to his saddle kept him from toppling to the mountain trail.

Knotting his fingers in the thick red hair, Weed lifted his head. "Kane! Can you hear me?"

The blood-smeared face was slack and pale, the eyes hidden under half-closed lids. His lips moved silently, but Weed could not tell whether there was recognition.

"Then again, he may not last the night even if we do stop somewhere," Braddeyas commented. "Fever's getting worse, I'd say."

"Kane!"

No response.

"He's been out of it since the fever set in," Braddeyas went on. "And he's lost a lot of blood—still losing some." Absently he scratched the dirty bandages that bound his own hairy forearm. Signs of recent and desperate combat marked each man of their small band.

"I don't like to stop," frowned Weed, assuming Kane's leadership. "They're too close on us to risk it."

Braddeyas drew his cloak tighter about his narrow shoulders. "Kane won't last till morning unless we rest."

"Pleddis won't push on through these mountains tonight," offered Darros, who had ridden back to join them.

"Why won't he?" Weed demanded. "He must know we're only hours ahead of him. The bastard's probably counting his bounty money right now!"

The dark-bearded crossbowman shook his head decisively. "Then he'll be counting it beside a roaring fire. You won't find nobody riding these trails tonight. Not with this moon. A man will risk his life for gold maybe, but not his soul."

Weed glanced toward the rising moon in sudden awareness. The long-limbed bandit was from the island Pellin, and not a native of Lartroxia. Nonetheless, years of raiding along the continent's hinterlands had made him familiar with the tales and legends of the Myceum Mountains. He looked at the red moon of autumn and remembered.

"The Demonlord's Moon," he whispered.

"Pleddis will have to make camp," Darros asserted. "His men won't ride past nightfall. He'll have to wait for dawn before he takes up our trail again."

"We can risk a halt, then," Weed surmised.

"We've no choice," commented Darros, his jaw set.

The two remaining members of their band, tall Frassos and crop-eared Seth, proclaimed agreement by their grim-faced silence.

"By the red moon of autumn, the Demonlord hunts;
His black hound beside him, he seeks along the ridges,
Hunting blood for demonhound, souls for Demonlord . . ."

"Shut up, Braddeyas!" growled Weed, his ragged nerves overstrung by the creeping sense of fear.

"We ain't going to make camp along the trail, are we?" mumbled Seth uneasily. "Kane's just dead weight, and that's only five of us to wait through the night."

"Any other ideas?" demanded Weed. "Night's coming on fast."

Kane's head did not lift from where he slumped against his horse's neck, but his voice slurred thickly: "Raven's Eyrie."

"What'd he say?" Weed asked.

"Raven's Eyrie," answered Braddeyas, bending close to Kane. He held water to their leader's cracked lips, then shook his head. "Still unconscious. Like he's saving up what strength he has. I've seen him do this before."

"Any idea what he meant?"

"Raven's Eyrie is an inn not far, maybe two miles from here," explained Darros, who knew the region well. "It overlooks the River Cotras and the road that runs along the river gorge. Used to be a major caravanserai, before Kane raided it years back. They never rebuilt the place, and my guess is it's all in ruins now."

Weed nodded. "Yeah, I remember Kane talking about that raid. Must have been about eight years back, because it happened just before I joined Kane."

"I was there," stated Braddeyas with crusty pride. He had raided these mountains even before Kane had come to them ten years before. His hair was grey-streaked and thinning now, which said something about the man, for the mountain outlaws seldom died in bed.

All too true for the others of Kane's once powerful band—men cut to pieces by mercenary swords when Pleddis encircled their camp. This handful had slashed their way through his trap, but three days of desperate flight still found the free-captain close on their heels. Nor was he likely to quit their trail. The Combine cities of Lartroxia's coastal plain had set a high bounty on Kane, and Pleddis meant to claim it.

"If its walls are standing, the inn will give us shelter until dawn," Frassos pointed out. He coughed thinly, wincing as pain shot through cracked ribs.

"You know the way, Darros, then lead us there," Weed decided. "Daylight's just about gone."

"It is that," someone muttered.

Night was closing over the mountains on great raven's wings. Shadow lay deep beneath the blue-grey pines and frost-fired hardwoods which shouldered over the narrow trail. Darkness hungrily swallowed the valleys and hollows that spread out below them—pools of gloom from which waves of mist rose to storm the wooded slopes and pour over the limestone ridges.

A battered, gut-weary handful of hunted men—ruthless, half-wild outlaws hounded by killers as remorseless as themselves. Shivering in their dirt and blood-caked bandages, they rode on in grim determination, thoughts numb to pain and fear—although both phantoms rode beside them—intent on nothing more than the deadly necessity of flight. Flight from the hired bounty killers who followed almost on the sound of their hoofbeats.

They were well mounted; their gear was chosen from the plunder of uncounted raids. But now their horses stumbled with fatigue, their gear was worn and travel-stained, their weapons notched and dulled from hard fighting. They were the last. The last on this side of Hell of those who had ridden behind Kane, as feared and daring an outlaw pack as had ever roamed the Myceum Mountains.

No more would they set upon travellers along the lonely mountain passes, pillage merchants' camps, terrorize isolated settlements. Never again would they sweep down from the dark-pined slopes and lay waste to villages of the coastal plains, then dart back into the secret fastness of the mountains where the Combine's cavalry dared not venture. Their comrades were dead, fed ravens in a forgotten valley countless twisted miles behind their bent shoulders. Their leader, whose infamous cunning and deadly sword at last had failed them, was dying in his saddle.

They were all dead men.

And night was upon them.

"Thoem! It's dark as the inside of a tomb!" cursed Weed, trying to follow the shadow-hidden trail. He glanced uneasily at the blood-hued disk rising above the ridges of autumn. The moon cast no light this night.

"We're almost there," Darros promised him from the darkness ahead.

Moments later the trail rose over a gap, and he called back, "There it is! And there's lights! The inn hasn't been deserted, after all."

Not quite, Weed observed. Even in the thick gloom, he could see that Raven's Eyrie lay half in ruins. The grey stone and black timber structure crouched on the edge of the deep valley below them, rising from a bluff overlooking the River Cotras. By the dim-eyed rows of windows, Weed noted that the main building of the sprawling caravanserai stood at least three storeys. The outlying wings of the inn appeared no more than fire-gutted walls. River mist hung over the blackened walls of Raven's Eyrie, and in the darkness below the limestone bluff, the Cotras thundered its unseen rush to the western coast.

Cautiously they urged their exhausted mounts down the twisting path that descended the ridge from the gap. The last grey ghost of twilight died away as they emerged from the pine-buried slope and reached the river road. Though wider than the path they had been following, the river road showed signs of neglect. New saplings speared through its hoof-beaten surface, and older trees reached out from the looming forest on either side. Men and horses had ridden by, and smaller hoofprints marked the passage of an occasional drover, but wagon ruts were few, and these old and eroded. Weed reflected that the depredations of Kane and his men probably explained the near abandonment of this once heavily travelled trace.

In darkness they approached the inn. Only a few of the outbuildings remained standing, but they could catch the smell and soft noises of horses and livestock. Several lighted windows of bull's-eye glass stared dimly toward the road. A pair of smoky lanterns hung beside the front entrance, but the thick timbered door had the look of being bolted. A wooden sign hung out above the lanterns, swnging slightly, though the wind was less raking here in the valley. Its paint was charred, and the panel bore blade scars, but Weed could make out the blocky Lartroxian letters: "Raven's Eyrie." On the sign above the letters perched a huge raven, in bas-relief and painted black. Someone had set a bit of red glass into the bird's eye, and lamplight glinted there. The raven seemed to watch their approach.

"How many would you say?" Weed asked Darros, after the other had ridden ahead for a closer look.

"Not very many, by all signs," the crossbowman replied. "Looks like just a few people are keeping the inn going. Them and maybe a few travellers, I'd guess. Strange their dogs haven't scented us."

"Shouldn't be much trouble, then." Weed turned in the darkness to give orders. Frassos did not respond when he called his name.

"Frassos?" he called again.

No reply. His riderless horse wandered forward instead.

They conferred in startled bewilderment. Frassos had ridden behind, guarding their rear. No one had heard him cry out; no one had heard the sound of a fall.

"We're all of us done in twice over," suggested Bradeyas. "Maybe he passed out and fell."

"We should have heard him if he did," Weed pointed out.

"Should we go back and look for him?"

The red moon burned down on them from the misty ridges. Weed shivered under its rusty glow, remembering the mountain legends he had heard of this night.

"Does anyone want the job?"

It was too dark to see their eyes, but Weed sensed that no one met his face.

"If Frassos is all right, he can catch up to us at the inn," muttered Seth. There was no confidence in his voice.

II

A Guest Returns

For the space of a dream, Klesst drifted in the restless sleep of fever. Shaken from her half-sleep by sudden angry stridor, she flung herself free of covers in frightened awakening.

The moon's burning eye stared at her through the rippled panes of her window, and Klesst threw her hand to her lips to stifle an outcry. From below in the inn, angry shouts, splintering clamour of overturned benches, a raw scream of pain.

Had the black hound at last found her? Had it broken past the door? Was it even now climbing the stairs to her room?

But the angry voices continued. The words were indistinct to her, but their tone was clear. Now more curious than afraid, Klesst decided she must see what had happened.

Dizzily she dropped her feet to the floor and held fast to the oak bedstead until steadiness returned to her limbs. The night's chill pierced her thin cotton shift, and she hurriedly wound about her shoulders the woolen coverlet Greshha had woven for her. For the moment, her fever had left her, and though suddenly cold, she felt a certain shaky strength in its wake. Her teeth chattered; the fire in her room had almost died, and no one had filled the woodbox.

The angry shouts had subsided by the time Klesst tiptoed down the narrow hallway to the balcony overlooking the inn's common room. Cautiously she crept through the shadows to the pine log railing and peered from behind a gnarled post.

She darted back in fear—then, certain that the shadows concealed her, risked a longer glance. Her eyes grew wide with a child's wondering stare.

The front door of the inn was flung open. Cold gusts slanted the lantern flames, spun curled leaves across the threshold. Strangers—wild, dangerous men—had burst into Raven's Eyrie. Death had entered with them.

A burly, black-bearded man held a cocked crossbow; his eyes searched the shadows of the common room and raked the balcony where Klesst crouched closer to the log railing. Another man with gangling limbs and mousy, straw-colored hair brandished a narrow blade of unusual length. He seemed to be in charge, for he snarled commands to someone outside the inn.

The inhabitants of the inn and its few guests stood frozen against the long bar. There was Mother, her expression unreadable, with Selle, the scrawny serving maid, cowering against her. Pot-bellied Cholos, who served her mother as tapster, licked his lips nervously and glanced sidelong at the hulking Mauderas, who kept the stables and saw to such heavy work as was ever done at Raven's Eyrie. Mauderas's eyes were sullen as he pressed a hand to his crimson-sodden sleeve. Two guests, apparently drovers, were backed against the bar as well. Another guest, whose green tunic identified him as a ranger, lay crumpled beside an overturned table, a crossbow bolt through his back.

Bandits! Klesst realized with a shudder, recalling the many lurid tales she had listened in on, safely crouched by the corner of the fireplace. The murderous outlaws who held sway over the mountain wilderness—who had laid waste to Raven's Eyrie one awful night before her birth.

There was a disturbance at the door. Two more bandits appeared, staggering under the burden of a third man. One was a wiry figure, partially bald and gap-toothed, though his hair was barely greyed. The other was a husky, swarthy-faced tough with cropped ears and battered nose. The man they shouldered between them was as large as the two together. His clothes were filthy with dirt and caked blood; matted red hair hung over his bearded, brutal face. Klesst remembered the stories she had heard of ogres and trolls that were said to haunt the mountains, lairing in hidden caves and creeping forth at night to pull down travellers and steal little girls from their beds.

Klesst had thought the big man unconscious. But as the outlaws supported him into the room, his knees suddenly straightened, and she heard him say, "I'll sit over there."

Somewhat impatiently he pulled free of their grasp and half fell onto a low-backed oak chair next to the fire. The crop-eared bandit righted the overturned table and shoved it before him, while the blond procured a thick bottle of brandy from the trembling Cholos and crossed the room. The red-haired giant mutely accepted the bottle and tilted it to his lips for a long swallow. When he thudded it to the table, the dark green glass was empty to half its depth.

Gingerly he brushed the tangled strands of hair from his face and settled his wolfskin cloak about his shoulders, his manner at once domineering. Fresh blood soaked crude bandages along the slashed side of his leather hacton, and a crusted wound on his scalp had streaked his face with dried blood. Beneath the rust of beard and caked gore, his face was white with fever.

His eyes seemed to glow with a strange blue light by the fire. Perhaps it was the fever. Almost casually his gaze wandered about the room, touched the shadowed balcony where Klesst crouched. For an instant his eyes met hers, and Klesst froze with fear. There was something unnatural about his eyes, she instantly realized—and something familiar. But while he must have seen her, his gaze did not pause in its quick surveillance of the common room.

Instead, his stare halted on her mother's face. Thoughtfully he studied her, as if searching for a memory.

"Good evening, Ionor," he greeted her then.

Mother's lips were a tight line, and Klesst could sense the tension in her unsmiling face. "Hello, Kane," she whispered, and quickly turned her eyes from his stare.

Klesst sucked in her breath, recognizing Kane from the countless tales she had overheard of the dread bandit leader. No wonder they stood frozen in fear at the bar. . . .

Then she heard Kane ask, "Weed, did you check to see

if there was anyone else in the upstairs rooms—other than that kid up there by the railing?"

The lanky blond outlaw started to reply, "Just checked the outbuildings so far—going to search the inn right now. They said there wasn't anybody else here. . . ."

"Be certain," ordered Kane. "And stick that kid in bed."

But Klesst had already fled to her room.

"How are you feeling?" asked Weed, more than a little surprised that Kane had regained consciousness. But then there always seemed to burn some last reserve of strength within his huge body.

Kane grunted noncommittally. "Damn fever comes and goes. Hard to know where I am part of the time. Could swear I wasn't wounded that bad—unless that quarrel was poisoned."

"Ought to have Braddeyas clean that hole in your side, put on a fresh dressing. Likely it's all festered along your ribs."

"Later, maybe. Don't want to start it bleeding again." Kane rubbed his forehead wearily, wiping away dried blood and greasy trickles of sweat. "Feel stronger once I get some food down, catch some sleep. Can't spare more than a few hours—Pleddis can't be far back."

"Figure we can risk it here till dawn. Darros says Pleddis will have to camp. Demonlord's Moon tonight." Weed paused, then added: "We lost Frassos coming down the ridge."

"No point looking for him," Kane concluded simply. "Not this night."

Seth came stomping down from the rooms overhead. "Nobody else here," he reported. "Just a skinny girl, and I locked her in her room. Second floor's pretty near empty, but there's a big room with a fire going on the third."

Kane nodded. It was hard to concentrate, and he could feel his strength ebbing once more. "Put a guard where he can watch outside, Weed," he ordered. "Another man stay awake to watch things here. There's a big storeroom past the kitchen there. Tie the men and lock them inside it—no point killing them if they stay in line. Toss that body in with them.

"Leave the women out to clean up this mess. Doubt if

anyone else will come along tonight, but if they do, we don't need to give alarm the instant they walk in. Then they can put together some food for us. Watch them closely, though."

His eyes returned to Ionor's drawn face. "But you wouldn't try to poison me, would you, Ionor?"

"It's a cleaner death than I'd wish for you, Kane," came her strained reply.

"Bring me another bottle," Kane told her mockingly. "And one of those hens I smell roasting." Grudgingly she complied. Kane watched the sway of her body as she stiffly came toward him; memory of her drew his lips in a cold smile.

"Sit down," he said. Since it was not an invitation, Ionor sat down across from him, taking the chair his boot dragged forward.

"Are your memories so bitter, Ionor?"

Her voice was cold, drained of anger—deceptive, for hate edged its timbre. "You and your bandits raided my father's inn, slaughtered our guests, murdered my family, looted and set fire to Raven's Eyrie. You gave my younger sisters to your men to rape until death was a mercy! I could hear their screams even as you had your way with me. I can still hear them. No, Kane! Bitter is too sweet a word for the memories I have of you!"

No emotion touched Kane's pallid face. "Shouldn't have run off on me like you did," he said, dividing the roasted fowl with curious delicacy. "I could have made you forget that night."

His eyes seemed to wander from focus, and Ionor smiled inwardly to see the fever that racked his giant body. "Nothing will ever erase that night!" she whispered.

A rough hand squeezed her shoulder and drew her from her seat. "Bring food for us," growled Seth, his mouth stuffed with meat he had scooped up from the dead ranger's plate.

"We'll talk more later, perhaps," Kane called after her. Her shoulders tensed, but she made no reply.

"Want some opium?" queried Braddeyas, once they had secured the men in the storeroom. "It'll take the sting out of your side to where you can sleep good. You'll need your strength."

"I can sleep," mumbled Kane, swallowing a mouthful of brandy. "Don't want to dull my wits, with Pleddis likely to catch us before the next ridge." His chin declined slowly toward his chest.

Then he jerked his head erect and stared fiercely about him. "Bring my sword from my saddle!" he demanded. "Pleddis on our necks, and I sit here like a besotted lord at his wedding feast. This is no time to sleep! Fix me a pipe to hold me awake."

Weed signed insistently to Braddeyas, and the broken-toothed outlaw began to fill a pipe with coarse tobacco, secretly stuffing a large crumb of opium into the bottom of the bowl. He lit the pipe with a wood splinter and handed it to Kane.

Darros reappeared at the door, carrying Kane's long sword in one hand, while he hastily drew the bolt with his other. "Thoem! I don't like that mist!" he muttered, not voicing his true thoughts.

Kane took the strangely-hilted blade from him and rested the scabbard against his leg. Hs fingers touched it, sensed its strength. Steel knew neither pain nor exhaustion, and its only fever was the warmth of an enemy's blood. Kane wished such unfeeling strength were his, for he was desperately tired, and he dared not rest. His vision blurred and cleared with the throbbing of his skull. "I've gone into battle in worse shape than this," he said defiantly, drawing at the harsh smoke that passed so easily into hs lungs.

When the pipe was out, Weed took it from his relaxed fingers. Kane's slumped head did not lift from his chest; his breathing was slow and regular, his eyes closed.

"He'll rest better like this," explained Weed. "Let's get him to a bed. Did you say there was a place ready upstairs?"

Staggering under Kane's weight, Seth and Darros hauled their unconscious leader up the narrow stairway to the inn's topmost floor. There a common room had been prepared for several of the guests; a fire burned on its hearth, and a straw-ticked bed was covered with a quilted blanket. They stretched Kane across the bed and threw the quilt over him.

"Go on and get some rest," advised Weed. "Braddeyas and I will take first watch."

He waited until they had quit the chamber, then bent over Kane's ear. "Kane," he whispered, "Kane, can you hear me?"

Kane made a noise in his throat that might not have signified anything.

Frowning, Weed bent closer. "Where did you hide it, Kane? Remember? You always cached part of your share of the loot. Where did you take it, Kane? You can tell me, Kane. I'm your friend. We'll find your cache and use it to escape. We can live like lords in some other land. Where is it, Kane?"

But the other man seemed too deep in sleep.

Sadly Weed rose from his side. "At least don't die and leave all that gold to rot," he begged.

Opening the lattice window a few inches—for the room was warm, and Weed feared this would increase Kane's fever—he wearily left to join Braddeyas.

III

Ravens Fly by Night

A shower of sparks started up from the fire and disappeared into the black cavern of the chimney. Weed grunted and shoved again with the poker, wedging the new logs closer to their charred predecessors. Perhaps the fire would burn brighter now. The huge fireplace of limestone blocks occupied most of one end of the common room. It should have warmed the entire area; instead its flames crawled dispiritedly over the smouldering logs, and an unseasonal chill for autumn crept through the room.

Wiping his hands, he turned from the hearth to gaze once more through the window. Though the full moon was rising higher above the ridges, thick mist rolled from the Cotras to cloak the valley beyond. There was little to see as Weed squinted through the whorled panes; only the neglected grounds of the inn, the leaf-paved roadway beyond. Above the doorway, the signboard swung with the wind. Its hinges squawled like a raven's croak, and against the inn's lights it flung a swaying shadow across the frosted earth like the shadow of raven's wings.

He examined the bolted door. There should be a man posted outside, he realized. Even on this night, even though Pleddis was certainly camped a safe distance back on their trail. Again he thought of Frassos's strange disappearance. It was not a night to venture beyond the security of bright lights and locked doors. Even as a stranger to these mountains, Weed sensed the presence of evil abroad beneath Demonlord's Moon.

Gloomily he sank onto a bench, his eyes toward the

door. Behind him he could hear sounds from the kitchen. The warm smell of roasting fowl carried from the cooking area beyond the bar. Braddeyas kept watch on the two women. Once food was prepared for the ride before them, the women could be bound and locked in with the others. Then perhaps he could get Braddeyas to stand guard outside the inn.

Weed dug his fingers into his eyes, more savagely than need be, for sleep was numbing his senses. Braddeyas might refuse. Weed wouldn't blame him; he doubted that he would accept the risk, either. And while Weed was second in command now, Braddeyas had been with Kane too many years to be bullied into obedience by the younger outlaw.

The noises from the kitchen seemed farther away, almost melodious. The fire was burning better now, and he could feel its heat on his side. Weed slapped his face stingingly, fighting off the deadly fatigue. Perhaps he should walk about the room.

Maybe he should walk through the door, mount his horse, and ride out. One man would stand a far better chance of escaping pursuit. Let Pleddis overtake Kane and the others. Kane was the reason for his relentless pursuit; he would not bother to press on after one bandit. The price on Weed's head was tempting for a single bounty hunter, but Pleddis had to pay his men; economics would save him. And yet, Kane might well win free. The bandit leader had done the incredible time and again before this. Perhaps Kane could elude the arrows of fate once more.

Weed felt a certain loyalty to Kane. He had fought beside Kane, followed his commands—and Kane had proved to be a highly capable and generous leader. Indeed, in the final battle Weed and the others had broken through Pleddis's ambush on the savage force of Kane's charge through the mercenary ranks. But Weed felt a greater loyalty to his own neck, and it appeared certain that Kane would never again hold power over the Myceum passes. There remained the secret cache of loot that Kane had hidden away—against a disaster such as this. At present Weed's possessions consisted of a sorehooved mount, a notched sword, and his battle-torn gear. If Kane would lead them to his cache . . .

The sweet-smoke scent of roasting hens wrapped about him, watering his mouth, though his belly was warm with wine and meat from the meal just eaten. His head fell downward onto his arm. He should get up before sleep claimed him.

And he did rise to his feet. Or he seemed to see his body stand, pace about the room, peer through the fogged bull's-eye panes. The shadows seemed to creep and hover in grotesque patterns as he paced . . .

With a sudden jarring crash, Weed fell to the floor.

In an instant of confused panic, he thrashed free of the overturned bench and tried to regain his feet, thinking dully that he had rolled off in his sleep. Then he became aware of the jeering face above the swordpoint levelled at his throat. Weed froze.

"Now there we went and woke him up," grinned Pleddis.

Weed swallowed and waited for death. Many hands jerked him to his feet, tore away his sword and dagger. A dozen or more of Pleddis's men were pouring into Raven's Eyrie—entering through the kitchen, where Braddeyas lay with a split skull. A sudden uproar, fierce but quickly stilled, echoed across the inn as the mercenaries burst in on Darros and Seth. They died where they slept.

Weed sweated. Pleddis's blade glinted before his throat.

The mercenary captain's face was jubilant, but his eyes were like the edge of his sword. "Where's Kane?" he demanded softly.

Scarcely comprehending that disaster had so swiftly overtaken them, Weed stood silent, swaying back from the blade. His mouth was dry.

"You got half a minute to tell me. And you've just about used that up."

Ionor appeared from the kitchen. Her face was flushed and her blouse disordered. "They carried him upstairs," she announced, hatred bright in her voice. "I'll show you where."

"Carried?"

"He's wounded near death, by the look of his side. He couldn't walk."

Pleddis smiled like a wolf at her words. "By Vaul, you were right about your aim, Stundorn! I'll double your share if it sure enough was your quarrel that brought the devil low. Quickly now, show us!"

Leaving Weed under guard, the captain and a number of his men followed Ionor up the stairs to the third level. Triumphantly she led them to the door of the room where Kane had been taken. Pleddis's smile split his leathery face. Inside this room lay the object of his pursuit, the successful conclusion of a dangerous campaign. And a bounty that would leave him a wealthy man.

Knowing Kane's cunning, their weapons were poised for whatever last trick he might have left. In the darkness outside, others of his men surrounded the inn. Kane would not escape. But even with a crippling wound, they feared the savage power of his sword.

Sucking in his breath, Pleddis kicked open the door. It was unlocked. Slammed back against the wall.

Only silence met them. Kane lay sprawled across the bed, unmoving. A chill wind eddied through the open window. Blood stained the blankets. Kane's arms lay at his sides, in the attitude in which his men had left him. His face was turned to one side; a tiny pool of dampness trickled past his partly opened lips. In the flickering firelight his face seemed unnaturally lax and pale.

Wary of tricks, Pleddis approached the bed. Kane did not move. Only when he reassured himself that no weapon lay near did Pleddis touch the silent figure. Kane's skin was cold as a snake's. Almost impatiently the captain shook his still form, found his body unnaturally rigid. Frowning, he felt for a pulse, then held his blade before the motionless nostrils. No moisture fogged the cold steel.

Pleddis stood up, almost with an air of disappointment. "He's dead."

IV

Hounds and Carrion Crows

Weed slumped against a table, his arms tightly bound behind his back, his mind seeking desperately for some hope of escape. With a sick chill in his belly, he realized his position was without hope. And cutting through the dull panic was the agonizing thought that he had thrown away his life to stay with a dead man.

Pleddis's men filled the common room, warming themselves with fire, food and drink, excited congratulations. He had pulled them all inside when it was evident that the bandits had been taken; they had rushed into the inn as if it were the last refuge against the mist-shrouded night. Maybe it was. There were more than twenty men milling about the room, wearing the motley gear of mercenary soldiers. With their stamping and loud laughter, they sounded like hunters just come in from a grueling and successful hunt. From their impersonal stares, Weed felt like a snared fox surrounded by a pack of baying hounds.

Seated by the fire, Pleddis was in high spirits. He drank wine from a sloshing cup and accepted the applause of his men, his weathered face almost flushed. There was little enough color to the man. His skin was pale and seamed, bleached instead of tanned by wind and sun. His hair was close-cropped and grey, his face clean-shaven; his eyes were of a peculiar washed-out blue so as to appear grey. He was of average height, but compactly built, giving him a deceptively stubby appearance. Gear of worn leather and chain mail tunic were nondescript as his person—and the same faded grey. But his teeth were straight and white, and he flashed them in a broad smile when he laughed, which was often—a rapid, mirthless bark.

He was laughing now.

"A fine last stand for Kane and his fearsome band of killers, eh? Trapped like rabbits in a hole, sleeping like they was in their mother's arms. One man snoring at his post, the other so busy trying to get under the mistress's skirts that he never noticed she'd unlatched the woodshed door to the outside. Vaul, what dreadful desperadoes! I'm going to feel silly asking for the bounty on the likes of you! But I'll still ask!" His men joined in his laughter.

Pleddis gulped down his wine, his shrill laugh muffled against the cup. "Of course, you must have figured Captain Pleddis would lie low tonight, sit shivering at his campfire, jumping every time an owl screamed. Did you now? Sure you did. You really thought I'd quit a trail not hours cold, and after three days of chasing after you! Well, I grew up on Thovnos, so I guess I didn't hear all the gruesome tales of Demonlord's Moon you mountain people like to shudder over. Same goes for most of my men, though some of them had their worries about riding on."

His face turned grim, and he stared contemptuously over their ranks. A number of them avoided his eyes. "But it wasn't too hard to make them see that a pack of devils was a better risk than crossing Pleddis, eh?" He laughed again.

"Huh! What about the two men we lost getting here?" grumbled a mercenary from the rear, who quickly ducked from Pleddis's searching scowl.

"You'll not see them again," a husky voice told them. "The Demonlord hunts beneath this moon, and you'll see no more of them his hound pulls down."

Pleddis made an annoyed grimace. "Well, he would have found a fat enough morsel in you, old woman."

"Greshha!" There was a strange hint of anger in Ionor's voice.

The older woman crept almost guiltily from behind the mass of soldiers whose entrance she had followed. The servant's plump cheeks were still ashen with fear, and she blinked and trembled as if dazed.

"So she does belong here," said Pleddis. "We found the old woman hanging back along the road. Seemed so glad to see us she came running into our arms. Couldn't talk two words of sense—something had her bad scared. Now I see it was her own bogey tales."

"She's a servant here," explained Ionor in a tight voice. "She had been given the night off, and I had supposed she would spend it with friends in the village near here." She jerked her hand toward the kitchen, and Greshha dumbly followed her gesture.

Meanwhile Eriall, one of Pleddis's lieutenants whose face Weed knew, had carried in a grisly burden. "Here they are," he announced, holding out both fists. Clenched by their scarlet-spattered hair, three heads dangled from his grip. Their jaws hung loosely, tongues lolling, eyes rolled upward in a fish stare behind half-closed lids.

"Recognize your friends?" laughed Pleddis. "Eriall, you're dribbling blood all over your hostess's floor. Where's your manners?"

The other grinned and showed the heads to Weed. "Maybe this piece of shit ought to lick the boards clean."

"Too bad the one's skull is busted near in half," mused Pleddis, mourning a damaged trophy. "Well, pack them good in salt with the others. They bring us five ounces of gold each in Nostoblet, and I doubt the Merchants' League will care if their purchases are a bit damaged in transit. Mind you cut off that earring there."

"Why don't I just take along his while I'm doing the rest?" suggested Eriall.

Pleddis stroked his jaw thoughtfully. "How about that, Weed? Want to ride back to Nostoblet all packed in salt? They set twenty ounces of gold on your head, but maybe they'll pay a little extra if we hand you over intact. You'd rate a public execution all to yourself. Be real nice. Which way do you want it now?"

"Let me kill him," snarled Ionor.

Pleddis considered her gravely. "Bloodthirsty is the lust of a woman," he misquoted. "But I'd like to carry one back alive to Nostoblet, so he can tell everyone there how Captain Pleddis ran them down and made raven food out of the whole damned wolfpack."

Ionor's face was twisted, her breath fast. Weed thought

of a hot-clefted slut who had been cheated of her climax. "Hang him from the railing then for me—I want to watch him die. It's my right. You caught them in my inn. You might still be trailing them if they hadn't stopped here."

Pleddis seemed to be weakening. "They might pay extra if he's alive."

"I've given you food and lodging here," argued Ionor. "The extra gold will be less than payment."

"But you owe me your lives for saving you from Kane's men," Pleddis pointed out. The game amused him.

"Should I add Kane's head to the others?'" broke in Eriall.

"Not when they'll pay me five hundred ounces of gold for Kane," Pleddis brayed. "For that I'll bring in the whole carcass. Bad as they want Kane, they'll likely pickle him in brine and put him on display. Bet they could charge admission just to see him. Bet they will, in fact!

"No, it's cold enough we can sling him over a horse, and he'll last until we can get back to Nostoblet. They won't care what he smells like there. Stundorn, take a few men and drag Kane's body down here. We'll leave him in the stables where the frost will keep him from getting ripe too fast. Watch that the dogs don't get at him."

They had left Kane where he lay when they found him dead. Several minutes had passed since then, in the confused aftermath of Pleddis's attack on the inn. But now the captain's attention returned to the prize quarry of his hunt. Stundorn and some others disappeared up the stairs.

"Weed, I'm still not sure what to do with you," he continued.

"Hang him," Ionor pleaded, her memory reliving a scene eight years back. A memory of familiar faces turning purple, of limbs thrashing a death dance from an impromptu gallows, while murder-crazed animals roared in laughter below.

"I suppose I can grant the request of a handsome lady," gallantly remarked Pleddis, thinking that his hostess had a definite beauty beneath the harsh mask of hatred.

Weed forced himself to speak with scornful assurance. "Grant it and be damned. I can't hope for any better in

Nostoblet. And I'll die with the secret of Kane's hidden cache of loot."

It was a foolish bluff, he realized in panic. But against imminent death, any respite would offer hope.

"Well, now . . ." began Pleddis, his eyes lighting with sudden interest.

Stundorn burst onto the balcony, his bearing totally shaken.

"Kane's gone!" he blurted.

V

To Chase the Dead

Kane breathed a silent curse as his boot slipped from its purchase on the limestone wall. For an instant he swung precariously in the darkness, only the steel grip of his fingers against the stone block saving him from a thirty-foot drop to the frosted earth below. The fall might not kill him, but it was crippling height for surety. Grimly he forced his scrambling boot back into a masonry crack and rested his arms from the tearing weight of his massive frame. His great strength now seemed scarcely sufficient to stand upright, and his wounded side was lancing agony—but at least the strain and the chill air had cleared his thoughts somewhat.

From the open window above him, Kane heard the startled shouts of Pleddis's soldiers. Baffled rage flamed within him. He had needed more time to descend the wall of the inn. Weakened as he was, he could never reach the ground before a frantic search revealed him to his enemies. Again his boot slipped as he sought to hurry his descent. The limestone blocks of the inn had been set flush in the wall originally—a precaution against athletic thieves or guests who cared not to settle their account. Only because mountain winds and winters had eroded the masonry over the years was Kane able to find purchase—such purchase as there was.

Not even extreme exhaustion and the mists of opium had completely dulled Kane's uncanny senses. The feral instincts that countless times had drawn him from sleep to full awareness of imminent danger had called to him once again. Kane had awakened to the brief clamour of Pleddis's attack, and almost instantly he had understood his position.

Even at peak condition Kane would have stood no chance against a score of seasoned mercenaries. And he knew he was trapped—knew without wasting a glance outside that a man of Pleddis's capability would have surrounded Raven's Eyrie before thrusting within. In another minute his enemies would be smashing down his door—unless he decided to make a suicidal rush down the stairs, or let an archer pick him off as he scrambled down the outside wall.

A desperate plan came to him then. Pleddis knew he was gravely injured. He would let the bounty hunter find him dead. Any number of risks suggested themselves to him instantly, but plainly there was no other course. Pleddis would lower his guard only if he believed his quarry dead.

It was not too difficult for one of Kane's knowledge. His appearance was ghastly enough for a corpse, and the cold draft through the window coupled with the chill sweat that had seized him would impart a convincing clamminess to his flesh. Over the centuries Kane had delved deeply into all manner of occult studies, and the discipline of imposing mental control over physical functions was known to students far less adept than Kane. For much of their ride, Kane had held himself in a near trance to conserve his strength, and now he withdrew his consciousness into a deeper coma, rigidly controlling breath and heart beat to so low an ebb as to appear lifeless to Pleddis's inspection.

Several minutes after his enemies had quit his bedside, Kane returned to full awareness. He realized he now had only a few minutes to escape—a short interval once Pleddis had ordered his men from their surveillance of the inn. They would celebrate the success of their long hunt; for a moment all would be jubilant confusion. Then for any of a hundred reasons someone would return to the dead man upstairs. By then Kane must be gone.

He had cut it close. Too close. Kane had barely lowered himself through the window when Stundorn entered the room. In another instant their stunned fright would leave them. Someone would peer out the open window.

And he could never reach the ground in time. Quickly Kane took the only course left to him. Another window was close at hand. Recklessly Kane clawed his way to the darkened aperture. Somehow he managed to maintain a hold long enough to rest his weight on the ledge. He pushed at the lattice.

It was secured.

Kane bit his lip and tore a knife from his belt. He jammed its blade into the crack between window and casement. His movements seemed panic-driven, but his haste was that of one experienced in his task. In only a few seconds the latch snapped free.

Swinging open the heavy lattice, Kane squeezed through the window. No sooner had his cloak and sword scabbard cleared the ledge than a shout from close by signalled that someone had looked outside.

"No one on the wall!" a soldier called out.

Kane grinned savagely and glared through the darkness of the room. He was not alone.

A small figure crouched on the room's narrow bed. Her wide eyes were almost luminous as she stared at him—a huge, menacing figure outlined in the moonlight at her window.

"Are you alive?" she whispered. His appearance was supernatural, and she had been listening to the shouts outside her door.

Kane made no comment. He had swung into the child's room, and he remembered that the door was locked from outside. His dagger still shone in his hand. "Don't make a sound!" he hissed.

Klesst's voice was grave. "I won't tell them you're here," she said, "Father."

"I remember one time down along the coast," Pleddis said, staring into the empty room. "It was late fall, and we were making camp for the night. Dragging in drift-wood for a fire, and one of the outfit hauls loose a big snag—and there's a swamp adder thick as your arm, all laid out and sluggish with cold. Kid was from the coast, knew what he had, so he just laid into it with the stick of wood he was carrying, not even wasting time to pull his sword. Must of hit it fifty times, till the stick busted and the snake was half flattened out. Had to be dead; we didn't think any more about it.

"Long about the end of second watch we all woke up —Vaul, it was a scream to chill your guts! There was the kid flopping out of his blanket roll, that damn black snake with its fangs buried in his neck. Hell, its head was bigger than your fist and full of venom, and I don't guess the kid lived long enough for us to stir up the fire.

"After that night I never trusted a dead snake. Always hack them to chunks, no matter how dead they look. Except just now," he concluded bitterly.

"He can't of got far," Eriall judged. "Hadn't had no time, and crippled up like he was."

Pleddis grunted and inspected the window casement. Lanterns flashed from the ground below. "What do you see?" he called down.

Nattios bawled back, "Nothing. No marks below. We're looking along the wall."

The mountaineer was no fool at tracking, Pleddis knew. "Well, look closer. There's blood on the ledge here."

"No. Nothing," came the reply after a pause.

"There's rocks down there," Eriall said, craning his squat neck to look down.

"Yeah, and there's frost, too," Nattios retorted gruffly. "Good as sand for leaving tracks. Ain't nothing."

"Well, Kane couldn't have crawled down that wall, anyway," the stocky lieutenant declared. "Man that big couldn't scale these stones even if he wasn't busted up. The blood's a false trail."

Pleddis's laugh returned. It was not pleasant. "Kane could have done it. He's not lying in bed there. He either went out the window or out the door. I got men at every exit, so if there's no tracks outside he has to be hiding inside. Won't do him any good, because we'll find him."

"Could be he got out somewhere else, mixed his trail in with our tracks," Eriall persisted. "We came in from all around the sides, you know."

"Could be. But I figure Kane didn't have the time to do anything too fancy. He's hiding in here somewhere. If he's not, we'll pick up his trail wth the dogs they got here. Long as we keep him from the horses, he won't get far."

Stundorn's stubbled face was strange. "Captain, you're sure he was just faking he was dead, then?"

Pleddis glared at him. "Dead men don't run out on you." Abruptly he scowled. "Unless some bastard slipped back and stole the corpse for the bounty!" He thought carefully. "No, I can account for all of us, and for the bunch that stay here, too. Still, if I find some bastard's pulling a fast one, there's going to be one more head in that salt pack, and it won't cost the Merchants' League a copper!"

But Stundorn remembered that his quarrel was supposed to have given Kane his death wound. "All the same, captain, it's the Demonlord's Moon. They say his powers hold sway over the mountains tonight. Maybe he could make the dead rise. And there's all kinds of black legends about Kane. We may be trailing a dead man, captain."

Pleddis stood a moment, face impassive. Then his laugh barked rustily. "Maybe so, Stundorn. But you just remember that corpse is worth five hundred ounces of yellow gold, and if he comes looking for you, just yell for me."

"Father!" exploded Kane, in a louder tone than he intended. He crossed the room to the girl's bed.

"Yes," Klesst whispered. "I saw you come in, and they said you were Kane. The children in the village call me Kane's bastard. They say you carried Mother away after you raided the inn, and after she escaped and came back she had me, and you were my father."

Kane stared at her.

"See. I have red hair like yours, and my eyes are blue like yours." Klesst did not flinch from Kane's stare. "I can even see in the dark better than the other children, like the stories tell about you."

"Your grandmother," Kane muttered, touching the child's face.

"So I won't tell those soldiers where you are," Klesst concluded.

"You should hate me." Her skin was feverish. As was his.

"No," declared Klesst. "The others hate me. But when

they hear stories about you, then they look frightened. I like to see them frightened. I like to think they're even a little frightened of me."

Kane shook his head. The excited shouts of his pursuers brought him back to the moment. Turning from her, he risked a glance through the window. Outside they were circling the inn with torches and lanterns. He knew they would find no trail. Then they would begin to search the inn. Digging grime from his boots, he smudged over the bright scratches made by his knife on the latch. There was no smear of blood on the casement that he could see.

Grimly he took stock of his chances. They were not good. All that his ruse had accomplished was to give him another few minutes. The end was inevitable, unless he could slip through their net. And even then . . .

Kane forced his mind to think clearly. For the moment, the threat of certain death had spurred him from exhaustion. Some final reserve of strength kept him moving when he should lie senseless, pushed back the black waves of fever and opium. The barricades must soon break.

"I knew you from my dream," his daughter told him. "But then I didn't know your name."

About to warn her to be silent, Kane stopped. "How can you dream of someone you've never seen?" he wondered, somewhat in awe of the child. Seeing her brought memories that he cared not to linger upon just now.

"I saw you," Klesst insisted. "And another man, all in black with a great black cloak. He has a great black hound. . . ."

Kane frantically signed for her to be silent. A number of men were coming down the hall. They were searching the rooms.

Kane's hand reached over his right shoulder, and the ancient blade of Carsultyal steel silently swung from its scabbard. It was a good weapon, Kane thought with grim pride. This one had been difficult to find—probably few like it still existed. Carsultyal lay buried by sand and sea and time. And the ancient city's last citizen would very shortly lie dead with its memory.

Again he glanced outside. They were watching from below. The soldiers in the hall—he might kill the first group to enter, but there were more to take their place, and Kane was trapped—wounded so that his last fight would not even be a good one.

The door was locked from outside. And there was Klesst. It might make them less thorough in their search; they would likely assume the child would cry out if Kane had somehow hidden inside her room.

A futile hope, probably. And the room was too small. Kane assumed it was one of the narrow single rooms for wealthy travellers who deigned not to share quarters with other guests. Such accommodations cost dear and were cramped, but at least a well-to-do traveller would not have to share a bed with three hog drovers.

The search was only a few doors away.

And there was no place to hide. Just a bare-timbered room. No chests, no tapestries. Kane's huge frame could never squeeze under Klesst's tiny bed. There was a closet. That in itself marked the room as once a luxury accommodation. Kane swung open its door. The closet was surprisingly large, considering the economy of space that an inn demanded. An oddly dank smell came from within. A few nondescript items of clothing hung from pegs along the interior.

It was worth a chance. At any event, Kane decided, when they opened the door he would hurl himself out, with luck cut down a couple of them before they could meet his rush. It was better than standing there like a condemned man in the middle of his death cell.

"What's your name?" he asked suddenly.

"Klesst."

"Well, Klesst, I'm going to step inside your closet. I want you to pull this latch down from outside, and then get back in bed. When the soldiers come in, just tell them no one's been in here. And if they don't believe you and look inside . . . well, afterwards you can tell them that I said I'd hurt you unless you did as I told you."

Klesst nodded, impressed by the important task he had given her. She smiled uncertainly as she shut the closet, then quickly shot the latch. She barely had time to scurry back to bed before they came to her door.

"This is the kid's room," someone observed. "Been locked."

"Well, open it, anyway," ordered a gruff voice.

A scraping of the bolt, then suspicious faces peered in from the hall.

The gruff voice belonged to a paunchy man with thick shoulders and a rolling gait. He carried an arbalest, his fingers near the trigger. "Hey, kid," he demanded, "anybody come in here?"

"No, sir," Klesst said, being polite to make hm trust her.

Their eyes carefully searched the shadows of the room.

"You sure?"

"Yes, sir."

"You been awake?"

"Yes, sir."

"You sure you ain't been asleep?"

"No . . . I mean, yes, sir."

The man with the arbalest entered the room. Several other men followed. Swords were bare in their fists.

A thin-faced mercenary examined the window. "It's locked, Stundorn. No sign of blood or anything," he stated in a nasal voice.

Stundorn shifted his arbalest. Klesst wondered why the steel bow didn't snap its string. "Might have been open before. This room is below Kane's, off to the side only a little. He might have climbed down."

He frowned at Klesst. "You see anything, kid?"

"No, sir."

"You wouldn't lie now, would you?"

"No, sir."

"Do you know what happens to little girls who lie?"

"Yes, sir." Klesst's imagnation grappled with the possibilities.

"And you haven't seen any sign of a big bandit with blood just pouring down his ribs where I shot him?"

"No, sir."

"Closet's latched from outside," someone noted.

"Now you aren't hiding my bandit inside your closet, are you?" Stundorn rumbled.

"No, sir." *What did happen to little girls who lied?*

"Do you know I got an itchy nose?"

"No, sir."

"It's a fact. My nose itches every time I hear a lie."

Klesst stared in horrid fascination.

"Now why do you suppose it's itching right now?"

"I don't know, sir," she answered shakily.

Stundorn stood back from the closet door. He brought his arbalest to his shoulder, sighted about chest height on the door. His fingers curled over its trigger.

"Now open that door, Profaka," he directed the thin-faced mercenary.

Gingerly Profaka reached across to the latch and drew it back.

He yanked open the door.

The closet was empty.

"This place is clean," Eriall informed his leader. "Been through it from attic to cellar, looked in every hole bigger than a chamber pot. Ain't no Kane, and that's a fact."

Pleddis nodded tiredly. He had overseen most of the work. "Yeah, and no one made a break for the outside; I had men out there watching every block of stone on this inn."

The captain banged his fist on the wall in anger. "Obviously, then, Kane somehow got outside before we realized his trick."

"But how? We pretty well proved he had to be inside."

"Well, we damn well just proved he's not inside! Now you tell me where that leaves us!"

Eriall was silent. He massaged his shaven skull. Pleddis's laugh startled him.

"Sure, I know what he did!" His white teeth flashed in a grin. "You just got to think like Kane thinks. Now Kane's smart, and he's got a lot of tricks. He went out the window, sure, but he didn't climb down. That's what he knew we'd think he'd do. So instead Kane climbed *up!* He was on the top floor, so getting to the roof was actually easier than climbing all the way to the ground.

"Kane must have worked his way along the roof up to where it abuts the burned-out north wing. Then he just climbed down onto the old walls and groped his way down into the gutted interior, and slipped through the rubble and into the night—while we were standing like fools wondering where his body had got to!"

"Then he's had a good start all this time we been looking under beds!" Eriall growled.

"Maybe," Pleddis admitted, still pleased with his cleverness. "But Kane don't have a horse. Wounded and on foot we'll run him down in an hour. Nattios! Find Ionor and tell her we'll need dogs for tracking! Hurry! What's the matter?"

"We're going to track Kane now?" the mountaineer queried uneasily. "It will soon be midnight. The Demonlord will hunt—"

"Move, damn you!" Pleddis hissed. "Yes, we're going to track him! Do you want the Demonlord to catch him? Lord Tloluvin don't need that gold!"

"Don't speak his name!" Nattios gasped. Seeing the vicious anger rise in Pleddis's eyes, he ran to find Ionor.

VI

In Seven Years You'll Hear a Bell . . .

Ionor turned on Greshha with thinly checked fury. "Why did you come back? I told you to take tonight off."

They were alone in the inn's great kitchen. Shouts close by told of Pleddis's fast-moving search of the rambling structure. The two drovers had joined in, and Ionor had ordered Cholos and Mauderas to help the mercenaries—even directing Sele to guide the searchers through the huge inn. Ionor felt certain Kane would be found if he were hiding within the walls of Raven's Eyrie. If not . . .

Her jaw tightened as she scowled at the older woman. Greshha was avoiding her eyes. "I said, why didn't you stay away?"

The servant woman took a deep breath. Her thick body shook. "I guess I know you didn't want me here," she mumbled, face downcast.

"What did you say?"

Greshha raised her chin; her eyes were shrewd. "I guess I know why you wanted me to stay away tonight," she stated in a louder voice, defiantly.

A hiss escaped Ionor's tightly drawn lips. She started to swing back her hand, then checked her arm. "What are you talking about?" Her voice was like a slap.

"I'm no fool. I can remember," Greshha stolidly told her. "I know you hate the child."

Ionor's long fingers clenched and opened, like a pantheress flexing her claws. She tossed her head, and her loose braid flicked over her shoulder, twitched down her back like an angry black tail.

The stout mountain woman did not quail before her mistress's obvious look of menace. "Poor Klesst. I can't blame you for hating her when she came. But after all these years! I kept taking care of her when it was your place, hoping you'd learn to love her. But you never did, Ionor. There's no loving left in you—only hate. Hate's eaten the soul out of your breast, so you can't even love your own flesh. . . ."

"Shut up, you fat fool! I've tolerated your meddling, but you've overstepped your place this time!"

"I never thought you'd go through with it. All this time I kept thinking you'd soften to her. But you're cold, burned out, Ionor. There's no heart left in you. I know now you mean to do it."

Ionor drew back against the cutting table, her lips twisted in a snarl. "What are you talking about?"

Ducking her head for breath, Greshha plunged on. Her round face took on an aspect of sullen determination. "I was here when you were birthing her, don't forget. I stayed with you when your screams and curses drove everyone else from your bed. I held you down and tried to comfort you when the midwife had to use the knife to bring her forth from your womb. And even while you screamed out things to make the gods turn away from you, I stayed with you and pitied you because no one thought you could live through the night.

"Seven years ago tonight, it was, Ionor. And they all said it was a miracle when both you and the child lived through. But only I knew what kind of miracle it was."

"You're an old fool, Greshha!"

"Old, but no fool. The things you was screaming weren't good to cry out—not with the Demonlord's Moon shining down through your window. They weren't good to hear, and that's why the others drew away from you that night. I'll confess it, I was afraid myself, and when the child was born, and the midwife had done what she could, and we thought the opium would let you ease into sleep . . . Well, I left you, too, and told myself to look to the child because her mother would be gone by daybreak.

"Then when the dogs began to howl and cringe, and the others all huddled by the fire and prayed . . . I couldn't leave you alone to die, not when the fires all burned low and blue under the shadows. I crept back to your room, praying each step, and afraid to think what it was we heard snuffling outside the inn..

"And I stopped at your door when I heard your voice, and when I heard that *other* voice answer, I knew who you was talking with, and I knew it was worse than death to open your door. I just froze there too scared to tremble, and the words you two spoke burned into my memory like hot iron into flesh. And after *he* left, I still stood there crying and praying and not making a sound. And when I finally took heart to look in the door, I saw you lying there asleep with a black smile on your lips, and I knew your strength would be back in the morning.

"But before the gods, Ionor, I never thought you'd do it! I swear I would have smothered you there as you lay if I had believed that. I kept thinking, she'll learn to love once she's held the child to her breast and she forgets the horror and the shame and the pain. But you never held the child to your breast, and you never learned to love her—because all that's left in you is hate, Ionor.

"So I knew why you wanted me gone tonight, and that's why I wouldn't go. And I'll not go. I'll not let you do it."

"You meddling old fool!" spat Ionor. "If you dare interfere . . . But what can you do?"

Greshha expanded her shoulders truculently. "There's soldiers here. Captain Pleddis has League authority. He won't let you do this thing."

Ionor laughed. "Pleddis is a cold-blooded bounty killer. His soldiers are hired thugs. He'll not care what I do. He only wants Kane."

"Maybe so. I guess I'll find out what he'll do."

"Don't be a bigger fool!"

"Maybe he'll be interested if I tell him he might not *get* Kane."

"I'm warning you!"

Greshha looked at her livid face and backed away. No longer was there doubt in her mind; instead there was fear. The servant woman started for the door to the common room; she could hear heavy boots approaching from there.

As she turned, Ionor's hand came away from the cutting

table. The sharpening steel in her fist made a rotten crunch as she brought it down over Greshha's skull. The mountain woman crumpled to the floor with no more sound than a dropped sack of grain.

Ignoring the huddled body, Ionor glared at the door. She had acted out of desperate rage, without forethought. And someone was entering the kitchen.

It was Mauderas. He halted at the threshold in surprise. His hulking figure blocked the doorway; behind him stretched the inn's bar, and beyond she could see several of Pleddis's men moving through the common room.

"Close that door!" she hissed. "Lock it!"

Mauderas obeyed, a stunned expression on his dark face. "What happened?"

"Never mind," Ionor told him. "I had to stop her from talking to Pleddis."

"She dead?"

"I think so. We can't let them find her."

Mauderas licked his mustache and surveyed the room. The outer doors were barred, but Pleddis's men were watching from outside. Fortunately the windows were shuttered on the back wall. No one had seen . . . yet.

"I don't see what Pleddis would care about—"

"Don't forget Captain Pleddis is a lawman!" she snapped. "Maybe he wouldn't use his authority, maybe he would. No point in tempting luck. I don't want to fool around with that bounty hunter right now. We'll have to hide her body—tell them she went back to the village, if anyone asks."

"How? She's too big to stuff under something, and Pleddis's men are all over the place. Someone's going to want to come in here any minute. They can't turn up Kane anywhere, and Pleddis was about to tear up the floorboards looking for hiding places."

"I know; they came through here twice before. Does it look like Kane left the inn, then?"

Mauderas nodded. "Pleddis figured out how. They'll be out scouring the ridges next."

Ionor thought carefully for a moment and came to a decision. "Then we'll do it the old way. Take her out the passage and sink her. That way it's certain they won't find her."

Mauderas put a broad hand on her shoulder. "Been a long time since I sunk anyone."

"I feel confident you haven't lost your touch."

"Passage hasn't been opened since the raid. Thought you wanted to forget the old days, keep the passage closed up."

"I know what I said. But I don't want to risk complications with Pleddis."

Mauderas shrugged. "Anyway you call it then, Ionor."

Stooping over the limp body, he arranged the loose limbs with the calm competence of one who knows his task. With a grunt he rose up again, Greshha's lax figure slung across his broad back. "The old woman weighs more than a side of beef," he grumbled.

But Ionor had left him. Descending the steps to the wine cellar, she paused to grasp a portion of the railing. With a sharp tug, the upright swung out from the banister like a lever. It was a lever. Somewhere below a counterbalance released, and a large section of the flagstone cellar floor rumbled smoothly into the outer wall.

A square of blackness opened in the cellar floor, from which a stale, damp wind welled up. It was like a breath from some slumbering behemoth. Indeed, the sound of muffled breathing seemed to emanate from within—a distant rushing moan.

Stairs of greasy limestone descended into the gloom. Mauderas took a lamp from Ionor, holding it clumsily under the weight of his burden. He eyed the passage doubtfully.

"Hurry! I think I hear someone calling for me!"

Mauderas grunted and put a boot on the top step. "Oh, I'll hurry. But I'll hurry back to keep you warm tonight."

Ionor made an impatient gesture. "Stay there for a while before you return to the inn—and leave by the other way. They'll believe me if I say you went to walk Greshha part way to the village. And later no one will question a disappearance on Demonlord's Moon."

"Anyway you call it, honey," Mauderas drawled, his voice rising from the darkness. "I'll be along to keep you warm directly."

Hurriedly Ionor swung the lever back to its upright position. The section of flagstones grated back into place. Pounding on the kitchen door was thunderous as she emerged from the cellar.

"Sorry. I was getting brandy," she explained, unbolting the door to admit Nattios and several of his fellows. "With that devil running loose, a lady likes to keep herself locked in safe."

VII

Raven's Secret

Satisfied that no bones were broken, Kane struggled to his feet. He would limp badly, but his high boots had reinforced his ankles so that the shock of impact had not resulted in a disabling sprain or worse. Or worse. He massaged his aching shoulder; his right arm had almost been torn from its socket. But by all rights he should be lying here with a broken neck.

Kane looked about him, reconstructing what had happened now that the scarlet bursts of pain were receding from his consciousness.

When Klesst had fastened the closet door, Kane had stepped back against its wall. He had a vague impression of reaching to steady himself. His groping fingers closed on something—had it been one of the pegs?—that had swung inward with his shove.

Then the section of closet floor on which he stood dropped away, and Kane felt himself plunging through darkness. Blindly he struck out. His fingers closed on wood—the rung of a ladder. But the rotted wood tore away under the wrenching force of Kane's three hundred pounds of bone and muscle.

Spun about by the jarring contact, Kane desperately clawed at the wall. Other mildewed rungs smashed against his grasp, splintered under his weight. But it was enough to check his hurtling body. Kane's steel-tendoned fingers locked onto the flashing rungs, almost bringing his fall short. Then the dragging mass of his body proved more than the weakened timbers could withstand. The ladder tore loose from its anchorage to the wall and careened to the stones below.

It had been enough to break his fall, Kane dropped the final eight or ten feet and struck the stones on his feet, the wreckage of the ladder splintering beneath him.

He lay for several minutes, semiconscious after the stunning impact. Above him stretched a seemingly endless shaft of blackness. Kane had no clear idea of how far he had fallen. He was in a chamber beneath the cellars of Raven's Eyrie. Klesst's room must be at least fifty feet above—probably more, since the sound of his fall seemed to have brought no response from his pursuers.

Patches of skin were abraded from his hands, and he dug out several large splinters. Gingerly he flexed his fingers, found they were otherwise uninjured. A smile twitched his bleeding lips, for a man with crippled hands was more helpless than if he had broken his leg. Casting about, he found his sword, its point buried inches in the damp limestone. He drew it out, reflecting he had narrowly missed being impaled on its tempered steel.

Once more he gazed up the pitch-dark shaft. He had triggered a trapdoor in the rear of the closet, somewhere above. Obviously a counterbalance had sprung the trap shut once again, otherwise he would see light and puzzled faces would be staring down at him. A ladder was anchored to one wall of the shaft, though it appeared unlikely he would be able to climb back up after the destruction his fall had caused.

Kane had just begun to form a guess as to the shaft's purpose, when he heard a grating rumble overhead. Light suddenly washed down from the roof of the chamber some fifty feet to his left. A section of stone had slid open, revealing a long flight of stone steps. Voices trickled down.

Baring his teeth in a snarl—*Had Pleddis's hounds sniffed him out even in this lost hole?*—Kane concealed himself behind a massive stone column. Sword in bleeding fist, he waited.

Instead of the anticipated rush of mercenaries, Kane saw only one man descend the steps—and then the door overhead slid shut. His eyes narrowed in calculation. The man he recognized as one of Ionor's servants; the dead woman he carried slung over his back Kane had never seen before. This turn of events was a mystery to him. More to the point, it meant that his presence here had not been discovered—on the contrary, the brawny servant seemed intent on a task which demanded secrecy.

The newcomer carried a lantern in his fist. Its light was hardly sufficient to disclose the walls of the chamber—tens of yards across, and in places shored and vaulted. Evidently the room was a natural cavern which at one time had been roughly restructured to serve as a hidden cellar. A damp breeze ghosted through the darkness, causing the lantern flame to dance, and Kane noted a narrow passage leading out of the cellar's far wall.

Mauderas glanced about the hidden cellar, his face showing more fear than suspicion. This was a place where countless dark crimes had bloodied the stones. It was not a wholesome spot to linger, particularly on the night of Demonlord's Moon.

"What the hell!" he muttered, raising his lantern suddenly. He tensed as the feeble light picked out the splintered ends of the ladder, pointing in all directions like the half-flexed fingers of a dead man's hand. The woman's body slid from his shoulders with a heavy flopping sound.

"That wasn't so rotten it would of collapsed by itself," Mauderas thought aloud. Drawing his sword, he shuffled toward the wreckage, the lantern thrust before him like a shield.

Which left him blind to anything outside the close circle of its light. As he crept past, Kane leaped from the shadow of the pillar. Mauderas sensed his rush and started to turn. Kane's heavy blade sheared off half his face as it passed down through his neck.

The lantern smashed against the floor. A pool of flame licked over the damp stone. Grotesque shadows writhed over the nitre-frosted walls, mocking killer and slain, as Kane wiped his blade clean of the dead man's gore.

"Kane . . ." A rasping voice called to him.

He spun on his heels, a curse exploding from his throat.

"Kane . . . is it you?" the eerie voice whispered.

Kane stalked toward the sound. In the rippling light he saw that the woman Mauderas had carried had raised herself weakly.

He knelt at her side. "I'm Kane," he told her, noting the blood that matted her hair.

Her ashen face was lax; her arms quivered spasmodically. Seemingly she had barely strength left to whisper. "The child, Kane . . . Save Klesst . . . She may be of your seed, but she's innocent."

"Why is Klesst in any danger, old woman?"

"Ionor . . . She birthed her seven years ago tonight. . . . Nothing but hate in her . . . She called out to him for vengeance that night. . . ."

"Called out to whom?"

"I heard him at her bedside. . . . His black hound was clawing at our door. . . . The Demonlord came to her. . . ."

Only willpower held life in the mountain woman's dying flesh. All strength had left her—only her eyes and lips showed trembling movement, like the final flickering of a lampwick when no more oil remains. Her voice was trailing off, and Kane anxiously bent his ear to her face.

"The Demonlord bargained with her that night. In seven years he'd draw you back to Raven's Eyrie. In seven years he'd come with his hound to drag your living flesh down to Hell. Ionor would see her vengeance fulfilled—but the price would be the child. Ionor must take Klesst to Raven's Bald where the Demonlord and his black hound wait. She must give the hellhound your spoor by throwing the child into its maw. . . .

"Then the black hound will come for you, Kane, to drag your evil soul down to everlasting torment in its master's realm . . . and there's no place you can hide from the hound of Hell! It's no worse than you deserve, but the child's done no wrong. Don't let her sacrifice Klesst. . . . There's naught but hate in—"

Greshha's whisper was no longer audible. Kane shook her still form, intent on learning more. And now her eyes and lips were fixed and silent. As they would be forevermore.

The pool of flaming oil crept into tiny islands of fire that one by one snapped and died. Kane arose from the dead woman, and the chamber was once more in darkness.

He stood wondering for a moment, while his uncanny

eyes adapted somewhat to the thick gloom. Numbness was stealing over his body. Fighting the pain and exhaustion that clouded his perception and dragged at his limbs, Kane limped toward the passage at the opposite wall. The damp and softly moaning breath issuing from the blackness indicated the passage must lead outward—and Kane had no desire to return to the inn, even if he could gain entrance without discovery.

The passage was cramped, with walls and floor of irregular masses of limestone. Kane judged that portions of the rock had been broken away to enlarge the natural tunnel. He had begun to form an idea of the hidden cellar's function, and when he reached the end of the passage, his suspicions were confirmed.

The tunnel opened onto a narrow ledge, jutting midway from the limestone bluff below Raven's Eyrie. The River Cotras rushed thunderously beneath the mists another hundred feet down. Close by the mouth of the passage lay a pile of fist-sized stones and broken rubble—harmless enough, but Kane read a more sinister interpretation.

Before the raid, Raven's Eyrie had been a prosperous caravanserai. But Ionor's family had gathered its great wealth by darker harvests than the hosting of trail-weary travellers. Kane suddenly realized that he had uncovered the chilling secret of Raven's Eyrie.

Such inns of terror were not rare along desolate roads through untilled wilderness. Kane had encountered them on occasion, although never on so grand a scale as Raven's Eyrie, whose dark secret had never been suspected. He wondered how many other hidden passages opened into guest's rooms like the one he had unwittingly stood over and tripped. How many black crimes, what heaps of stolen riches, had this hidden cellar known? Studying the cairn of fist-sized rocks, Kane thought of the nameless travellers who had been secretly dragged from their beds to this unhallowed cellar, where here, their bellies ripped open and weighted with stones, their corpses were thrown from the ledge to sink forever in the deep current far below.

No doubt their disappearance, if noted, would have been laid to marauding gangs of outlaws; some of the crimes, Kane bitterly reflected, were probably laid to his name. But now the passage showed evidence of long disuse, and Kane wondered why. Did wealthy travellers no longer risk these trails; were their guests too few to disappear without notice? Or was Ionor of a less murderous temperament than her predecessors here? Remembering the hatred in her eyes tonight, Kane doubted this last.

He dismissed the matter; it was of no concern. Instead there was Pleddis to deal with. And the words of the dying woman. Truth or madness? Kane dared not disregard her whispered warning. He knew the power of hate.

Klesst—he must get to Klesst. For the child was the key to the doom Ionor intended for him. But the ladder in the shaft was hopelessly damaged; even if Kane could somehow bridge the missing section, he doubted that it would bear his weight. And Pleddis held the inn. There were other secret doors, he knew, but it would be impossible to evade detection if he returned to the inn. His escape from there had taken the limit of his strength and guile—and then it was chance that had saved him. He could not hope for this a second time.

Kane's head felt light, dizzy. It was death to get to Klesst. But if he could not reach the child, Ionor would seal her pact with the Demonlord. Then Pleddis and his hired killers would show him far greater mercy than the doom which would certainly claim him.

It was hard to concentrate. Kane's strength ebbed, as pain and fatigue racked his flesh, fever and drug mists swirled through his brain. Raven's Knob, the old woman had whispered—there Ionor was to seal her unhallowed bargain. Kane had a memory of that jutting spur of barren rock and lightning-blasted trees. Rising from the bleak crest of a high ridge, it was a landmark in the region and the setting for any number of dark legends. No sane man would approach Raven's Knob when the Demonlord's Moon rose behind it. Possibly not even Pleddis could force his men to carry their search to its slopes.

Ionor would take Klesst there. Kane knew he must reach Raven's Knob first. But he had no idea how much time remained to him. He had heard Ionor's voice when Mauderas entered the hidden cellar. Very little time had passed. Ionor, however, would take a straight course for Raven's Knob. Kane, weakened and uncertain of the path, must elude Pleddis's searchers in order to reach the point. And the night held dangers far more sinister than mercenary steel.

There was no other way. Cold anger seethed in Kane's heart. He had been driven across the land, ensnared in this deadly web, each step of his course seemingly predetermined. He would not be the blind pawn in some dark game fate played.

The ledge seemed to twist downward at a steep slant from the mouth of the passage. Clumps of laurel anchored to cracks and folds in the almost sheer face of the bluff; their roots held crumbling shelves of soil and broken rock. They were treacherous footholds under the best conditions; tonight Kane could not imagine worse. Presumably, though, he could work his way to the riverbank along this deadly pretense of a path. If he slipped . . .

There was no other way.

Fighting the weakness that gnawed at him, the vertigo that already blurred his mind, Kane set his boots against the slippery ledge.

VIII

And That Will Be Your Call to Hell . . .

"Stundorn, you know better than to hit an unconscious man," Pleddis told him. "Wait until he comes to again so he can feel it!" He threw back his head with braying laughter.

The paunch-gutted mercenary spat and unwound the cestus from his fist. "May be a while."

"He'll keep," grinned Pleddis, critically studying Weed's broken face. It took some of the frustrated pain from his belly to picture Kane hanging there instead.

Weed's battered body slowly spun about. The bandit's arms had been tied behind his back. Then a longer rope had been tied to his wrists, its other end wound around the balcony railing. They had hoisted him above the floor in this manner, his toes only inches from support. While he hung there, his shoulders threatening to tear from their sockets, Stundorn had worked him over with the cestus.

"When we come back with Kane, he'll tell us the truth about this cache of loot," Pleddis promised. "Because he knows this is just a taste of what will happen if he lies to us just once. Only way to make a man tell the truth when he expects death in return—you got to make him want to die."

He smiled jovially at Ionor. "Now he *is* going to be alive when I get back, isn't he?"

"This is better than killing him," she said flatly, watching Weed's tortured body as it slowly spun from the force of the last blow.

Pleddis laughed appreciatively. "Don't think I'd want you for my enemy—no, I don't! Well, then, we'll let you and that fat tavern keeper guard him close—and your man Mauderas when he comes back. Of course, I've got some of my men posted here inside, in case Kane doubles back, and there's more guarding the horses. Personally, I expect to find him crawling along the mountainside not even a mile from here, but with Kane you best keep all bets covered. He comes back, there's a welcome here for him."

A harried Nattios pounded in from outside. "Captain Pleddis, it's no use!" he blurted. "I can't do a damn thing with them hounds. You got to drag them out of their kennel, and then they just scrounch down on their bellies and whimper. Hell, one damn near chewed old Usporris's arm off trying to drag his tail back inside! They're too scared to piss, captain. They ain't good for so much as barking at a thief if he was to step over them—ain't no way we're going to use them to trail!"

"So." Pleddis shrugged his shoulders, affecting nonchalance he did not feel. "Then we trail without dogs. Didn't need them before now. I know damn well you can track a man on foot over this short a field."

He glared at the long-nosed mountaineer. "Unless you're too damn scared to do your job. And you and any others who feel that way know what I think about a man who won't do his job."

Nattios nodded unhappily. He knew. They all knew.

"Stundorn—you aren't afraid to chase down a fortune in gold."

"No, captain," he lied, face pale beneath stubble beard.

"See, Nattios. Stundorn's not afraid."

"You find where Kane's trail leads off, I'll take you to him," Nattios promised sullenly.

"I'll hold you to your word." Pleddis's teeth gleamed brightly. "Now let's not waste any more time."

When the sounds of the hunters had been swallowed by the night, Ionor moved from the window and took down her hooded cloak. The dark brown wool would be almost invisible in the night, which was to her liking. An encounter with Pleddis's soldiers was something she wished to avoid—although it was not for Pleddis to question her coming and going, nor for any man to hold her back from the path she had set foot on seven years before.

Klesst's wide eyes greeted her when she opened the door. Perhaps if her eyes had not reminded her of Kane . . . if her hair had not been red like his . . .

"You're awake," Ionor stated in automatic reproof.

"I couldn't sleep with everything happening, Mother. And I've slept so much of the day." She wanted to ask if the soldiers had captured Kane, but she dared not show interest. But Kane was magic, for he had vanished from her closet. They couldn't catch a sorcerer, could they?

"That's all right. Put your clothes on now, Klesst. We're going to go for a short walk."

"Why, Mother? Tonight's the Demonlord's Moon." She felt a thrill of bewildered fright.

"That's all right. The soldiers will protect us from any bad things. The night air will break your fever. Just get dressed now."

"I think my fever is gone now." Could soldiers protect her from the black hound?

"Just get dressed."

She wondered if Mother had a surprise for her birthday. One of the girls in the village told her how she was taken out to the stable on the night of her birthday, and there was a baby colt just born, and she got to have him because he was born on her birthday. But Mother never gave her surprises on her birthday. Sometimes Greshha did, and pretended that they were gifts from Mother, too, but Klesst knew better, because once she saw Greshha embroidering the birthday skirt with her own hands.

"Did I hear one of the soldiers say that Greshha came back?"

"No, Klesst. Why are you dawdling?"

"Which skirt shall I wear, Mother?"

"It doesn't— Wear the dark blue one."

That was her best one. "Can I wear my good linen blouse?" Maybe it *was* a birthday surprise.

"Yes. Hurry, Klesst." Ionor fidgeted with her fingers, subconsciously seeking to speed her dressing, but not wanting to touch the girl. Her body felt tense as she watched Klesst hurry on her clothes, struggle to push her feet into buskins she had outgrown. She would need a new pair soon. . . .

Ionor pushed the thought from her mind. It was too late to turn back; she knew that when Kane returned to

Raven's Eyrie. Pleddis's appearance had made her think briefly that the Demonlord could be cheated of his bargain. Yet while this thought might have stirred a phantom of hope, far greater was her anger at the chance that her vengeance would not be fulfilled. But the Demonlord would not be cheated. The game was his, and this was only another cat-and-mouse cruelty of his dark humor. She had struggled seven years to quell any love for the child, knowing the unholy bargain she had sworn to consummate. And yet, if Pleddis had taken Kane, might she have learned in time to . . .

Then surged stronger the screaming vision of seven years past—the death and horror of Kane's raid, the shame of her captivity, the tearing agony later in the ruins of her home. . . .

"Mother, I'm ready now. Why is your face so strange?" Wrapped in her woolen shawl, Klesst looked up at her anxiously.

Ionor shook her head and closed her eyes for a moment. "Nothing's wrong, Klesst. Now come along quickly."

IX

Broken Barricades

The mass of laurel roots sagged beneath his weight. Bits of rock and humus crumbled away from where the bush anchored itself to the bluff. He heard the trickling sound of its fall. With painstaking care Kane transferred his weight to another shelf of rock and inched forward against the bluff. No handholds here—just the desperate pressure of his body against the bare rock.

Mist rose from the river far below, breathing a damp film upon the slippery rocks. At times the mist completely obscured the tiny ledge Kane followed, so that he became uncertain which fragmentary path led down to the riverbank, or ended instead several yards beyond in a sheer drop. Time and again he had to backtrack over some perilous section of blind trail which moments before had required all his effort to negotiate. No longer was Kane sure whether he actually followed the path to the river—or even if such a trail existed. The fog held its secrets well, and often he had to rely solely on touch to discover the next foothold.

The mist writhed through his mind as well. Kane lost note of time; it seemed he had been crawling for ages across the treacherous bluff, never coming closer to either summit or base. And in truth he was lost. The rudimentary path he struggled along wormed across the escarpment above the River Cotras for miles beyond the point where Kane had hoped to descend. This path was only a broken ledge along a series of faults in the strata—a deadly trail no mountain man would attempt even by day. Pleddis, who was scouring the gravel beds between river and cliff, never considered that his wounded quarry would be rash enough to crawl along the escarpment where no path existed. And so Kane passed beyond the line of his pursuers, although the crumbling ledge that had saved him from capture threatened at any instant to cast him headlong into the mist-wreathed darkness.

He seemed to move in a dream. The mist crawled in phantom shapes; spectral hands clawed out to tear him from the ledge. Even the cold, sweating rock seemed unreal, insubstantial. Kane knew this was no dream, but he had to force himself to be aware of his reality. Otherwise he would lose concentration, no longer care whether a tangled clump of laurel would bear his weight or crumble beneath his boot. He ground his bleeding hands against the rock and savagely pressed down on his limping ankle, using the pain to drive back the sense of dream.

But the phantoms waxed more substantial, the lichen-garbed stones less real. And no further could the agony of his body overcome the fever in his mind. Somehow Kane managed to lurch on toward where the ledge seemed to broaden—or was that, too, a trick of his faltering senses? Unable to determine, he sprawled heavily onto the dank shelf of rock.

His limbs were nerveless. His exhausted body ached for air, but his chest seemed too weakened to draw breath fast enough. Kane shuddered; great spasms shook his sweat-slimed frame.

He lay like one dead, while he fought to hold consciousness. Vertigo shivered through his brain. The ledge he pressed against tilted, spun away, dissolved. . . .

And then the rocks dissolved.

And the stone became transparent, clearer than the finest diamond.

And the mountains opened to Kane.

And Kane looked within the mountains.

He saw the treasures of the hills locked in their crypts of primal stone—veins of gold and silver, raw gemstones, buried crowns, and chests of coins—and the grim guardians who watched over them.

He saw the graves of the hills, where forgotten skeletons mouldered into dust, and lost tombs whose corpses lay unquiet and imprisoned, and their rotted eyes burned with blue flames as they writhed to return his stare.

He saw the graveless dead of River Cotras—who had been claimed by the river's fury, who had thrown themselves into its flood in futile search for oblivion, who had been flung into its depths to hide the fruits of murder—white scattered bones, and current-tossed skulls, and moss-crusted lairs for fishes and wriggling things.

He saw the lost mines of the ancients, and that which they mined and that which they buried—that which they sought after and did not find, and that which they feared and could not flee—and the knowledge made him close his eyes and cry out.

He saw caverns that crawled downward and downward, and the blind flapping things that dwelled within them—and the cities that were raised there, where no light would even burn—and the misshapen faces that peered fearfully from slitted windows in towers for which there were no doors.

He saw the black flames of the far abyss, toward which monstrous worms gnawed chaotic tunnels through the rock, seeking the flames of Hell, where as obscene moths they would burst forth to wheel and dart, until their smouldering wings would fail and they would plunge like meteors into the lake of fire.

He saw the hidden creatures of the mountains, risen from their secret dens to hunt by the Demonlord's Moon. Huge, bloated toads that hopped through the fog, flicking forth searching tongues from reeking jaws of acid-venomed fangs. Lonely abandoned cabins, inviting a traveller to shelter—that were neither cabins nor abandoned, and their invitation was not for refuge. Glowing-eyed creatures shaped somewhat like men, who ran on furred limbs, and showed wolves' fangs when they howled. Shambling giants like misshapen apes, yellow-toothed and shovel-taloned—some shaggy as bears, some scaled like snakes—bestial descendants of those who first claimed man's image. Creeping from caverns, naked creatures no longer quite human—filthy, scabrous packs of men, women and mewing children, not half so hideous as the hunger that brought them forth. And that which follows lonely travellers in the dark of the woods, until at last they look behind, and in that moment die (Kane looked upon its face, and terror scarred his soul).

There were others....

And Kane moaned and gnawed his tongue, crushed his fists to his eyes. Until the visions faded into grey, and only the knowledge remained.

He opened his eyes. The rock was solid about him. The fever had broken.

And now a steaming, fetid breath snuffled his body. Eyes like red glowing stars stared balefully down upon his upturned face.

"No, Serberys," said a voice, "Kane is not ours . . . yet."

Kane snarled and flung himself aside. Larger and blacker than any bear of these mountains, the hound of Hell snarled back at him.

"Now we've spoiled his dream," came the sardonic laugh. "Were you dreaming, Kane?" The Demonlord's onyx-taloned hand rested on his hound's hackled neck. He stood tall and lean and muscular; his garments were black and finely cut to the current mode—full-sleeved shirt and tight trousers, knee boots of soft leather, and a long sword at his belt. A wide black cloak seemed to flap about his shoulders, but Kane knew it was not a cloak.

Kane glared at the majestically evil face and the unwinking black eyes. "If you've come for me, Sathonys, you'll find my steel as ready as ever."

The Demonlord smiled; mockery robbed his expression of any warmth. "We've met on friendlier terms in past years, Kane. Why do you show your fangs now?"

"We'll play this game no longer," growled Kane, edging back along the ledge so that the face of the cliff was close behind him. Serberys's squat bulk completely blocked the trail before him; black tongue licked smoking jowls. He flexed the cramped pain from his sword arm, but did not yet draw his blade.

"But a vassal plays his lord's game for so long as the master wills," mocked Lord Tloluvin, his cloak billowing about him.

"I'm not your vassal." Kane's fists clenched like rocks.

"But you've served me well in the past." The night winds moaned along the escarpment, but his cloak did not swirl in obedience to the wind's caress.

"And you've served me better—and we've fought side by side. But Kane owes allegiance to neither god nor demon, and I'll not be your pawn in this game you play now."

"If not pawn, perhaps prize," the Demonlord laughed. "And yet, you must surely understand that all mortals are but pawns."

"Nor am I mortal."

"Perhaps before dawn you'll be proven wrong on both counts."

"This may be my last night, but who comes for me will find no pawn!" warned Kane, the fury of his blue eyes as hellish a flame as the Demonlord's own.

Lord Tloluvin studied the death in Kane's stare. "I've cause enough to respect you, Kane, true, and admire you. At times our battles have been in the same cause."

"You show little gratitude for a comrade in arms."

"Kane! You know better!" protested Lord Tloluvin in sardonic reproof. "I only follow my nature—one you well understand. Sathonys, Tloluvin, Lato, by whatever name—my nature is the same. Only a fool expects loyalty in the Demonlord's friendship."

"Perhaps then you, too, are only a pawn—to your nature, or whatever laws you obey."

The Demonlord's smile was sudenly menacing. Serberys growled like brazen thunder and took half a stride forward on the ledge. "Your wit is as bold as your arrogance, Kane. We'll argue this later, I think.

"But stop to consider my game, since I doubt its nature confuses you. You must admit I've set the gameboard well. For seven years Ionor's festering hate has poisoned this wounded land—twisted her soul and tainted the spirits of those about her. And now to seal her pact of vengeance she will give me the child, the daughter she has tortured herself to keep hating for seven years. Is it not a work of art, Kane? You can admire art such as this, I know. Or do you better appreciate the mastery with which I drew you to me here tonight—held by bonds of fever like a chained sacrifice, with greed and ruthless cruelty like a snarling pack to drive you—and a trail of death and ruin to mark the passage of the hunt."

"If you've set the gameboard for this night, Sathonys," Kane spat back, "you still cannot manipulate all the pieces. Other men you may use as pawns, but not Kane!

I'll yield to no predestined fate, and if I fall, I'll die hard and I'll die a free man!"

"Still shaking your bloodstained fist at fate, Kane? But I suppose that is your nature, and I return your accusation. Before dawn comes we'll speak further on free will, and then I think we'll know better whether this arrogance is vain boast or desperate faith."

Serberys raised his sooty muzzle and bayed. The ravenous howl sent echoes of terror resounding through the night.

Lord Tloluvin stroked his massive shoulders. "Yes, Serberys, I sense it, too. Ionor approaches Raven's Bald with the child, and we must go await her."

His smile was agelessly cruel. "By your leave, Kane—but while we've tarried here, the seeds sown seven years ago in hate, and so carefully nurtured since, are about to flower beneath my moon.

"And did you know that this trail you've so desperately followed ends in a sheer precipice only a short way from here?"

Thunder smashed down over the ledge, like deafening laughter.

Kane stood alone.

X

Demonlord's Moon

At first Kane hoped that the Demonlord had lied. As rage fired new strength through his muscles, he plunged recklessly along the now wider trail. For some distance the ledge offered a secure path along the face of the cliff. Kane realized now that he was not on the trail he had thought to follow, but at the same time he was headed in the direction of Raven's Bald. Lord Tloluvin would have known this—had he then lied to make Kane turn back?

The Demonlord had not lied this time.

Kane skidded to a halt, as before him the ledge abruptly fell away. Here the fault in the strata had broken loose, and a great section of the escarpment had sheared off into the River Cotras far below. No trail crossed the black chasm.

Straining to pierce the river mist, Kane peered upward. Above him the cliff marched into the night; below he could hear the muffled roar of River Cotras. From what he remembered of the river gorge in this region, this ledge must be at least a hundred feet from the crest. He was trapped here, unless . . .

Examining the chasm, he thought he discerned a narrow crack which appeared to lead to the area of the fall. If he could find handholds along this crevice, he *might* be able to reach the slide, where the broken rock *might* provide an avenue to scale the bluff.

There was, of course, no hope in turning back.

Am I truly a pawn in the Demonlord's game?

The crack in the rock ran perhaps fifty feet—a sheer plummet—before it reached the slide rubble. The stone was damp and slippery, white with frost in places. Bits of splintered rock plugged the crevice every few inches. There scarcely seemed space enough to dig his fingers.

Stretching out, Kane forced his powerful hands into the crevice. He heaved his massive body off the ledge and into space. His giant shoulders bunched and strained; his legs scuffed against the rock, while the river mist swirled up about him from far below.

His movements were rapid, for he knew his overtaxed strength would falter in another moment. Like a great ape, he swung across the escarpment, driving his body on by force of will. Death awaited his first misjudged grip.

The crevice slowly narrowed. Kane found he must support his weight solely by his clawing fingers—and still the crack tightened. Until there was no longer space to thrust his fingers.

Kane's breath grunted an inarticulate curse, but with each second a killing agony, he wasted no time. Hanging perilously by one arm, Kane quickly drew a dagger from his boot. Its flat balanced blade was designed for throwing; whether its steel would support his bulk, Kane had only one way of determining. Using the knife for a piton, Kane jammed it into the crevice and tried his weight.

The tempered steel shivered and grated; the hilt seemed to bend slightly under the tearing stress. But it held. Clinging desperately to the sweaty hilt, Kane jerked its mate from his other boot. He thrust it into the crevice, then swung out with the other blade. Two insignificant hafts of steel and leather were all that supported him above the deadly abyss. It seemed the blades could never endure the strain. They did; Kane's desperate gamble succeeded.

With these makeshift pitons, he struggled across the final few yards to what was relative safety. Reaching the rubble left by the avalanche, he gratefully rested his boots on an outjutting boulder. An hour's rest would seem lifesaving now, but he knew there was not a minute to spare. Grimly he began to scale the chaos of broken rock which marked the slide.

Stundorn was ill at ease. The blocky mercenary distrusted the strange swirling mist that cloaked, then revealed, the autumnal ridges. Nor did he like the eerie shadows that seemed to flash along in the darkness on all sides of them, although time and again a sudden frightened challenge had revealed nothing. *But would shadows make sounds?*

Once more he tried to fight down gnawing fear. He had lost hope of finding Kane in the night—already they had hunted farther than Pleddis had been prepared to. Pleddis had overstretched their lines, spread the search too far. Now they wandered through the darkness in small bands. Stundorn glanced ahead on the ridge as the Demonlord's Moon rose high over Raven's Knob. Dread chilled his spirit. This trail skirting the river gorge was no place to linger tonight.

"Are you sure you know what you're doing?" he demanded of Nattios.

The mountaineer's nerves were, if anything, worse. "There's the tracks. Look at them yourself, and tell me what we're doing. Woman and a child, and not too far ahead. I'll kiss your ass if it's not the woman from the inn and her kid."

"But why would she be on the trail to Raven's Knob?" the other persisted. "No sane errand would take her there tonight of all nights. Hell, you know the stories they tell."

"I didn't say she was going *to* Raven's Knob," Nattios argued. "I said this trail leads *past* Raven's Knob. We don't know where she's really headed."

"Then why don't we turn back?" grumbled one of the other half-dozen men in their party. "Damn woman wants to take her kid and risk what's out here tonight, that's her business."

"None of that talk," growled Stundorn, thinking the man had a valid point. But no, he would have to face Pleddis, and his captain took a harsh view of cowardice.

"Ionor's out here, she's got to have a good reason," he explained. "Could be she's gone to meet Kane. That kid's got hair like Kane, and those blue eyes. Didn't get them from her mother, and we don't know who she calls father. Might be it's Kane—he's been through this range of hills before."

"Seemed ready enough to drink his blood back at the inn," the grumbler persisted.

"Could have been fake," guessed Stundorn. "Kane decided to hole up at Raven's Eyrie after all—and she was fixing them food. Could be Kane's more welcome there than anyone guessed. Might explain how he managed to slip out of the inn without our knowing it."

"Well, there's something sure funny about that inn," Nattios contributed. Talk drowned out the night's eerie sounds. He hoped the conversation would continue.

They shuffled on a bit farther in silence. The movement from the corner of their eyes seemed to increase; the night sounds edged closer at hand. Bolder.

"How close are we to Raven's Knob?" Stundorn asked, uneasily gazing at the bald spur of rock on the crest of the ridge.

"Pretty close—maybe a mile or so by trail," the tracker hazarded. "Stundorn, you suppose Kane knows you shot him?"

"That ain't certain," protested the man with the arbalest, who had earlier boasted of it.

"Because maybe Kane's dead after all. We ain't none of us seen him since the first. There's some damn weird things you hear about Kane, and if he died tonight . . . Well, there's been dead men before that didn't lie in their graves."

"Shut up!" Stundorn cursed him, thinking that a dead man would surely take vengeance on his slayer if he could return from the grave.

"I just wondered if you knew for sure you shot him, and if you knew where the quarrel hit him, that's all. Then maybe we'd know whether Kane's just crippled, or whether up ahead somewhere there's a dead man waiting. . . ."

"I said, shut up! Keep your mind on the trail."

"Ain't nothing there to keep my mind on. A blind man could read these tracks—they're leading straight along the trail to Raven's Knob."

"Vaul! What's that?" someone gasped.

They froze in their stances to listen. A scraping, scrambling sound, not far away . . .

"It's something climbing up from the river!" another cried out.

"Fool! That's a sheer drop!" Nattios swore.

"It's closer!"

"Then what . . . ?"

With a bloodcurdling howl, Kane flung himself over the last shelf of rock. A man screamed in terror.

Kane's face was battered, his body and clothing torn, filthy, stained with blood. His sword flashed from the scabbard as he cleared the precipice, a yell of animal ferocity twisting his lips. He had sprung out of the abyss as if by sorcery—a vengeful phantom who loomed to giant stature in the terror of that moment. The Demonlord's Moon cast its red glare upon him, and his killer's eyes blazed with the sure promise of death.

Stundorn's shot was wild, for only fear had triggered his weapon. "Kane!" someone bawled in panic. The bounty hunters broke and fled.

With a roar of insane fury, Kane lunged after them. With no thought of danger, he drove them before him. Too long had he been hounded by jackals; the wounded lion had turned to kill.

Stundorn wasted an instant trying to crank the cocking rachet of his arbalest. The reflex was fatal now, for his comrades had left him to stand alone. As he dropped the useless weapon and groped for his sword, Kane's hell-driven blade split him almost in half. The others made no attempt to stand before his rush. In frantic haste to escape the bellowing demon, Nattios misjudged the edge of the cliff; his screams were swallowed in the river mists.

Kane ravened after them. Another mercenary died with Kane's sword sunk to the hilt through his spine. The survivors split from the trail to plunge into the forest, and Kane leaped after them to tackle the last man. Brutally he pounded the mercenary's skull against the rocks, again and again, until his fists held only pulp.

Then the red mists of rage parted, and Kane rose from his gory work. From the black trees he heard another man scream once and break off. Under the dark pines, shadows rustled to close on the echo of death. Kane coughed and shook his head. As the killing rage left him, awareness of his danger returned.

Had Pleddis heard the cries, the fury of Kane's attack? Had someone escaped to warn him of Kane's presence? The problems seemed only of minor importance; Kane knew a far deadlier menace was closing about him. He stared defiantly at the ridge before him.

There before the red moon rose Raven's Knob. And

this trail climbed toward it. Ahead was Ionor with the child—*but how far ahead?*

Kane paused only to snatch up and recock Stundorn's arbalest—for the steel-bowed weapon was accurate to kill at over one hundred fifty yards, and he might still get close enough. . . .

Throwing his last strength into his stride, Kane pounded up the trail to Raven's Knob. His sense of hideous danger all but drowned the agony that shrieked through his frame with every step.

Klesst suddenly stopped and tugged at Ionor's cloak. "Mother, let's not walk any farther. I'm tired now."

"Come on, Klesst. It isn't much farther. If you don't stop this whining, I'll slap you."

Mother's slaps stung all the worse because the girl sensed the anger in her blow. "But Mother, I'm frightened out here. The soldiers are way behind us."

"I said, come on!" Ionor jerked her arm forward, then released her hand once Klesst started to follow. She had always tried to keep from touching her. . . . It was better that way.

"Mother, I think I remember this place."

"Surely you've played near here often before."

"Never. The other children are afraid to come here, and I don't like to be alone so far in the woods."

Ionor walked resolutely on, impatiently slackening her quick stride to let the child stay beside her. It was not as if Klesst were hers. She was Kane's—and a stolen part of her own flesh. Stolen. Raped and shamed and stolen. Klesst wasn't her daughter—she had been determined on that from the first. She was a cancer which Kane had implanted within her body, and in pain she had been purged of the cancer. Almost. The child was something apart from her. If there had ever been love this would be different, but there had never been love; there never would be love. She would feel no more guilt for Klesst than for a cancer that a surgeon excised and destroyed.

It would be over in another few minutes. Seven years of hate. Klesst would not suffer. Not like she had . . .

"Mother, I think this is the place in my dream."

"Hush, Klesst."

"No, Mother! I know it's the same place. That great big

rock up there is where the black dog first appears, and the black man who walks behind him." Klesst's voice rose in sharp fear.

Ionor frowned at the girl. She had hoped to avoid physical contact—*physical force*—with the child, though she had a length of cord under her cloak if she needed it. "Don't be afraid, Klesst. When you get to that big rock and see that there's no black hound and his master, then you won't have those silly nightmares any more."

"I'm still scared," Klesst whispered, her eyes round and frightened.

"Come on, quickly now."

Klesst walked slowly on. She did not want to anger Mother. She used to think that if she never made Mother angry again, then Mother might forget the awful thing she once had done—although what this crime might have been, she never understood. Of late Klesst had lost hope of making Mother ever forget.

Then her owl-like eyes stared at the barren spur of rock. Ionor had forgotten—if she ever knew—how well Klesst could see in the dark.

"Mother!" screamed Klesst, breaking away. "I can see them! It's the black dog and the black man! They're waiting in the shadow of those big rocks up ahead! Mother! The black dog sees me, too! Can't you see how red his eyes glow?"

"Come here, damn you!" shouted Ionor, reaching for the cord. In her urgent need to catch the terrified girl, she lunged and stumbled over a root. "Come here!" she yelled, as she sprawled after the retreating child.

It was the last fragment of horror for Klesst. She whirled and dashed back down the trail, utter panic lending horrible impetus to her childish stride.

Ionor called once more, then saved her breath for overtaking Klesst. The girl could not stay ahead of her for very long.

But terror gave her strength, so that Klesst flew headlong down the path, running faster than she ever had. She could hear Ionor's boots drawing closer from behind, and in her mind Mother, the black hound, and its master all merged into one onrushing phantom of dread.

A giant, diseased apple tree overhung the trail. The last of a blighted orchard that once had stood along this slope, the huge tree reached over the path with grotesque and nightmarish limbs. The sick-sweet odor of rotting apples hung under its shadow like the smell of stale flowers in a graveyard. It had frightened Klesst when first they passed beneath its clutching branches.

Now as she rushed past it, her feet skidded on the rotted fruit. Klesst howled and pitched flying onto the decay-strewn ground. The jar of her fall left her no breath to cry out.

Desperately she tried to scramble back up to run. Too late. A frenzy of motion in the darkness, and Ionor's cold hand knotted in her disordered hair. Still trying to draw breath, Klesst was yanked to her feet.

Ionor slapped her, hard. "Now I'll show you what good it is to run!" she panted. And she drew the girl's wrists together, fumbled with the cord.

Klesst watched mutely as her hands were tied, still too terrified to grasp what was happening to her. She wondered if Mother meant to whip her like once she did Sele.

There was a scuff of boot on stone, then another silhouette joined the apple tree's contorted shadow.

It's the black man, thought Klesst. *He's come with his hound. Mother will give me to him. . . .*

"Kane!" snarled Ionor, leaping up in fury.

There was fury in Kane's eyes.

The arbalest in his arms shuddered.

Ionor shrieked in clawing agony as the iron-barbed quarrel tore into her belly and flung her back against the tree. She should have fallen then; instead she hung there, writhing in torment. At point-blank range the quarrel had drilled through her spine and sunk into the gnarled trunk.

She struggled frantically to break free, but her strength suddenly failed. Hate was slower to desert her, and she spat curses through her bubbling lips as she died. And finally there was an end even to her hate. Her slumped figure hung limply from the apple tree, impaled on the iron spike like a shrike's prey on a thorn.

Clumsily—for his chest pounded with agony, and scarlet mists blurred his vision—Kane gathered up his sobbing child and wrapped her in his wolfskin cloak.

"Well played, Kane!" came sardonic congratulations. "I had thought the game won."

Klesst buried her face in Kane's shoulder. Kane warily

shifted his burden away from swordhilt. The Demonlord and his hound stood before him on the trail.

"Do you still say I'm your pawn?" he growled. "There stands your pawn. Your pact is forfeit, and you'll have to play at my game if you think to claim this prize!"

"Your game, Kane?" mocked Sathonys. "I think not. And perhaps I was wrong to call you a pawn. We'll play the game another day, and then we'll see whether Kane is truly master of his fate, or simply fool of luck.

"Still, I won't say this outcome displeases me. Our souls are like matched blades fired in the same forge, Kane. After all these centuries, I believe I'd miss you, and you've served me well so many times."

Kane's eyes blazed in anger.

"As an ally, of course," the Demonlord amended, with a sarcastic salute.

He touched the hound's misshapened head. "Come, Serberys. The moon is growing old, and our friend Kane has led so many souls into our domain tonight. We must not delay our hunt any longer, as I see my creatures have become quite hungry."

Serberys opened his slavering jaws in a baying note of horror.

Hound and master vanished into the night.

Kane almost found pity for those who had dared to pursue him beneath the Demonlord's Moon. But pity was too rare in Kane to bestow upon his enemies.

Through the throbbing haze of pain, Weed felt himself lowered to the floor. He waited blindly for the torture to take some new direction, only thankful that the agony of his wrenched shoulders had let up. Then a knife sheared through his bonds.

He opened his swollen eyes. It was Kane, although it took a moment to be sure. The outlaw leader was a grisly sight to see this side of Hell.

Kane pushed a bottle of brandy into his mouth. Weed tried to take it in his hands but found them too numb to respond. The brandy was fire on his torn lips and broken teeth, but he swallowed greedily as Kane tipped the flask.

In a moment he had come to himself enough to note the torn bodies of his guards strewn about the room.

Kane had descended on them in a murderous rush of fury, but Weed had hung unconscious through it all.

"Can you ride?" Kane demanded.

Weed glanced at Kane's face, then quickly looked away. "I guess so," he grunted, feeling cracked ribs as he struggled to stand. "I guess so. Give me a minute to get my breath."

"There're horses saddled and ready in the stable," Kane told him. "The guards won't bother you."

"Thoem! What's happened?" muttered Weed, swaying for balance. "Where's Pleddis and all his men? They all went out to look for you. . . ."

A chilling howl stirred the night winds. It sounded like the bay of a hound as he closes on his quarry. It was not pleasant to hear.

"I think they found other hunters already out there," said Kane.

He thrust a bulging scrip into Weed's hands. It was heavy, but the weight of gold was one that Weed's tingling fingers found strength to close upon. "Here's gold," Kane told him. "Use it as you need it. When you're strong enough to ride, take Klesst here and go. Dawn will soon break, and you'll be safe enough—besides, Sathonys owes me for a game. Take Klesst with you to Obray's Station—that's well north of the Combine's authority, and no one will follow. Take good care of the girl, and when I join you shortly, I'll share my cache with you. I know that interests you."

Weed wiped the blood from his face, not realizing until later that Kane had known his designs. "Sure, Kane. Whatever you say. But what about you? Pleddis is going to return any minute now. . . ."

"I'll see to my end," Kane grimly vowed. "You make damn certain about yours."

Dawn was greying the skies, the Demonlord's Moon had plunged beneath the black ridges, when Pleddis pushed open the door of Raven's Eyrie. He staggered into the common room, his garments ragged and bloody, his face more colorless than ever. His limbs trembled, and there was gore on his sword no human veins had spilled. He had lost his laugh.

"Demons!" he blurted out with a choked voice. In a

dazed stupor, he lurched across the center of the room. "Devils from the hills! Vaul! The things were everywhere! Snapping, clawing, leaping out on you from the trees and the shadows and the rocks! Too many—reaching out from all around us! Couldn't make a stand!"

His eyes still shone with horror. "And that hound! That hideous black hound! I saw it drag Eriall down as he ran! Vaul! I can still hear its baying! Drove me like a hunted fox across the ridges—but I outran it, made it back alive!"

He paused for breath, and awareness of his surroundings came to him. The huge inn lay in total silence.

"Where—where is everyone?" Pleddis called out.

"I'm right here," said Kane, rising out of the shadow.

LYNORTIS REPRISE

Prologue

High above the blighted wasteland Lynortis broods in gloomy majesty. Lofty eyrie on a fang of sandstone, the fallen citadel stares out over the silent wilderness of desolation far below. Lynortis. Fortress city whose walls no army could overwhelm. Tyrant lord of the limitless forestlands sprawled at its feet.

Lynortis, your eyes are sightless now, and the rich rolling valley over which you reigned is the boneyard of two hundred thousand souls. Lynortis is dead, and there are no mourners. No longer do carrion hawks nest in your gutted halls; even the jackals have abandoned your dunes of bleached bones. Alone and silent, you are the funeral obelisk for your unburied tens of thousands—and for the bones of your conqueror. When slayer kills slayer, all are one with the slain.

Two nations died here, although one was hailed victor. Ask the dead whose side won the war.

I

Hunters in the Forest

The girl's breath came in ragged sobs, and her stride was a broken stumble. Hours before, her long legs had run swift, sure as a deer beneath the misshapen trees. A deer is swift, but hounds are patient. Since noon they had hunted her through that insane nightmare of moss-grown destruction. Now her tanned legs were scratched and bruised as they pumped wearily beneath the thorn-laced branches, and her bare feet left smears of blood upon the gnarled roots. Her long brown hair was disordered with twigs and moss; her thigh-length shapeless gown hung in grimy tatters about her lithe figure. The only sound she uttered was the jagged rhythm of her breath.

"Not here!" The hoarse drawl came dimly from a hundred yards to her right.

"Not here!" An answering hail from her left, and closer. There echoed a stamp of hooves and jingle of harness.

She darted into the wreckage of a huge trebuchet. A tent of saw-briar overgrew the rotting beam of its counterweight, and the shadowy shelter within was tiger-striped by the declining sun. Heedless of tearing thorns, she wriggled closer to the charred timbers of the mammoth siege machine. Smeared with soot and leaf mould, her tanned limbs and shift of coarse brown cloth merged with the rotting timbers of the apparatus. Against her thin face her brown eyes seemed large as those of some nocturnal creature. She froze—motionless save the fast rise and fall of her high breasts and the quick, hunted flicker of her eyes.

At first there had been hounds. They had almost caught her then. But she had slithered breathlessly through a debris-choked tunnel, and when the baying pack had followed, the rotted shoring had given way. Now men's eyes had to search out her trail, and it was enough to hold a scant lead.

A moss-grown skull stared up at her, the rest of its bones still crushed beneath the throwing arm of the trebuchet. Two skeletons in rotting mail lay half-buried in the earthworks, ensnared in a nest of saw-briar. Near her feet lay a rust-pitted dagger; a mouldering swordhilt protruded from beneath the wreckage of the throwing arm. The rusted weapons gave her comfort no more than the rotted bones caused her fear. Her terror was of the present, and of the savage men who hunted her.

"Here! Fresh blood!"

From behind her—and close. She had been unable to hide her trail. Her concealment was no refuge.

Hopelessly she broke from cover, flinging herself past the shroud of thorns. Their excited shouts were close—in a few seconds they would reach the ruined siege engine. Rank brush and twisted second-growth trees promised scarce cover to hide her flight.

"Yo! That's her!"

Terror urged another burst of strength to her aching legs. She dashed headlong through this graveyard of a battle three decades silent. Each breath was agony, and still her lungs could not draw breath enough.

They were following close to her heels, confused in the war-scarred forest, making too much noise themselves to catch the sound of her flight. But they had horses.

She hurtled the fallen beams of a smashed springald, stumbling over the piled rusted fragments of its iron-headed bolts. It brought her up just short of a weed-grown trench that lay hidden a step beyond. But this was a region of the battleground she did not recognize, and she dared not chance shelter that might instead be a cul-de-sac.

A tangle of yellowed bones filled its bottom, she saw as she leaped scrambling across. Then into a brush-grown ravine a dozen painful strides beyond. Wriggle snake-like down its slope, where bones line the eroded dirt like cobblestones. They are stopping by the trench, making certain their quarry doesn't hide there. . . .

The gully emptied into a wash of detritus and sparse scrub. Beyond lay a thick stand of broken trees—cover, if she could reach it. She darted onto the wash, keeping low.

"Yee-hee!"

She skidded on the loose rubble of the clearing. Half a dozen horsemen broke through the patch of woods ahead. They had encircled her.

"Here! We got her!" They pounded toward her.

She spun, but there was no escape behind. The others were pelting down from beside the ravine she had quitted. She stood in full sight in the low scrub of the wash. Again she whirled. She was trapped.

Fear twisted her face. They laughed as they closed on her, this band of forest outlaws who would take their time before letting her die. Hard-faced killers whose plundered gear was as mismatched as the men who wore it. They moved in slowly, tempting her to try to run through their circle.

She sobbed a curse at them—half-crouched, backing away as one moved closer, spinning about as another crept still closer from behind. They were playing with the prey who had cost them so much toil. A circle of grinning wolfish faces, casually moving in across the space of washed stone and dry bones.

The lead horse of the group that had waited in the timber stalked toward her. Its fat rider was the bandit chief, Grey—who had let his men drive his quarry into his dread grasp. His blubbery lips twitched in a triumphant grin.

Then his horse stumbled, its hoof breaking through the gravelled crust with an eerie brittle smash.

Man and steed screamed in tearing agony. From the splintered bubble beneath the wash erupted a spewing mist of black vapor, flowing heavily across the barren space.

The horse plunged to the ground, spilling its rider in a writhing heap that spared him the mercy of a broken neck. She could see the blackened skin slough away from blistered features as the outlaw leader screamed mindlessly for a moment longer. And already the black mist had billowed over those who were with him.

Those who yet could, fled in desperate panic. The black vapor swirled like a hell-driven cloud, flowing across the wash—breathing its searing death upon all who were near.

The wind was blowing back toward the ravine, she saw, and carefully gauged the spreading cloud. Of those with Grey, all lay shrieking on the bone-strewn gravel. Those who had hounded her were trying to outrace the mist, in their terror forgetting their prey.

Somewhere she found strength for a final burst of speed. Perilously skirting the advancing cloud of vapor, she escaped its withering tendrils and reached the patch of forest that lay upwind. The vapor would slowly dissipate, but by the time the survivors regrouped it would be dark—if any still had heart for their game.

On failing legs she stumbled into the shelter of the gnarled trees. And into the grasp of the man who stood watching from their shadow.

She opened her mouth to scream, but already one spade-like hand smothered her lips, while the other enclosed her wrists. With desperate strength she struggled against him, but he held her fast with casual strength.

"Quiet!" His voice rumbled in her ear. "I won't hurt you!"

She shuddered and hung limp in his arms. Her heart hammered painfully, but it was useless to try to break away.

He removed his hand from her lips, but retained his grip on her wrists. "Don't worry, I'm not with them," he told her. "Let's just rest easy now, and let the survivors put distance between us. I think they're too demoralized for any more of this."

He added, "What's your name?"

"Sesi," she admitted, after a pause. She twisted about to get her first good look at the man who held her.

No wonder she had not seen him as she plunged into the trees—he might have been one of the gnarled and massive trunks come to life. While he was not much above the average height of a big man, he was built on the solid scale of an ancient oak. Chest and torso broad and hard as some mighty bole, pillar-like legs, arms thick with corded muscle—all gave him an aura of massiveness more than size, of awesome and irresistible strength. The long-fingered hand that pinned her wrists was large and sinewed; coarse red hair furred its back and the thick forearm. He wore a leather vest trimmed with tufted wolf fur and silver conchos, laced half-open, and a shirt of light mail beneath. Tight leather trousers flared to cover high riding boots. A heavy knife was sheathed at his belt, and the curiously wrought hilt of a broadsword protruded from behind his right shoulder. Sesi had never known a man to carry his sword strapped diagonally behind his back, and she judged him an outlander.

A short beard rusted his coarse-featured face, and nape-length red hair was tied by a leather band sewn with bright bits of girasole above the craggy brow. His eyes . . . Sesi shivered. Cold, blue. Eyes of a killer . . . eyes that had watched many a man die, had absorbed a fragment of each death, and the essence of death flamed within their blue depths.

"I am called Kane."

And Sesi tore her eyes away, wondered for a moment whether her escape from her pursuers had been good fortune.

Kane released her, and she pulled away from him. Her wide eyes regarded him nervously, as she tried to gather the edges of a tear that opened her shift halfway up her side.

"Who were they?" He asked casually.

"Bandits. Scavengers. Their sort prey on travellers in the mountains nearby. Sometimes they slink into the battlefield to steal from the dead. Masale decreed that this all be left untouched as a monument to his victory—but no one guards the field, and the vultures creep in for what they can steal. There is iron, gold. . . ."

"I see bones."

"There are bones."

"Why were they chasing you?"

Sesi knotted the frayed edges of her gown over the tanned curve of her hip. "Can't you guess?"

He studied her, then shrugged, face impassive. She could not read his thoughts. "They went to great effort."

"You saw?" She combed fingers through her tangled mane.

"I was curious to know why a gang of petty killers was so desperately searching the forest."

"Why are you here? This land is forbidden to all."

"Do you live here?" he asked instead.

"There are a few of us," she told him uneasily.

"Then I'll take you there."

"I can find my way."

Kane shook his head. "It's growing dark, and this land is treacherous with overgrown pits and unexploded shells—as those who hunted you learned. My horse is not far."

Sesi shrugged wearily and followed the stranger. It seemed dangerous to trust a man with eyes like Kane's, but then she had little choice.

II

The Key

The fire-blackened stone walls stood roofless beneath greying skies. Ragged gaps in the masonry evidenced the impact of stone missiles flung from mammoth siege engines from the fortress high above. One wing lay in a smashed jumble of weed-grown debris; the main hall was gutted to bare walls. Incongruously spared amidst splintered stone, a stained glass rose window flamed red, gold, and blue in the dying light.

Once the wooded plain at Lynortis's feet had known many stately manor houses such as this. Two years of unleashed hell had smashed the land and its people like a princess's doll-things in the path of a mad stampede. The marvel was that this much of the mansion yet stood one stone upon another.

A far wing—once kitchens and servants' quarters—showed a streak of smoke from a broken chimney. Yellow light leaked through chinks in the boarded windows, and the broken roof showed crude repairs. A gaunt-ribbed cur snarled from the shelter of a wall as Kane approached.

"Let me down. They'll want to know," Sesi slipped from Kane's saddle and limped toward the low stone building.

Kane sat on his horse, sensing the eyes that watched from within. Casually his fingers freed the clasp that held his scabbard to his left hip. A tug on the hilt would pivot the scabbard on its shoulder swivel, freeing the blade in an instant.

"Hranal!" She pushed at the door. "It's all right. Let me in."

The dog—he wasn't growling a challenge. He was snarling in fear. Kane realized it just as the door was flung open.

Her scream and the scrape of Kane's blade clearing the scabbard shivered in the air at the same instant. Kane spurred his mount toward the door, but already strong arms had yanked Sesi inside.

The door was too low, or Kane would have bolted through—with room to maneuver, a mounted swordsman could break up any free-for-all. Instead Kane leaped from his saddle and squinted into the dimness within—warily holding onto the reins. Several shadowy shapes struggled inside the low-ceilinged room. Kane started for the door, and a tall figure barred his way.

"Kane! Wait!" the man shouted. "This isn't your fight!"

Kane paused, watching the other's poised blade. Inside, the struggle subsided. The figure stepped from the doorway—a broad-shouldered blond man in silver-studded mail.

"Kane! By the Seven! I said that has to be Kane when I saw you ride up!"

"Hello, Jeresen." There were lines of hard living and a long scar that had not been there fifteen years before, but the face was one he knew well. A suggestion of paunch and shadows beneath his eyes indicated the mercenary captain had lived well before hard times left their recent mark.

The big blond-bearded man grinned and sheathed his sword. "Been a long time, Kane, since you and me put Roderic on his brother's throne."

Kane nodded, casually lowering his swordpoint. "That was a good fight, Jeresen. What eventually happened after I had to leave?"

Jeresen chuckled. "After Roderic calmed down, I got your old job. Now and again someone would have doubts as to the justice of Roderic's claim to the throne—enough to keep it interesting, and remind Roderic he needed me and my men. Few years back, Roderic bit into a kidney pie with some unsuspected spices in it. After that, all hell broke loose, and when we finally cut our way out of there, there wasn't much left of us. Since then we've done one thing or another. Yourself?"

"One thing or another."

Jeresen eyed him suspiciously. "What are you doing here?"

"Going from one place to another. Lynortis is a good place to pass through when you don't care to meet anyone."

"Yeah, I'll bet." grinned Jeresen. "What were you doing with the girl?"

"Picked her up along the battlefield. She was running from a gang of bandits, until their leader's horse smashed an unexploded gas bomb. I was carrying her back here hoping for shelter for the night."

Jeresen swore exultantly. "That was that son of a bitch, Grey! So the goddam fool busted open an old Lynortian gas bomb, did he? Wish I'd seen it! The bastard was trying to steal the key to a fortune right out of my grasp!"

"Key to a fortune?"

"Yeah, that's what you had cozied up on your saddle with you just now. Hell, come on in, and I'll tell it over a few bottles. There's gold enough in this to share with all my old comrades."

Kane returned his sword to its scabbard and followed Jeresen into the ruined wing. Inside were maybe ten armed men—blond Waldann mercenaries under Jeresen's command. Kane recognized a few faces and exchanged greetings. He guessed there must be others who had not joined them—unless this battered handful were all that remained of the once formidable troop that had followed Jeresen northward to earn a living by their blades.

Sesi, her arms tied behind her back, hunched miserably in a chair. Her eyes sought Kane in desperate hope. There was blood on the stones of the floor, and the old couple who cowered in one corner of the kitchen would not help her. Neither would the heavyset man who lay in the center of the crimson stain. Kane looked away and sat down at the long table.

"Hranal! Wine!" Jeresen yelled to the elderly man, who was dabbing at his smashed lip. "Wine for us now—then have your woman cook meat. Make it good, or you know what to expect. Laddos, go with him."

He sat across from Kane. "The place is a ruin, but the cellar still has bottles of rare vintage unbroken by the siege. So you're only passing through. There's a coincidence."

Kane declined to press matters. "A fortune, you were saying."

The Waldann captain grunted. "Silver, gold, gems—as much as every man can carry if we're quick."

"How quick?"

"We'd better be out of here by daylight."

"There's nothing here but the bones of two armies."

"More than that if you know where to look," Jeresen assured him. "Been near thirty years since Lynortis fell, but what we're looking for won't have rotted."

The old man returned with dusty bottles of wine. Jeresen watched him pour with relish, warming to his tale. "Hell, Kane, you know the story as well as I do, probably. How Masale of Wesvetin gathered together an army from the slopes of the Myceum range and marched with a hundred thousand men to carve an empire from the lands of North Lartroxia. In the path of conquest stood Lynortis, a fortress city carved from the top of a mountain and said to be unassailable. The lords of Lynortis ruled the great valley stretched below, and the citadel had for centuries considered Lartroxia's plains its fief. Masale knew Lynortis had to fall. He ravaged the towns and holdings at the city's feet, then laid siege to Lynortis itself. A hundred thousand men against a single fortress.

"It wasn't battle; it was endless slaughter. Unassailable walls atop a sheer pinnacle of rock. Gods! How many thousands died in senseless assaults! Two years Masale besieged Lynortis. Two years his giant siege machines hurled rocks, spears, and flaming balls of pitch at the fortress, and the catapults of Lynortis returned the barrage undaunted—and rained death in glass shells of burning phosphorus and deadly vapors fashioned by the wizards of Lynortis from secrets they found under the earth. Plague and famine slew thousands more. The conqueror's army rotted away before his eyes; the entire land became a desert of destruction—still Lynortis withstood Masale's siege. Masale, who had never lost a battle, could not bring the fortress to its knees, not by might of arms, not by starvation—for Lynortis somehow was provisioned.

"At last the fortress fell by treachery. There were passages through the rock spire that opened onto the valley below. After two years of siege, someone showed Masale the way through the mountain—led the conqueror and the remnant of his army secretly into Lynortis on one moonless night. The final battle was a hard one, but the city was taken unaware, and two years of siege had left its defenders weakened. By dawn Masale was in command of a city of the dead, and the rocks far below were splattered with broken bodies of all those who had escaped his army's steel.

"Masale left Lynortis in flames, boasting that he had spared not one life of all within. But his dream of empire died at Lynortis as well, for scarcely twenty thousand remained of his army of conquest. Masale returned to Wesvetin with nothing to show for his dream but a land drained white of its blood and its wealth."

Jeresen paused for a huge swallow of wine. Kane waited for him to recount something not common knowledge.

"He brought back one survivor as part of the plunder of Lynortis—Reallis, the young daughter of Yosahcora, its last ruler. It gave him some bitter satisfaction to have his enemy's child as slave and whore. Often when despair was upon him he amused himself with Reallis, until at length it seemed she would bear his bastard. Masale meant to kill her then, it's said—but the girl disappeared. Escaped, Masale thundered, and his people wondered why he bothered to lie.

"But Reallis did escape somehow. Survivors of Lynortis, or enemies who sought to use his bastard against him? Who knows? For Reallis was never heard from again. Now, twenty years later, word comes to Masale that Reallis had escaped to hide among the few refugees who live among the ruins of the battleground—and that Reallis had given birth to a daughter. Word got out finally through some drifter who'd been holed up here. Took a fancy to the daughter, but couldn't get to her because she was always inside tending to her mother, who was dying of fever. One night he sneaked in and got close enough to overhear Reallis on her deathbed telling the daughter all about a secret room piled high with gold and jewels hidden somewhere in the caverns beneath Lynortis. He couldn't get close enough to hear where the treasure was hidden, but the daughter was there until the end and heard it all. Next night he tried to get to the girl, but they caught him and beat him half to death. So he limped off and came to Masale with his story—figuring on sharing in the treasure when Masale got his hands on it. Masale sweated him pretty hard before he was certain it wasn't some trick. The bastard talked a lot and loud on the rack. Not everyone who listened was as hard to convince as Masale."

Jeresen drained his cup with a flourish and pointed. "Word reached me through Bonaec there. He was hired to Masale, but after what he heard he shipped out and came running back to his old captain for help in beating Masale to the treasure. Bastard in my own outfit then sold out to Grey for a bigger cut of the gold. Grey's boys got here a hair before we did, and now I'm certain Masale is hard on our heels."

All eyes were fixed on Sesi. She stared hopelessly at the floor, uttering no sound.

"Just a matter of getting her to talk." Jeresen grinned. "We'll grab what we can carry and make a run. You'll have equal share, too, Kane. Not that I'm doing it all for old times' sake. We may have to fight past Masale, and I know what you're worth in a fight. Agreed?"

"Of course," Kane said, draining his own cup.

Jeresen grunted and clapped Kane's thick shoulder. "Well, enough, then. And time to move." He smiled wolfishly at the bound girl. "You see we know what the score is, Sesi. Tell us quick where the treasure lies hidden, and I'll take you with us beyond Masale's reach—and your lap'll be heaped high with gold. It's the only choice you have."

Her voice was almost too low to hear. "I don't suppose it would do any good to tell you I don't know what you're talking about."

Jeresen hit her without seeming to move. Her head flew back. Blood started from her nose. The circle of eyes watched mercilessly.

"All right," Sesi said shakily. "But I can't describe the place. Give me a horse, and I'll lead you there."

"Very smart," Jeresen congratulated. "Bonaec, make a noose for her neck. Sesi, I hope you don't think you can slip away in the dark. We really don't have time to waste."

He watched Bonaec haul the girl to her feet and snug a noose to her throat. The stocky mercenary paid out several feet of slack and tied the other end to his thick wrist.

"The first time you cause me to find fault with you," Jeresen told the girl, "I'll tell Bonaec to cut off your ears. Bonaec will enjoy that. So will I. So make sure you don't make us wait too long to get to that gold."

III

As Night Closes

There had been more of the Waldanns—another thirty men left with the horses a distance from the ruined manor. Jersen had not expected resistance from the few refugees who lived there, and more men might have warned Sesi away. The girl was lifted onto a saddle, and the others swiftly mounted to follow her lead. Night was fast closing over the battle-scarred forest, and, Kane noted, there would be no moon tonight.

"I don't understand how Masale could have missed a room full of gold," Kane remarked to Jeresen.

The Waldann captain paused to shout an order. "It was hidden in the caverns beneath Lynortis. Few knew its secret, and Masale took no prisoners when the city fell. It was a treasure Yosahcora had amassed to buy an army to break the siege. There were those who didn't care to see Masale continue his march to empire. The treasure was to persuade them to attack Masale and lift the siege—Yosahcora had planned to send part of the gold out through the secret passageways with a few trusted agents. But Lynortis fell before his plan could be tried, and Reallis was the only one left alive who knew of the treasure. She wasn't inclined to share the secret with Masale."

Kane nodded. "Sounds plausible. And you're certain Sesi knows the secret?"

"She'd better," Jeresen stated. "I need this gold, Kane. The years don't seem to have bothered you, but I'm pushing fifty. You don't get much older in this game, and I've nothing to show for my years of living close to death but a few beat-up veterans to follow me and less gold between us than a lord squanders on his whores on a night of slumming."

He broke off and studied the shattered terrain. "Maybe we'd better light torches. It's getting dark, and there's no trails through this damn junk pile."

Shadows lay thick over the nightmarish tangle of blasted trees, rotting siege machines, weed-grown embankments. Ahead of them loomed a huge ballista, its giant timbers charred and frozen as if the phosphorus bomb that seared its catapult and the crew had struck only hours ago. Charred skeletons yet manned its broken arm. Touch a man with fire hot enough, mused Kane, and his bones will last forever.

High above them Lynortis looked down—a ruined fortress atop a spike of sandstone thousands of feet high. Kane could barely make out the narrow roadway carved into the face of the stone, spiralling the pinnacle to a dizzying summit. Stones hurled from that height had gouged craters into the earth as deep as a man was tall.

Cautiously they worked around the earthworks of the ruined ballista. Trenches and craters scarred the terrain, and where the earth was not barren from some still virulent poison, scrub growth of three decades made their passage almost impossible.

"Can't you find a better trail?" Jeresen demanded of his captive.

Sesi shook her head. Her horse and Bonaec's led the way. "We are following a trail of sorts. You forget that the battlefield has been deserted these many years."

"Well, something's been going through here," Jeresen pointed out. "There's tunnels running through the scrub."

Sesi's horse screamed and plunged forward—its hooves breaking through the crumbling sides of an unseen trench. Wrists bound behind her back, Sesi fell from her saddle. Her neck jerked back with the throttling halter as the falling horse carried her into the hidden trench.

Kane's sword slashed across the tethering rope just as the slack snapped taut. The strands parted with a crack an instant before the noose could break her neck, and Sesi rolled away from her stricken mount, into the weed-buried earthworks. Her legs flashed white as she wriggled head first into cover.

"Get her!" Jeresen yelled. Bonaec leaped from his saddle and dove into the trench after her. Its leg broken, the foundered horse lay on its back at the bottom, hooves thrashing dangerously. The thickset Waldann skidded around it and plunged through the brush where the girl's long legs had disappeared. Farther back, the others milled in confusion, not knowing what had happened in the thick gloom.

Jeresen bawled orders for his men to encircle the trench. Horses crashed and stumbled as cursing riders tried to force them through the twilight wasteland.

"If she gets away in the darkness . . ." snarled Jeresen in a rage.

"She can't run far with her hands tied," Kane said. "She would have told us nothing with a broken neck."

"Hell, you did the only thing . . ." Jeresen started to say.

A scream echoed eerily from the bottom of the trench. Bonaec. He only screamed once.

Someone finally lit a torch. Men dropped into the trench and forced their way into the tunneled path through the thick scrub. In a moment they backed out, dragging Bonaec by his heels. They didn't find the mercenary's head. Nor did they find Sesi.

"There's a tunnel down here!" someone announced, as their blades hacked away the cover of undergrowth. "This animal trail runs straight into an old tunnel!"

"Then follow it!" Jeresen yelled, and swore as they slowly obeyed him. Farther down the line of the trench, his riders were finding no sign of the girl.

"She knew it was here," Kane decided. "Rode her horse into the trench and chanced it. Masale's army spent two years digging tunnels and earthworks against the counterbombardment. If Sesi knows the battlefield, she could be crawling off to hide where we'll never find her."

"Found an old blade down there, too," Jeresen surmised gloomily. "Sawed her hands free and lopped old Bonaec's head off when he crawled after her."

"Must have been a dull blade," observed Kane. "From the stump of his neck I'd say his head was chewed off."

IV

The Hand of Kane

"I wouldn't be out there tonight for a pile of gold as high as Lynortis," grumbled Hranal, handing Kane a platter of boiled meat. "Too many men died out there."

"Oh?" said Kane, jerking his hand away from the steaming meat. After an hour of scouting around the site of Sesi's disappearance, Kane had decided the girl had made good her escape—at least until daylight. Leaving the problem to Jeresen, he returned to the ruined manor for a long-deferred meal. If Jeresen wanted his men to risk their necks in a pointless search, that was between the Waldanns and their leader.

"Too many died," Hranal repeated. "Too many to stay dead on nights like this. I've seen things moving around the old battleground in the dark of the moon, and I've stayed behind bolted doors since."

"You're full of crap, old man," muttered Laddos, who had remained behind to watch the manor and its tenants. "Dead men stay dead—unless there's sorcery at work. Ain't nothing but bones here." He dug a grimy hand into the platter.

The old man stared at the mercenary without anger. He and his wife had shown little emotion after their initial terror, serving the Waldanns' wants in docile silence. "You may have seen many a man die," he stated, "but you never were in a battle like this one. There never was a battle like the siege of Lynortis. They died here by the thousands. Suicide assaults to storm the fortress walls—when the roadway was buried under crushed bodies twenty deep. Then the months and months of siege—stones and springald bolts dropping down day and night, bodies smashed and skewered. And the glass bombs of phosphorus and black vapor bursting over the trenches—they died by the hundreds then, burnt to the bone and screaming their insides out. You can see whole sections of the battlefield at night ghost-lit where the phosphorus bombs struck."

"I've been through sieges," Laddos growled.

"Not like this one. There never was a siege like this one. Masale was determined to take Lynortis—kept bringing in new troops as fast as they could die. He came here with a hundred thousand men, and he must have brought in at least that many more as the siege wore on—no one knows how many. And plague set in when the countless dead were piled in heaps as high as Lynortis. They couldn't bury that many dead, they couldn't burn that many dead, they couldn't carry that many off. For two years the air was foul with death, and the survivors fought on behind breastworks of the dead.

"Then the night Lynortis fell. You could hear their screams all through the night, and at dawn the pinnacle was red with blood, and the earth beneath was piled with smashed bodies more than a hundred deep. They died by the tens of thousands that night, and you can see their broken bones piled like snow drifted against an oak at the base of Lynortis. Lynortis cost Masale his empire, but Masale made Lynortis pay with its life.

"Who can say who won the war? Who can number the dead here? Masale left the field a graveyard, and the bones of two nations bleach unburied here amidst the ruins of war. And they don't rest easy, my friend—take the word of a man who's lived through it all."

Laddos cursed him and gnawed at the stringy meat. His gaze wandered to the bolted door.

"You've lived here ever since?" Kane asked. "Why?"

The scarecrow figure gestured weakly. "Where else to go? The woman and I served the master before Masale swept upon us. No one kills the servants. For a space Masale himself made this house his quarters, but when the trebuchets found the range, he moved back. Sometimes his generals quartered here, sometimes his surgeons worked over bodies too broken to fight again. We served them all. And when the missiles fell about the house, we hid in the cellar until it stopped for a while, and when we crawled out we'd find our masters buried beneath the walls and ceilings, and then new masters would come.

"We hid the night Lynortis fell, and when Masale marched his broken army away, there were no more masters. Where else to go? Who else to serve? We remained here in the wreckage with a few others who survived, lived off what we could scavenge, and shivered through nights when the ghouls and ghosts marched around the manor and pounded at our door. . . ."

From somewhere in the cellars beneath them, a dog began to bark frantically. Laddos and Kane exchanged glances.

"A rat," explained Hranal, as the two men started to their feet. "He likes to chase them."

The dog yelped in pain, howled in sudden fear. The sound rolled eerily through the ruined halls beyond.

"Big rat," observed Kane, wiping grease from his hands. He headed for the cellar.

"I'll just come with you," Laddos decided.

"Thought Jeresen said to watch the old man."

The Waldann's broken nose jutted truculently. "Hell, they ain't going nowhere. I want to see what scared that dog."

The cellar beneath the kitchen was clean and well kept. Shelves of wine bottles and foodstuffs were neatly ordered along the walls. One end was curtained off, and behind was a small bed and plain furnishings, a broken mirror and a few items of woman's clothing laid over an old trunk. Sesi's quarters, guessed Kane. The others slept upstairs.

A heavy door opened into the cellars beneath the main house. The door was ajar.

"This been open?" asked Kane.

"How should I know?" Laddos shrugged, edging the lantern into the room.

The floor of the gutted halls overhead had been broken through by falling stones. Sections had caved in under the weight of rubble. A few stars could be seen through the jagged apertures. Dust and decay and broken walls. The ruin was complete.

"There'll be another cellar beneath the far wing,"

Kane surmised. "Probably at least one subcellar beneath this one. Over there, steps go down."

"Where?" Laddos raised the lantern, stepping cautiously around the shadowy piles of debris. "Gods, if there's a weak place in the floor here . . ."

Kane crossed to the steps that led below. "Something's disturbed the dust here."

"Jeresen searched the place pretty thorough when we got here. I don't hear that dog no more." Laddos kept glancing over his shoulder.

"Paw prints in the dust, too. Something else I can't figure—too blurred and blotchy." Kane started for the stairs.

"Let's forget it. The dog had a rat."

"Give me the lantern if you're going back."

Laddos swore and followed him down the narrow steps.

Something growled from below.

"Watch it!" Kane's blade wavered.

Laddos hurried with the light. Twin circles of fire glared at them. The dog was backed into a corner at the foot of the stairs. Hackles raised, fangs bared, tail between his legs in paralyzed terror. He didn't seem to see them until they reached the base of the steps—then he bolted between them and dashed madly off into the ruins above.

The two nervously surveyed the subcellar. Its ceiling had not given way, but the chamber was cluttered with mouldering debris of uncertain nature. In the lamplight Kane saw a skeleton still sprawled across a rotting pallet, both legs clipped off at mid-femur. A torture chamber or hospital; the distinction seemed meaningless, as he glanced over the cobweb-shrouded tables and implements, noted the dry bones asleep under blankets of dust. A gas bomb, Kane guessed. It would have lingered for days in this low place.

"What's that?" Laddos hissed.

Something scurried crab-like away from the circle of lamplight. Kane had the impression of a misshapen spider the size of a hound. He started for it, but the creature scrambled agilely beneath a mound of overturned furnishings and vanished before he could get a good look at it.

Something squat and shaggy, with a gait impossible to describe.

"There's a burrow here!" pointed Laddos.

Kane nodded. He had seen one like it in the trench where Sesi had escaped. A cramped burrow through which an agile youth might wriggle, piercing the wall of the sub-cellar.

"Did Masale have trenchworks connected to the manor?" Laddos demanded.

"I don't know."

"Then what . . . ?"

"I don't know."

A broken-legged chair toppled over with a crash from a mound of rubble close to the burrow. Laddos whirled with a curse—then dropped his sword and thrust his arm beneath an overturned table.

"Got you—you goddam bitch!" The mercenary yanked the snarling girl out from where she crouched, his arm gashed where her dagger had struck. He flung her sprawling onto the stones and kicked the blade from her hand.

"Hold her, Kane! Jeresen's going to—"

Laddos didn't finish. Kane caught the lantern from his nerveless hand as the mercenary sprawled forward.

Sesi stared without comprehension as Kane wiped the blood from his swordblade.

Slowly she came to her feet—eyes on Kane as she straightened the torn edges of her short gown over her scratched and muddy thighs. "That's three times you've interceded, Kane. Whose hand do you play? Not Grey's; not Jeresen's. Is it Masale's?"

"I play Kane's hand," said Kane. "Does it matter?"

Sesi grimaced. "I suppose not—in the end."

"Don't edge any closer to that tunnel, or I'll pin your foot to the floor," warned Kane.

Sesi halted her stealthy retreat. "What now? Do you call Jeresen?" Her voice was cool for the terror that shone in her eyes.

"Should I?"

Sesi glanced at Laddos's body. "So Kane means to share Lynortis's treasure with no one. What difference will it make to me?"

"You'll find me kinder than Jeresen. If this treasure exists, it's useless knowledge unless you have someone who can arrange to get both you and the gold out of this devil-haunted graveyard."

"Is that why you think I haven't made use of my secret before now?"

"There's some reason why you haven't. Could be you needed time to think it out. The gold is useless to you here, but to get it out you'd need someone you could trust."

"Meaning you." Her voice was sarcastic.

"That's right."

"Suppose I told you I didn't know of any secret treasure?"

Kane shrugged. "It might be. But the story the old folks tell of your mother's coming here corroborates Jeresen's account. Was Reallis your mother?"

"She was—but that doesn't prove she told me of any hidden treasure."

"You'll never prove that to Jeresen."

Her shoulders sagged. "I know. Or to anyone."

She stood a moment slumped in despair, her lips pressed tight. Kane wondered that she had no tears. Then her hands caught the hem of her shift. With a quick movement she pulled the gown over her head and tossed it to the floor.

Her tousled brunette mane and her defiance were all that clothed her. Her flesh was a warm tan, her breasts high and proud. The dirt that smeared her lithe limbs and piquant face was a contrast to the clean lines of her hips and torso.

"This is all I have to give you, Kane. Whether you believe that or not, you're the only hope I have. Get me out of this, and I'll give to you the only thing I can offer."

Not original, and nothing he couldn't take by force, but Kane liked the set of her jaw as much as he approved of the rest.

"All right," he said. "We'll take this up again later. Right now there's Jeresen to think about. How'd you get back here?"

Sesi slithered into her ragged shift. "I grew up here; I know the battlefield well. When I led Jeresen to the trenches I thought it would either be a chance to escape or a quick death. When you cut my halter, I dove into the tunnel at the end of the trench. When you have to, you can wriggle pretty fast, even with your hands tied. I came out in the brush farther down, slipped away in the darkness and crept back here through the ruined wing. I thought Jeresen wouldn't think to search here again."

"Your hands were tied? What killed Bonaec?"

Sesi started. "Was that the scream? It must have been one of the half-men. There was one in here just before you came down. I was afraid to move or cry out, with Jeresen's men upstairs. I don't think they'd hurt me, but they terrify me."

"Half-men?" Kane remembered the misshapen crab-like skulker.

"They live in the ruins of Lynortis—the other survivors of the battle. They don't like to be seen."

It was time to get away, Kane decided. Jeresen might swing back to the manor at any minute, and it would not be good for them to be here.

"We'll slip out the way you came in," Kane told her. "Let Jeresen puzzle it out. If we can hide in Lynortis, Masale and Jeresen can fight it out while we make our break."

Sesi nodded. "This way, then." Kane followed her back up the stairs and into the night outside.

Behind them in the darkness there were scurrying, scraping sounds from the burrow.

V

Hunters in the Night

"How much of what Jeresen said was true?" Kane asked. They were close to the summit, and Kane judged it safe to rest for a moment. In the darkness it had been easy to steal across the battleground, although twice the search had come close. Once on the spiral road, the danger increased. Horses had passed this way, and if they encountered Jeresen's men here . . . On one side rose the sandstone cliff, on the other there was only emptiness. Nowhere to hide—it would have to be stand and fight.

"True? You're asking me?" Sesi was fighting for breath. She leaned against the low wall on the road's outer edge, watching the shifting torchlight far below. Jeresen had spread his men out as best he could. In places huge bonfires served as beacons to guide their search. It was a desperate search, even for that many men—but Jeresen had no choice.

Kane moved beside her, studying the lights below. They had crept through the tangled wreckage of the battlefield not daring to show the lantern. Sesi wondered time and again as Kane uncannily avoided unseen obstacles and pitfalls that even with her familiarity with the field she would have blundered into. When she realized her companion could see in the dark, she almost turned and fled. But Kane, enigmatic and menacing, was her one uncertain hope.

Kane was speaking. "I mean about someone overhearing your mother tell you about the treasure and going to Masale with that knowledge."

Sesi tried to see his face in the darkness. "That

would have been Amenit. Drifters pass through from time to time—drifters like yourself, if that much is true about you. If you don't mind stealing from the dead—and Amenit didn't—there are many dead here. Mother never was very strong; she died a month ago. Before she died we talked of things. Several nights later, Amenit was drunk. He crept in and tried to force himself upon me. Orsis beat him rather badly, and the next morning Amenit was gone. Poor Orsis—he was a protector for us both. Jeresen had to kill him."

"And you say Reallis never spoke to you of treasure?"

"Not a word. You have to believe me, Kane!"

Kane shrugged. "Something doesn't add up, I'll grant you. But we need to reach Lynortis. Got your wind back?"

The once imposing gates of Lynortis had been torn from their hinges and the bronze doors thrown from the summit, after the city had fallen from within. The citadel's dark streets were blocked with rubble. The skyline was one of foreshortened horizons, broken towers, gutted buildings, and fire-blackened walls.

Kane paused at the empty gateway, peering across the open plaza beyond. Sesi pressed close against his massive body. "Almost no one ever comes up here," she whispered. "And never at night. Only the half-men."

"I thought I saw something move over across there," Kane murmured, straining to see. Sesi could discern nothing but thick shadow.

"The half-men are other survivors?" he asked. "How many are there?"

"I don't know. There aren't many of them left. I've seen some of them creeping about the battlefield at night. They never tried to hurt me, but I never waited to find out."

Kane frowned uneasily. "I don't like this—but we've got to reach cover. Let's try it." He started across the open plaza for the shadowy streets beyond.

"Here she is!" bawled someone from the darkness. A blurred figure stirred from the wreckage of a petrary. "Kane's got her! Here!"

Kane snarled and threw his knife at the onrushing Waldann. The man cried out and pitched backward from the force of his throw. Kane retrieved the heavy dagger from the mercenary's chest as he dashed past. But the damage had been done.

Hooves and boots stamped across the plaza at the shout—indistinct shapes rushing toward them. A torch flared to life, another. Jeresen had posted men to guard the entrance to Lynortis. The Waldanns closed in on the fugitives like wolves for the kill—how many, Kane couldn't tell. It was enough.

Kane cursed his luck and broke into a run. If he could cut through the first to reach them, he and the girl stood a chance of losing the others in the chaotic ruins of the city. .

Halfway to the safety of the rubble-strewn streets, Sesi cried out and fell headlong across the stones. Kane spun about to help her. She writhed in pain, clutching her leg.

"Kane! My knee! It's broken!"

Kane hauled the girl to her feet. Sesi gasped as her injured leg buckled. He'd have to carry her. And they wouldn't make it.

. "Kane! Go on!" Sesi hissed, trying to crawl for the shelter she'd never reach.

But now it was too late for Kane to get clear. The first horsemen were upon them, hooves striking sparks as they drew rein.

They weren't certain about Kane in the initial surprise. Kane's knife caught one rider in the throat, spilling him from the saddle. His horse broke away as Kane lunged for its reins. The other mercenary reacted instantly, taking Kane's swordstroke across his buckler. He yelled out a warning and slashed down at Kane's face. Kane parried, at disadvantage against a mounted foe. The horseman did not press his attack—waiting for the others to close in.

It was hopeless, and Kane knew it. In seconds they would ring him with steel. In the open he had no chance against mounted veterans; if he broke for cover they would ride him down. It would be good sport for them, but a game quickly finished. Sesi was tugging Kane's knife from the fallen mercenary, whether for defense or a quick death, Kane had no time to speculate. The circle had closed.

Angry faces snarled down at him as the horsemen pressed in. Kane parried one blow, hamstrung the horse as it bolted past. Its rider died as he fell. That made the others more cautious. Their prey was certain, but the first to reach him would die. For a heartbeat they milled about, each waiting for someone else to rush in.

Another horse screamed and fell, hamstrung from behind. Its rider vaulted clear, landed heavily. Steel flashed low to the ground, and the mercenary's head rolled free.

The man nearest swung his torch. In its flaring light something spider-like scuttled back into the shadow. It was a man—or half of a man. He ran on his hands, legless torso swinging between his thickly muscled arms. He clutched a heavy knife in his teeth; there was blood on its blade.

Then an arrow sprouted from the torchbearer's chest. The link dropped from his hand, struck the stones, and went out.

Kane lunged for the horseman nearest him. Stunned, the Waldann remembered his shield an instant too late. Kane's upward thrust disembowelled him.

Another scream of pain from the darkness. Kane caught a glimpse of a mercenary on foot being dragged down by a twisted shape that rose from the darkness of a fallen wall.

"Down!" a bass voice yelled.

Kane dropped as a springald snapped. A wooden shaft as thick as his arm drove its iron head through the mail of the Waldann opposite him, scarcely slowing as it lifted the man from his saddle and carried him back into the darkness. Another arrow hissed past, and the remaining torch was smothered beneath its bearer's toppling body. In the darkness another man shrieked, more in terror than pain; his second outcry was cut short.

Two horsemen remained. Kane went for them, but they had had enough. They bolted past him, driving for the gate. One of the riders made it. His hoofbeats clattered for a long while up the winding roadway.

Kane could still hear their echo as the half-men gathered about them.

VI

In the Temple of Peace

On the ground a fallen torch snapped and flickered to life, spreading a pool of wan yellow light. Sesi shivered against Kane's arm, leaning heavily on it for support. The sword in Kane's left hand was poised to strike.

"Get the torch," he grated.

Sesi hopped quickly to the sputtering link, scrambled back to Kane. Her leg was badly lamed, but she was able to limp. Kane judged her knee had not been broken, only wrenched and numbed by her fall.

"You can put down your sword," said a voice from beyond the ring of light. "We're allies, it seems."

The speaker stepped into the light. Kane thought for an instant it was a two-headed hunchback. The figure came closer and Kane saw it was one man carrying another—or part of another man. Walking toward him was a tall, heavily muscled man, who appeared quite normal except for the eyeless mass of scar that was his face. Over his shoulder peered the head of the other man—a limbless torso slung in a harness to the blind man's back.

"Stop here, Semoth," he spoke in his bearer's ear. "We've saved their lives, but they're still not certain we are allies."

Behind the blind giant scampered the man without legs, his knife sheathed in a sling behind his neck. No, this man was beardless; the one Kane had glimpsed earlier was shaggy as a bear. Another man stepped toward them —the archer, from his bow and quiver. His face and arms were misshapen knots of burned scar, though an upflung arm had spared his eyes from the spewing phosphorus.

Another man joined them. Kane thought him a dwarf, but he had not been born with wooden clogs on the stumps of his thighs, or a steel hook where his right arm should have been. Others moved about in the shadow—maimed, twisted things whose misfortune had been not to die from the hideous wounds that had transformed men into freaks.

"We have overheard much," the limbless torso spoke. "It's easy to hide and watch when when you're only half a man." Several others joined his mirthless laughter.

"Who are you?" Kane asked.

"I am Byr," said the torso. "In my other life I was Captain of the First Guard. Masale's soldiers left me for dead beneath a fallen wall, and gangrene did the rest. My friend Semoth commanded a trebuchet crew, until a chance stone struck the throwing arm as they were loading a phosphorus bomb.

"We all have similar stories as to who we were in past lives, and how we became creatures who must shun the sight of men. We are the creatures of war, the veterans for whom there was no victory, no spoils, no poems and parades. Our comrades who are past caring are the honored dead, while we who must live are the despised and pitied cripples."

"You've lived here since the battle?"

"We have. Though we fought on opposite sides, the aftermath of war found us a nation of the maimed—united by our afflictions. And where would you have us live? When we returned to our homes, our wives and children cringed from us; our neighbors laughed and threw stones when we entered our old towns. How could we live? As beggars or as freaks to amuse the crowds? No, we chose to dwell in Lynortis, where no man ever comes—to live out our wretched lives in dignity where our fellows would not jeer and pity.

"And is it not better? Once we were men and enemies, who hated and killed. Now we are half-men and comrades, and we live here in peace."

"Your peace has ended," Kane told him. "Jeresen will be up here in force in another hour."

"To all things must come an ending," Byr stated heavily. "It is the law of nature. Even to the war there was an ending, although I think there was no victor. The war was the ending for three hundred thousand. Tonight may be the ending for the handful who have survived."

"Masale is coming back to Lynortis."

"We know." Byr's smile was quiet, but not serene. "Masale is already here."

"Here! How can you know?"

"We watch where no man sees us," the legless man snickered. "In thirty years we know every hole and mound of rubble here. The Crawler saw Masale's scouts sneak in two hours ago. He told Ghot," he nodded to an armless man, "and Ghot brought word to us."

Kane warily stepped past them. Sesi limping at his side, he climbed to the parapet and looked down. There were more torches now, many more. In places the motes of light rushed together; sometimes one winked out.

Semoth climbed after him, Byr guiding his blind steps. "Masale always was a good general," Byr commented without admiration. "He learned the Waldanns' position from his scouts, then encircled them in the dark—using no betraying light. They'll fight for a while between themselves, and at dawn those who are left will doubtless come to Lynortis."

"What will you do? They'll take Lynortis apart stone by stone looking for Sesi."

"We will not hide from them." Semoth spoke for the first time. "Sesi is our queen. Masale shall not have her."

"This is hardly a time for idealism," Kane protested. "The passage through the mountain is still open—Masale may not have it guarded yet."

"Where would we flee?" asked the blind man.

"To all things there must be an ending," Byr repeated.

"You'll be butchered," Kane stated. "And aren't some of you Masale's old soldiers?"

"That was in our other lives," Byr said calmly. "Now we are outcasts—half-men. Lynortis is our home, and Sesi is our queen. Outcast and hunted, she shares in our suffering, and Lynortis is her home. The war has not ended for us, nor has it ended for Masale. Now there will be a final battle and a victor, for that which began thirty years ago must have an ending."

"You're all mad."

"Yes, we're all mad."

Kane swore in exasperation.

"Come with us to the Temple of Peace," Byr invited gently. "It may help you to understand."

Kane considered his chances of getting Sesi away from Lynortis. The roadway would certainly be guarded now, and Masale had brought more than a hundred men, by their torches. The outlook was grim. Lynortis was shelter for the moment, but Lynortis was also a trap.

Since there was nothing he could do for the moment, Kane followed the half-men to where they all now were going. Sesi limped painfully while holding his arm; she could walk, but without a horse they were not going to outrun any pursuit.

"This is the Temple of Peace?" Kane queried, as the half-men entered the featureless basalt monolith that squatted in an open court not far beyond the city's gate.

"It is now," Byr declared. "The old days, the old gods are no more—they died with Lynortis. We who survive worship a new god."

"The darklings . . . ?"

"The darklings are no more—fled down into the nether regions from which they came, and only their burrows remain. A thousand screaming sacrifices were given to them, but their hell-spawned vials of killing vapor and searing phosphorus would not bring us victory. We rolled their poisons and fires back down into their burrows, and now we worship the god of Peace."

Nerves on edge, Kane followed the half-men past the wreckage of the temple doors and into the black stone temple. Its walls were stark and barren of any embellishment, drab and somber as an unmarked tomb. Once inside, the featureless walls were as claustrophobically oppressive as the inside of a sepulcher.

Within the sanctum several torches flared brightly. Here had once yawned an open pit into which uncounted sacrifices had been drawn down to Hell. Now the tunnel mouth was closed with great blocks of stone—an altar. And from the altar rose the statue of a man—a giant in battle dress, sword upraised in fierce challenge. The statue's face had been obliterated.

"The Peacemaker!" intoned Byr.

"The Peacemaker!" echoed the others.

"Kane! What is it?' Sesi whispered anxiously, as Kane balked inside the sanctum.

"The Peacemaker—our god," Byr told her. "The bringer of peace."

"But that's the statue of a warrior!" Sesi protested.

"A special warrior!" Byr explained. "He is the man who led Masale's army up through the passages of the mountain. His face is missing, for no man knows his face."

"You worship the man who betrayed Lynortis!" Sesi exploded in disbelief.

"We are soldiers from either side of that battle—and are we not equally maimed? The soldiers never win in any battle—only their leaders are victors. The soldiers fight and suffer; some live, some die—many like us don't quite die, but must live on as miserable human wreckage, while our leaders grow old in the luxury we suffered to win for them. Generals and princes live in glory, but the soldier dies in pain."

Byr's braids flew as he shook his head fiercely. "No, the Peacemaker did not betray us. He brought a swift end to two years of nightmare."

"But tens of thousands died because of him!"

"Tens of thousands died below, and died here. Who can say how many more would have died had the siege dragged on for two more years—for ten more years—with Yosahcora bartering wealth and souls for men and weapons, and Masale whipping thousands more of his subjects to add their bones to their brothers'?

"The Peacemaker brought an end to this, and for this we give him thanks."

Byr's face was calm, for all the hate and anger of his words. "But now we shall worship for what may be a final time. Take me to the altar, Semoth."

The blind man obeyed. The burned archer helped him with the harness, and Semoth carefully propped Byr's limbless trunk at the foot of the statue.

"Hail to the Peacemaker!" Byr's bass voice intoned. The assembled half-men echoed his chant.

"Hail to the Bringer of Peace!"

"Hail to the Bringer of Death!"

"Hail to the Bringer of the End!"

"Bring to us now an Ending!"

Kane grabbed Sesi's arm and steered her out of the Temple of Peace.

"There may be a way out. We can make a break while

the half-men engage Masale. It may draw men away from the passage through the mountain. Masale will be confident and attack up the roadway."

"Kane, I can't run any more," Sesi said wearily.

"You sure as hell can't wait here!"

"Does it matter? If Masale defeats them, he'll hound me wherever I run."

"If I can get us out of his lands, he'll never find our trail."

Sesi glanced at her swollen knee. "We'd never make it. You know that. It's me they all want. You can get away by yourself."

"I can try it with us both."

"It's hopeless. My best chance is to stay here with the half-men. If they can drive back Masale—"

"Sesi, they aren't going to defeat Masale! They're too few, too old, too crippled—and they're mad! You are, too, if you don't come with me."

"Stay and fight with them."

"Dead I can't spend that gold."

Sesi bit her lip. "Kane, damn you—there isn't any gold!"

Kane stared at her without expression.

"If I knew the secret of a hidden treasure room, do you think I'd be in this wretched situation?"

"You might—if you hadn't had time to figure out how to make use of that knowledge. You couldn't just pick up a chest of gold and go walking off to the nearest city."

"Kane, my life hasn't been much, but I want to keep living, and I can't stand pain. Jeresen could have had the secret on his terms—if I only knew it."

"We've been over this, Sesi. Someone's lying somewhere."

"I don't know what Amenit made out of what he heard. I think he liked to sneak around and watch me undress—he jammed the bolt and came into my room through the main cellar the night Orsis beat him and drove him away. Mother was out of her head as the fever got worse. She talked a lot about her girlhood in Lynortis. Not much of it made sense. Several times she tried to tell me about a room filled with gold, where she'd taken her own necklace to add to the pile. But she never said where it was or what it was all about. Kane, she wasn't ten when Lynortis fell!"

"Is that the truth?" Kane asked finally.

"Damn you, Kane! Of course it is! I've wanted to tell everyone this from the start! Only everyone knew I was lying when I wouldn't say what they wanted to hear."

Kane seemed lost in thought. Sesi could not read the feelings in his face.

"Look," she pressed him. "If I knew the secret of the treasure, I'd tell you before I'll tell those who have hounded me. You've done all in your power for me—I'd tell you now. No, I'd hold the secret over your head to make you throw your life away against Masale's attack. Kane, believe me—I don't know the secret of any hidden treasure!"

"I believe you," said Kane softly. "Massale won't."

Sesi shuddered and clung to him. "When Jeresen's men surrounded us on the plaza, I got your dagger. I thought I wouldn't let them take me, but I don't think I could have done it. I don't want to die, Kane."

"For all things there must be an ending," croaked a grotesque voice from the shadows.

Sesi screamed. Kane whirled in the direction of the voice.

The creature on the stones had once been a man—though it took imagination to recognize that. He had no more legs than Byr, but enough of his arms remained to make stubby flippers. Wrapped in a shaggy fur sack, he scooted over the stones like a seal. His jaws had been torn away, and in answer to some morbid whim he had had the broken mandibles fitted with snoutlike jaws of razor-fanged steel. There was blood on the polished fangs.

"The Crawler is back!" shouted the armless man called Ghot. He ran out of the temple to help the steel-jawed amputee—pushing him with his foot as the Crawler rolled up the low steps.

The other half-men emerged from the sanctum. "What is it, Crawler?" Byr demanded.

"The roadway is guarded, but they never saw me," the Crawler announced in his barely intelligible voice. "I came as fast as I could, but they'll be here any minute. Jeresen and Masale agreed to a truce after only a skirmish. Word came down of our presence here from one of Jeresen's men you let get away. He was scared out of his wits—enough to convince them. Jeresen and Masale had a council, and when I left, Masale was arguing final terms to hire Jeresen and his mercenaries to help him storm Lynortis. Instead of fighting it out, they're going to attack together!"

Byr yelled frantic orders. The half-men rushed about to prepare their defense.

"That does it," Kane said grimly. "Let's try to get out of this."

"Kane, I meant what I said. I'm staying with them."

There was that set to her jaw he admired. Kane shrugged. "All right, then. I'm not."

Sesi started to call out to him as he turned. The words would not come.

VII

Echoes

Kane leaned against the merlon of a deserted bartizan atop the fortress wall. At a distance much farther down, the half-men were preparing to defend the broken portals of Lynortis. In the darkness he could only glimpse vague shapes scurrying around the plaza before the barbican. Below he could see the line of torches writhing like a serpent up the spiral road to the citadel.

He knew he should be going, finding cover until this was over, until there was a chance for escape. Kane cursed the girl's stubbornness. He might have been able to win free with her. By himself he was confident of escape; Sesi was the only one they wanted—to lead them to a treasure she could never find. Kane regretted her loss. But this way was best. He'd have taken any risk for the secret of the treasure, but one piece of gold would buy a bedmate far more accomplished than Sesi. He should be going.

From the distance echoed a clashing roar. Kane knew the sound. Boulders hurled down the steep grade of the roadway. He could vaguely make out struggling knots of the half-men rolling the huge stones onto the road—like ants swarming over a beetle. Once started down the slope, the boulders plummeted downward with gathering speed—striking sparks as they caromed from the face of the mountain, glancing from the outer wall with sharp thunder. There was no room to avoid their avalanche for those on the roadway.

But Masale had endured two years of countless attacks and counterattacks along this bloodstained road—and he knew to expect resistance from the ruined citadel. Like phantom echoes through the night came the shouts of men, the splintering crash of falling boulders—then the brazen clangour of stone against armor. Masale advanced behind a mantlet hastily pieced together from relics strewn over the field below.

Men yelled, horses screamed as the avalanche of boulders struck the armored framework of the mantlet. Kane could see nothing of what took place on the road. Listening to the cries and crashes, watching the torchlit line waver and fall back, seeing rows of torches suddenly snuff out and fall spinning into the night, he could envision the chaos below. Rocks bounded over the wall to plummet down upon those on the tier below Boulders smashed into the advancing mantlet, splintering hastily repaired timbers, flinging shards of stone and broken armor over those who crouched behind. And when the rumble of the rockslide echoed away, the line of torches continued its advance.

Masale's troops were closer now. Kane heard the clatter of hooves, the roar of warcries. Then the creak of ancient siege machinery. The springald smacked viciously, and Kane knew its heavy bolt was arching downward. He heard the rasp and recoil of an onager, flinging its basket of fist-sized stones. Against one torchlit barbican he saw an archer firing into the advancing line. More stones rattled down the slope from the mangonel on the opposite barbican.

Frantically the half-men worked over the few light siege weapons they could bring to bear at this close range. Masale's column pressed inexorably upward, although time and again sections of torches were swept away to oblivion. Kane felt admiration for the half-men's determination—a handful of cripples fighting with a few pieces of outworn weaponry. Given enough men and weapons to defend the entire perimeter of Lynortis, Masale would never have a chance. As it was, the half-men were forced to concentrate all their defense on the section of the mountain directly below the gateway. Thus, as they advanced upward on the spiral road, only a fraction of Masale's troops came under attack at one time. There was no stopping his ascent to the open portal.

Now they were within a hundred yards of the gateway, and Kane could make out white smears of faces in the flaring torchlight. The smashed mantlet had been discarded, and they advanced in testudo formation—footmen in the van, mounted farther back. In minutes the van would force past the empty gates, and the horsemen would sweep through to annihilate all in the plaza. Arrows and rocks still rained on upraised shields; a springald bolt tore a path through their ranks. But now they advanced at a run, and Masale's archers were raining death amidst the city's defenders.

Farther back across the plaza a scorpion recoiled with a deadly slam—the heaviest siege engine Kane had noticed that was still operational. Daylight suddenly burst over the steep slopes before the citadel's gates. Kane threw up his arm, dazzled by the white-hot blast. A phosphorus bomb—the half-men had uncovered an unexploded shell somewhere. Spewing tentacles of incandescent death blossomed over the roadway. Where it struck, men flamed into cinder. Searing fragments reached out like lethal fingers, burning all they touched. Men and horses shrieked in pain and terror, bolted over the outer wall in blind panic. Flaming bodies pitched over the edge, falling like stars into the darkness far below.

The advance was broken. The scorpion bucked again, and another phosphorus bomb spread searing hell across the slope farther down. Masale's troops milled in terror. Another few bombs and their assault would be routed.

The scorpion lashed out a third time, but Kane saw no sunburst below. Far at the end of Masale's column, a score of torches were snuffed out. From cries in the night below, Kane guessed that a gas shell had struck there—too far down hill for the heavy vapor to have reached the main force.

Masale's troops were disciplined. Death before and behind them, they regrouped in the shelter of the far side, beyond the range of the defenders. Again they advanced—now in a headlong rush over the blackened bodies of their fellows.

The half-men waited with their last shell until the first of Masale's troops burst past the open portal. The phosphorus bomb exploded full in their ranks—turning the gateway into a screaming hell of death.

For a moment the gateway was blocked with charred and writhing bodies. Then the rest of the column surged over the fuming barrier, carrying the battle to Lynortis's last defenders. The phosphorus flames died, and darkness swallowed the final battle.

But Kane no longer watched the death struggle before Lynortis's gates. He stood frozen, looking out over the crenel, his eyes seeing a battle of three decades past.

He saw Lynortis before the fall—ten thousand men defending its walls against ten thousand more who struggled up the road to reach the citadel above them. He saw a hundred siege engines fire at once, hurling death down upon those below. The night was alight with starbursts of phosphorus flaming across the forests thousands of feet below. And from the attackers arched missiles and stones to smash through the towers of Lynortis and crush those who could not hide.

Nowhere was there a place to hide.

Fire raged across the city where flaming balls of pitch and naphtha splashed. In the valley below, lethal clouds of black vapor drifted, slaying all in their breath. Women and children fought in the streets for the pitiable rations of food and water that were spared them. Plague stalked them all, in the valley and on the pinnacle. And the cries of the maimed and the dying were as a ceaseless moan of wind.

On and ever on the nightmare continued, while days of horror merged with nights of terror like the flapping of batwings. Death glutted himself here, taxing even death's insatiable greed, and the breath of corruption was scented with the acrid perfume of burning. In high Lynortis and on the plain below, hundreds of thousands died in fear and violence, and death was the only peace in this endless vision of hell.

At last all was quiet. The flames, the cries were no more. A dead city looked over a dead valley, where only those moved who sated themselves among the endless rows and piles and pits and mountains of the dead.

Kane could see the dead stirring now. See the smashed and burned and torn and fever-pocked and famine-eroded bodies rise from the moraine of unnumbered bones. See their spectral hordes march across the war-blasted forest, rise from the talus of boken bones below, drift through the shattered towers and rubble-choked streets, dance a writhing spiral about the obelisk of Lynortis.

Kane moaned and shook himself awake from his trance. He stared about him in a daze. The night was still, close and cold in the darkest hour before dawn. The battle was over, then. Masale's men had overrun the last defense.

It was time to be going.

VIII

The Bringer of Peace

Kane moved like a ghost through the empty streets of Lynortis. His stealth was needless; there were none to bid him halt. The gates of Lynortis were guarded only by the slain. His path to escape was open, but Kane paused on the threshold.

The half-men had fought well, and in the end had died well. Masale had lost heavily on the assault up the roadway; scores more lay dead upon the stones of the plaza. With nothing to live for, the half-men had slain without fear for their lives. The price of Masale's victory had been costly, and from the strewn corpses of both his soldiers and the mercenaries not many had won past the plaza.

The Crawler lay smashed like a slug, his ghastly steel jaws still clamped in a throat. The blind giant Semoth sprawled with his face over a heap of Masale's soldiers. The others were there, too. Kane didn't see Byr at first, until he heard his name whispered.

Kane turned. A heavy bolt from the springald had been rammed butt-first into a mound of rubble. The leader of the half-men was impaled on its iron head.

"No! Don't touch me!" Byr warned him when Kane wanted to lift him free. "I'm bleeding inside. Only have a few breaths left to me."

Kane stood back and gazed at the carnage.

"So you came back," Byr said.

Kane studied his drawn face and knew what the man meant. "So you know me, then."

"I know you. None of us ever knew for certain, but I guessed."

"You fought well here."

"Not well enough. Masale and the Waldann captain fought past, with maybe ten or fifteen of their men. They have Sesi."

"I'm sorry for that."

"Why, Kane?" Byr whispered. "Was it for gold?"

Kane shrugged, his face hidden in shadow. "The gold had long ago been spent—even Reallis's necklace. I grew tired of the senseless slaughter . . . I wanted it to end."

Byr coughed a frothy beard of blood. "For me it ends now. But the war that has festered here for thirty years still goes on. Kane, bring to us now an Ending."

He lived just long enough to see Kane walk past him, away from the open gateway.

A pair of guards lounged at the entrance to the Temple of Peace. They mistook Kane for a Waldann straggler until it was too late. Kane let their bodies fall quietly, then walked into the torchlit sanctum.

Sesi hung naked from an overhead support—a dozen merciless faces intent on her. Her wrists were tied behind her back, and her arms drawn over her head by a rope thrown over the roof support. When the full weight of her body pulled down, the agony was excruciating and in time her shoulders would be torn from their sockets. A second rope made a noose about her throat, slowly strangling her whenever the rope that held her wrists was allowed to go slack. Her tanned flesh was crisscrossed with livid welts.

Jeresen was drawing up the slack on her bound wrists when Kane entered. One of Masale's men was carefully paring resinous splinters from a torch. Sesi stared down at Kane through pain-glazed eyes.

The Waldann captain was first to see him. His face twisted into a sneer. "You got balls coming back now, Kane! I know all about how you tried to steal this little bitch for yourself."

Masale started at his words. He spun and stared at Kane in wonder. "You!" he shouted.

"That's right." Kane smiled coldly.

The would-be conqueror touched his scarred and lined face, his grey locks of hair. His hooked nose had always made him look like an eagle, but he was an old and tired eagle now. His eyes were rimmed and haunted; his warrior's body showed the effects of dissipation beneath his splendid mail.

Masale shook his head in disbelief. "You amaze me, Kane. After thirty years you stand before me once again —yet on my oath, you haven't aged a year since that night you disappeared after leading me through the mountain passage into Lynortis!"

"By the Seven, that fits with some of the tales I heard about Kane when we fought together under Roderic!" Jeresen growled. "Some whispered he was a sorcerer—or demon—a deathless bringer of doom whose name figures in a hundred legends! Kill him, I say!"

"I give orders here!" Masale snarled. "Kane has served me well in the past. If he serves me again, he'll share in the gold."

The legendary warrior-king considered the red-bearded giant with the uncanny eyes. Masale had never cared to look into Kane's eyes. He liked it even less just now. "Well, Kane. Have you come to share in the gold?"

"You've chased a shadow," Kane laughed. "Sesi knows of no gold."

"We have plenty of time to question her," Masale stated. "If you don't think she knows of hidden treasure, why then have you come back?"

"Because to all things must come an ending, Masale—even to this war. And you have no time left."

Masale sensed his meaning, but already Kane's left hand had found his sword.

Masale bellows a warning and its echo floats on the air. Seconds of time move dreamlike, for they are final seconds—and all that happens in that instant before the brain knows that it is dead is like the passage of a lifetime.

Jeresen has dropped the strappado rope. Sesi's wrists fall to her back, and the noose closes on her throat. The crossbow—cocked and ready—Jeresen reaches for it. Kane's right hand flicks out—there's a knife—glittering across the room—through Jeresen's eye.

And Kane's sword lifts clear of his shoulder scabbard. His fingers have just touched its hilt, but its blade continues its outward arc. A soldier sees his belly spilled open, his comrade's hand sprinning in the air. There is a ribbon of crimson, and Kane's blade is still moving.

Now behind Kane—they rush him. His blade turns to meet them. A Waldann head lifts into the air along with the falling hand. His companion takes the swordpoint through his heart.

Kane pulls his blade free—his right hand catches the dead man's fallen sword. Kane whirls. He has a sword in each hand. In his powerful grasp they are no more than knives to him. Kane's twin blades carve flashing scarlet runes—parry and thrust—slash, parry, and thrust. Attack, Kane—you've no time to defend. His forearm is bleeding—there's a gash across his side. Five more lives lie sprawled at Kane's feet.

All together they're on him now. No wall for Kane's back. They're trying to circle. Rush in and be next to die—will it be you? Another man dies. The man with the axe—try to block its swing. Kane's right hand holds a broken sword—the axe-wielder holds an armload of his entrails. From the right flashes a spear, goring Kane's thigh. Kane staggers—hurls the broken sword at the spear-thrower's face. Jagged steel rips his eyes—the spearman never sees the swordblow that cleaves through his ribs.

They fall away now. Fear twists cruel faces for perhaps the first time. Kane seizes another blade in his bleeding right hand. A blond skull is split open, a leg is but a stump—and now the last few would flee. One dies with Kane's steel through his back—the other can only stumble to the door before the blood spurting from where his arm was is suddenly a trickle.

Masale stands alone now, face livid with rage. For Masale there has never been retreat, and he thinks only to slay this gore-splattered demon who has wreaked carnage among his men. He lunges for Kane, his blade a blue flicker. Kane moves faster, his blade faster still. Masale knows fear—then he knows nothing more.

And the echo of Masale's warning floats away into the night.

Kane stood reeling on the crimson-splashed stones. About him were only the dead and the dying. He glowered through the red haze of killing lust that throbbed through his huge frame. There were no more to kill. It was over.

Sesi's nude figure writhed at the end of the strangling

noose. Her neck had not snapped, since there had been no drop, but her face was turning dark from the throttling coil.

Kane lunged quickly. His blade flashed above her head. The rope snapped like a bowstring, and Sesi's limp body tumbled into his arms.

He removed the noose and cut the rope at her wrists. Sesi lay weakly in his arms, gasping for breath. She moaned when he touched her bruised, bleeding flesh, but there were still no tears.

"There are horses for the taking," Kane told her, wrapping a cloak about her shoulders. It was cold just before dawn. "We'll stop to pick up whatever you want to take with you. The war is finally over here."

"Who won the war, Kane?"

"I did."

"You didn't win a thing, Kane. You only survived."

"It means the same thing."

"But there must be more to victory than just survival."

Kane nodded to the fallen as he carried her from the temple. "Ask them now. Ask me in a hundred years."

SING A LAST SONG OF VALDESE

1

The Girl Beneath the Oak

"Reverence! Hold up a moment!"

The burly priest drew rein in a swirl of autumn leaves. Calloused fingers touched the plain hilt of the sword strapped to his saddle as his cowled head bent in the direction of her call.

Raven-black hair twining in the autumn wind, the girl stepped out from the gnarled oaks that shouldered the mountain trail. Bright black eyes smiled up at him from her wide-browed, strong-boned face. Her mouth was wide as well, and smiled.

"You ride fast this evening, reverence."

"Because the shadows grow deeper, and I have a good way to ride to reach the inn ahead." His voice was impatient.

"There's an inn not more than a mile from here." She swayed closer, and he saw how her full figure swelled against her long-skirted dress.

The priest followed her gesture. Just ahead the trail forked, the left winding alongside the mountain river, the right cutting along the base of the ridge. While the river road bore signs of regular travel, the other trail showed an aspect of disuse. Toward this the girl was pointing.

"That trail leads toward Rader," he told her, shifting in his saddle. "My business is in Carrasahl.

"Besides," he added, "I was told the inn near the fork of the road had long been abandoned. Few have cause to travel to Rader since the wool fair was shifted south to Enseljos."

"The old inn has lately been reopened."

"That may be. But my path lies to Carrasahl."

She pouted. "I was hoping you might carry me with you to the inn yonder."

"Climb up and I'll take you to the inn on the Carrasahl road."

"But my path lies to Rader."

The priest shrugged thick shoulders beneath his cassock. "Then you'd best be going."

"But reverence," her voice pleaded. "It will be dark long before I reach the inn, and I'm afraid to walk this trail at night. Won't you take me there on your horse? It won't take you far from your way, and you can lodge the night there just as well."

Shadows were lengthening, merging into dusk along the foot of the ridges. The declining sun shed only a dusty rubrous haze across the hilltops, highlighting tall hardwoods already fired by autumn's touch. Streaked with mist, the valleys beyond were swallowed in twilight.

Night was fast overtaking him, the rider saw. He recalled the warnings of villagers miles behind, who for his blessing had given him food and sour wine. They had answered his questions concerning the road ahead, then warned him to keep to the trail if night caught him and on no account make camp by himself. The priest had not been certain whether they warned him of robbers or some darker threat.

His horse stamped impatiently.

"I could make it worth your while to ride out of your way."

About to ride off, he glanced back down at her. Her smile was impish. Hidden by the cowl, his face could not be read.

She touched the ties of her embroidered bodice. "I would see that you had a most pleasant stay at Vald's Cove Inn, reverence." There was witchery in her voice. The bodice loosened, parted across her breasts.

"Though I can't see your face, I can see there's a man beneath that priest's cassock. Would you like to enjoy a mountain flower tonight? You'll remember her sweetness when you grow old in some musty temple."

Her breasts were firm and well shaped. Against their whiteness the tan flesh of her nipples matched the color of the swirling oak leaves.

Whatever his interest in her, the priest carried gold beneath his robe. The girl's eagerness to draw him onto a little-frequented trail aroused deep suspicion.

"The lure of wanton flesh is nothing to a priest of Thoem," he intoned.

"Then bugger yourself!" she spat, and lunged with a shrill scream for his horse's face. Sharp claws raked blood across his nose.

Already nervous, the horse screamed and reared. Caught by surprise, the priest lost his stirrups. Cassock flapping about his limbs, he scrambled for balance, then was thrown from the terrified mount. He fell heavily, somehow landing half on his feet, and cursed as his ankle turned under him.

The rearing horse bolted down the trail, took the right fork toward Rader, and disappeared. With mocking laughter, the girl ran after.

Limping badly, the priest stumbled after her, cursing with blasphemous invective. But the darkness quickly swallowed the flash of her white legs, though her laughter taunted him invisibly still.

II

The Inn by the Side of the Road

The lights of the inn were smoky yellow through the thick, leaded panes. The night winds caught the smoke and smell of horses, drove it down the road to Rader, so that the priest came upon the inn all at once.

He noted the many horses tethered in the outlying stables. There were a number of travellers at the inn to-night, and it seemed less likely that the girl meant to lead him into a trap. Or had her confederates lain in wait along the trail, probably they were content to steal his horse and gear. The priest swore angrily, decided he had been too suspicious.

His ankle stabbed with pain, but at least it bore his weight. His boots had probably prevented worse injury. He damned the voluminous grey cassock as it flapped about his trousered legs. It was slitted front and back from ankle to midthigh, and while that enabled him to straddle a horse, he blamed the clumsy garment for his fall.

The two-storey square log structure was a welcome sight. The autumn night grew chill; mist flowed like waves across the ridges. A night spent in the open would be uncomfortable at best. Worse, he had been warned of danger, and his sword was strapped to his saddle somewhere in the darkened hills.

A sign hung over the door: Vald's Cove Inn. The carving seemed of recent work, the priest noted as he climbed up to the door. The latch was not out, though the hour was not late. Hearing voices within, he knocked loudly.

He was about to knock a third time, when the door

was opened. Light and voices and the smell of warmth spilled out into the night.

A narrow, beardless face frowned out at him from the half-open doorway. "Who . . . what do you want . . . reverence?" His voice was thin and nervous, and he spoke in half-whisper.

"Food and lodging," the priest rumbled impatiently. "This *is* an inn, I believe."

"I'm sorry. There's no more room. You'll have to go elsewhere." He made to close the door.

The priest's huge fist checked him. "Are you a fool? Where is the innkeeper?" he demanded, suspicious at the man's show of anxious confusion.

"I'm master here," the other snapped in annoyance. "I'm sorry, reverence. I've no more room, and you'll have to—"

"Look, damn you!" The priest's bulk shouldered onto the threshold. "My horse threw me, and I've hobbled for miles already to get here. Now I'll have food and lodging if it's no more than floor space near the fire!"

The skeletal innkeeper did not quail before the bigger man. His narrow jaw clamped in anger; he clenched his black-gloved hands.

"What is this, man?" demanded a voice from within. "Do I hear you denying lodging to a brother servant of Thoem! What manner of innkeeper are you?"

The innkeeper started, then cringed effusively. "Forgive me, eminence. I only meant that my accommodations were not sufficient for one of his reverence's—"

"Let him in, you idiot! Turn away a priest of Thoem, would you! I see it's true how sadly you mountain folk have fallen in your respect for the true god! Let him in, do you hear?"

The priest pushed past the suddenly solicitous innkeeper. "Thank you, eminence. The manners of these folk are pitiable."

There were several people in the common room of the inn. Seated alone at one of several small tables was a tall, thin man whose scarlet cassock identified him as an abbot in the priesthood of Thoem. Like the priest, his face was hidden by the cowled garment. He waved to the other man with a finely groomed, blue-veined hand.

"Come join me by the fire and have some wine," he invited. "I see you're limping somewhat. Did I hear you say your horse threw you? That's bad luck. Our host must send his servants out to find it. Are you badly hurt?"

"Thoem saved me from serious harm, eminence, though I'd rather not walk another mile on it tonight."

"I'm certain. More wine, innkeeper! And hurry with that roast! Would you starve your guests? Sit down here, please. Have we met? I am Passlo, on my way in the service of Thoem to take charge of the abbey at Rader."

"A pleasure to meet you, Eminent Passlo." The priest touched hands as he seated himself. "I am Callistratis, journeying in the service of Thoem to Carrasahl. I've heard the abbey at Rader has fallen to the Dualists in these evil times."

The abbot scowled. "Certain rumors have reached us in the South. Word that there are certain rebel priests in the northern provinces who would contend that Thoem and Vaul are but dual expressions of the same deity. No doubt these heretics consider it prudent to align themselves with the god of these northern barbarians, now that the empire drifts into civil war."

The priest poured wine and drank hunched forward so that his lips were hidden in the shadow of his cowl. "I have heard such attempts to vindicate the Dualist heresy. It may be that our errands are the same, Eminent Passlo."

"Well, Revered Callistratis, that doesn't surprise me. I'd sensed immediately that there was a presence about you that argued for more than the simple priest. But I'll not intrude further on one whose mission requires that he travel incognito. But tell me, though, how would you deal with the Dualists?"

"By the prescribed formula for any heresy. They should all suffer impalement, their bodies left for night beasts and carrion birds."

The abbot clapped him on the shoulder. "Splendid, Revered Callistratis! We are of one accord! It pleases me to know that those who believe unswervingly in Thoem's sacred precepts have not all passed from the priesthood! I foresee a pleasant evening of theological discussion."

"Come, revered gentlemen, don't judge too harshly.

After all, there is precedent for Dualism in the history of your priesthood."

A short, stocky gentleman with a fine grey beard looked gravely at the priests. He straightened from the fire where he had stooped to light his pipe. A silver medallion embossed with a university seal depended from a chain about his thick neck.

"Precedent?" the abbot snapped.

The short man nodded through a puff of smoke. "Yes. I refer to the dogma formalized under the reign of King Halbros I that Thro'ellet and Tloluvin are but dual identities of the evil principle. No one in the days of the monarchy considered such doctrine heretical, although ancient beliefs plainly ascribe separate identities to these demon-lords."

The abbot paused to consider. "An interesting point," he conceded grudgingly, "although the manifold embodiments of evil are certainly acknowledged by our doctrine. Nonetheless, your argument does not hold in this instance, for there is but one true cosmic principle of good, whom true believers worship as Thoem. May I inquire, sir . . . ?"

The grey-bearded gentleman blew smoke in a flourish. "I am Claesna, of the Imperial University at Chrosanthe. Your proposal of theological debate caught my ear, eminence. The prospect of intelligent discussion promises salvation from what I had previously feared would be a dull evening in a backwoods tavern. May I join you?"

"Claesna?" The abbot's tone was surprise. "Yes, I've heard a great deal of you, sir. Please join us! Why does a scholar of your high renown pass through these dismal mountains?"

Claesna smiled acknowledgment. "I'm headed for Rader myself, actually. I've heard of certain inscriptions on what are said to be prehuman ruins near there. If so, I'd like to copy them for study and comparison with others that I've seen."

"So it's true that you plan to supplement Nentali's *Interpretation of Elder Glyphics*?" suggested the grey-cowled priest.

Claesna lifted a bushy eyebrow. "*Supplant*, not *supplement*, Revered Callistratis. Well, I see you are an extraordinarily well-informed man yourself. This *does* promise to be an illuminating evening."

"Oh, please, learned gentlemen," mimicked a sneering voice from the corner. "Don't bore us all to death with such learned discussions."

"Shut up, Hef!" A gruff voice cut him off. "You'll find a neater death than boredom when we get to Rader!"

The other made an obscene reply. An open fist slapped on flesh, then sounded the clash of chains, subdued cursing.

"Ranvyas, you son of a pox-eaten whore, you busted that tooth half out of my head. Takes guts for a pissant bounty hunter like you to bust a man all chained up."

"You had an even chance before the chains went on, Hef," growled Ranvyas. "And you won't need that tooth once I get you to Rader."

"We'll see, Ranvyas. Oh, we'll see, won't we? There was other smart bastards all set to count their bounty money, but ain't one of them lived to touch a coin of it."

Claesna indicated the two men in the near corner. One was a tall, lantern-jawed swordsman with iron-grey hair who wore the green tunic of a ranger. The other, his prisoner, was a wiry man with pinched face and stained yellow beard, whose blue eyes seemed startlingly innocent for one weighed down with wrist and leg irons.

"That's Mad Hef over there, whose black fame ought to be known even to you, revered sirs. Looks harmless enough, though I doubt all the prayers of your priesthood could cleanse his soul of the deeds he's committed here in the mountains. They were talking about it before you came in. The ranger finally tracked him to the cave where he laired, and if he succeeds where so many other brave men have failed, the public executioner at Rader is due for a strenuous afternoon."

From the rooms above came the echoing moan of a woman in agony.

The priest started from his chair, then halted half-crouched when none of the room's other occupants seemed to pay heed.

Again the cry of pain ripped through the panelled hallway above, down the narrow log stairway. A door slammed at the foot of the stairs, muffled the outcry.

Two other travellers exchanged glances. One, grotesquely fat, shrugged and continued to devour an apple pastry. His smaller companion shuddered and buried his chinless face in his hands.

"Pray Thoem, make her stop!" he moaned.

The fat man wiped his slobbery lips and reached for another pastry. "Drink more wine, Dordron. Good for the nerves."

Passlo's hand pulled at the priest's arm. "Don't be alarmed, Revered Callistratis. The merchant's young wife is giving birth upstairs. No one thought to mention it. As you see, the father is untroubled. Only his brother seems a bit shaken."

"The fat blob is a half-wit!" sneered Claesna. "I judge his mind is rotten with pox. I pity his wife, poor child. If our host hadn't sent a serving girl to stay with her, these swine would certainly have left her to labor alone."

"The mystery of birth," quoted the abbot, "where pain is joyful duty."

Now the innkeeper moved among them, setting before each guest a wooden trencher and loaf of black bread. Behind him walked a swarthy, bristle-bearded dwarf, the first servant the priest had noted in the inn. His squat, powerful arms carried a great platter of roast meat, which he presented to each guest that he might serve himself as he desired. The fat merchant growled impatiently when the dwarf halted first before the abbot and his two table companions.

"Please, Jarcos!" his brother begged. "Don't offend these revered sirs!"

Hef giggled. "Don't eat it all now! Save a nice hefty bone for poor toothless Hef!"

From overhead the screams, distant through the thick boards, sounded now at closer intervals.

The innkeeper smiled nervously and wrung his black-gloved hands. "I'll bring out more wine, Bodger," he told the dwarf. "Bring out your mandolin and play for them."

The dwarf grinned and scuttled into the back rooms. He cavorted out again in a moment, wearing a flop-brim hat with a feather and carrying a black-stained mandolin. His strangely pointed fingers struck the strings like dagger tips, and he began to caper about the room, singing comic ballads in a bullfrog voice.

The moans from upstairs continued monotonously, and soon the travellers forgot to listen to them, or to notice when they ceased.

III

"Do You Know the Song of Valdese?"

"Then, just as the hunter spun around at the sound, the werewolf leaped down from the roof of his cabin! He clawed for the silver dagger at his belt, but the sheath was empty! Too late he remembered the old man's warning! And as he died, he saw that the beast at his throat had the sun-colored eyes of his wife!"

Claesna leaned back against his chair and blew smoke at the listeners circled about the fire.

"Bravo!" squealed Jarcos, the fat merchant. "Oh, that was good! Do you mean that the werewolf was really his wife, then?"

Claesna did not deign to reply, instead nodded acceptance of the others' applause.

The meal was a scattering of picked bones and cheese rinds. The autumn night tightened its chill around the inn, where inside the travellers shared the companionship of wine and a warm fire. The hour grew late, but no one yet sought his bed. Pulling chairs in a rough circle about the glowing hearth, they had listened to the ballads of Bodger the dwarf, and as the night wore on someone had suggested that each tell a story.

"The mountains of Halbrosn seem haunted with all manner of inhuman fiends," Dordron remarked with a shiver. "Jarcos, why did you insist we make this journey to Rader? You know the wool market there has been dead for years."

"My astrologer agreed this was a wise venture. Let me worry about our business, little brother." Jarcos contrived to shape his rolls of chins into a resolute expression.

"Not only 'inhuman fiends' to watch for," Ranvyas commented, jerking a gnarled thumb toward his prisoner. "Up until two days ago there was Mad Hef here. Thoem knows how many poor travellers he's waylaid and murdered. Had a favorite trick of crawling out onto the road all covered with blood and moaning he was one of Mad Hef's victims. Too damn many good-hearted folks left their bones in the rocks for the mice to nest in. And I'd as soon forget if I could some of the things I seen back in that cave where he was laired."

Hef snickered and shook his chains against the post. "Got a special niche for your skull there, Ranvyas dear. Old man like you should've brought help along, 'stead of trying to sneak after me all alone. You're just too brave for your—"

Ranvyas raised his fist; Hef broke off in an angry mutter.

"There have been human monsters in these mountains worse than this carrion-eater," the abbot said.

"Oh? Do you know this region, eminence?" asked the innkeeper, who had joined them at the fire.

"Only from my learning. I dare say that the old provinces of the Halbros kings have figured so prominently in our history and literature that all of us know some tale of their mountains—though we are all strangers here."

He glanced around at the others. "Perhaps you observed the stone ruins that crest the ridge along the gap ahead. Quite striking against the sunset, I thought. That was the fortress from which Kane held these mountains in thrall for a hundred years. He ruled the land with a bloody fist, exacted tribute from all who passed through, fought back every expedition led against him. Some say he had made a pact with the forces of evil by which they granted him eternal youth and victory in return for the innocent blood he sacrificed each dark of the moon.

"For a while he aided Halbros-Serrantho in the imperial wars, but even the great emperor sickened of Kane's depravity and finally used the combined armies of the new empire to pull the tyrant's citadel down on his head. They say his evil ghost haunts the ruins to this day."

"A tale somewhat garbled by popular superstition," Claesna remarked. "Actually the legend of Kane has far darker implications. His name, I have observed, reappears in all ages and all lands. The literature of the occult recurrently alludes to him. In fact, there is an ancient compendium of prehuman glyphics that Kane is said to have authored. If it exists, I'd give a fortune to read it."

"A rather long-lived villain, this Kane," said Passlo drily.

"Some occult authors contend that Kane was one of the first true men, damned to eternal wandering for some dark act of rebellion against mankind's creator."

"I doubt Thoem would have damned a blasphemer to immortality," scoffed the abbot. "Doubtless his legend appeals to certain evil types who take his name for their own."

"Then they steal his physical appearance, as well," Claesna countered. "Legend describes him as a man of powerful build, seemingly a warrior in his prime years. His hair is red and he is left-handed."

"So are many others."

"But his eyes are his mark. The eyes of Kane are blue, and in them glows the mad gaze of a ruthless killer. No man may look into Kane's eyes and not know him."

Ranvyas started. "There's talk of an assassin who's behind these murders that are pushing the empire into civil war. Said to be an outlander brought in by Eypurin to remove those who oppose his false claim to the throne. His name is reportedly Kane, and what little is known of him answers to your description. Did this Kane die in the fall of his citadel?"

Passlo looked startled. "Why, of course . . . I suppose. Yes, he must have. That was centuries ago, man!"

"I had been warned against staying the night in the open," suggested the priest. "While nothing definite was said, I can see that these mountains have more sinister legends than the road has turns."

"That's so, Revered Callistratis," affirmed the ranger, running a hand over his short-croped hair. "You say you lost your horse on the trail? Lucky for you you didn't meet Valdese while you was limping along in the dark."

"Valdese?"

"A lamia, reverence," explained the innkeeper. "A most beautiful spectre, Valdese is—and most malevolent. Legend says she haunts the mountain trails at night. Entices travellers into her arms and leaves them bloodless beneath the moon."

Suddenly it had grown very quiet. Leaves rustled against the frosted windowpanes.

The innkeeper sensed the unease of his guests. "Had you not heard that legend, gentlemen? But I forget—you're strangers here, all of you. Still I thought you must have heard her song. Do you know the Song of Valdese?"

He raised a black-gloved hand. "Come out, Bodger. Sing Valdese's song for our guests."

The dwarf scuttled out of the shadow with his mandolin. Bowing to his audience, he began to sing, his voice comic no longer.

In the dark hills of Halbros' land,
There dwelled a lovely maid—
The brightest flower, the rarest jewel,
Shone dull in Valdese's hand.

Her father's inn stood beside the road,
Great was his wealth of gold—
But the choicest treasure of the land,
Was the heart of fair Valdese.

Then came brash suitors to her door,
Six bright and bold young men—
Said they had come to win the hand,
Of the maiden called Valdese.

"Sirs," she said, "don't think me cruel,
For I love another youth—
He must be gone for seven long years,
To study in a hidden school."

And when she told them the suitors laughed,
"Oh, your beauty is not for him—
Choose instead from one of our band,
And not some wizard's fool."

Then came her lover in a cloak of grey,
Returning from the hidden school—
Said, "I've been gone these seven long years,
Now I've come for the love of Valdese."

"Oh no," swore the suitors in jealousy,
"You'll not steal our prize"—
And with cruel knives they took his life,
And the heart of Valdése after.

Now Valdese lies in the cold, cold ground,
And her spirit haunts these hills—
But her lover was sworn in the Grey Lord's name,
To serve seven times seven years.

"That's terrifying!" breathed Dordron, when the dwarf stopped singing. "So uncanny an ending, that last verse!"

"Perhaps the last verse hasn't been written," the innkeeper suggested. "Bodger, see how things are upstairs. It's grown strangely quiet up there."

"Well, at least we servants of Thoem have nothing to fear from lamiae!" muttered the abbot stoutly. "Do we not, Revered Callistratis?"

"To be certain, eminence," the priest assured him. "Thoem protects his servants from all creatures of evil."

Passlo suddenly drew a crystal-hilted dagger from the folds of his cassock. "And for added protection in these shadow-haunted hills I carry with me this sacred blade. It was shaped from star-metal by priests long dead, and the runes on its blade give it power over evil's foul servants." He did not add that he had stolen the blade from the abbey vaults.

"Seven years in a hidden school," mused the priest. "That can only mean one thing."

Claesna nodded. "He was apprenticed to the cult of the Seven Nameless—and sworn to the Grey Lord."

"Thoem grant that we someday see the extinction of that black cult of devil worshippers!" growled Passlo.

"The cult is far older than your own religion," Claesna informed him. "And it isn't devil worship, strictly speaking."

"Well, they're devils they worship!" Jarcos said shrilly.

"No. The Seven Nameless are elder gods. Or 'protogods,' more accurately, since they exist beyond the ordered universe of good and evil forces. Their realm is one of timeless chaos, a limbo of unformed creation and ultimate dissolution—opposite forces that somehow exist simultaneously."

Claesna preened his beard. "Their entire worship is structured on the energy of opposing systems. Little is known of the cult, since its devotees worship in secret. New initiates must study seven years in a 'hidden school' to master the secret powers of the cult; then each is sworn to one of the Seven for the space of forty-nine years. The names of the Seven are secret, for should the uninitiate utter them he would evoke the god without having power over him. A rather hideous fate, it's said. Korjonos was sworn to the Grey Lord, who is the most feared of the Seven."

"Korjonos? Was that the young wizard's name?" the priest inquired.

Claesna bit his pipestem testily. "Yes, I believe so. After all, the ballad was based on true events. Happened a century ago, I believe."

"Not at all," corrected the innkeeper. "Not quite fifty years ago. And very near here."

"Indeed?" Dordron's voice was strained.

"In fact, at this very inn."

The eyes of the travellers bored back into their host's smiling face.

"Why, yes. But I forgot you gentlemen are strangers here. Would you like to know the story behind Valdese's song?"

No one spoke. He went on as if there were no tension in the room.

"Valdese and Korjonos were childhood lovers. She was the daughter of one of the richest men in Halbrosn, while he was the son of a servant at his inn. They were both barely past ten when Korjonos was orphaned. Penniless, he left the inn to study at a hidden school and vowed to return for her in seven years, with the wealth and power that his wisdom would bring him.

"Valdese waited for him. But there were others. Six coarse young louts from the settlements close by. They lusted for her beauty, and more for the gold she would inherit. Valdese would not have them, but they argued and waited, for the time was near when Korjonos had promised to return.

"And after seven years he did return. To their brutish

anger, Valdese's love for the young wizard had not diminished with time. They were married that night at her father's inn.

"But hate was black in the hearts of her rejected suitors, and they drank long into the night."

A log burst apart in a shower of sparks, cast light over the circle of nervous faces.

"The guests were gone; her father they slew with the few others who were there. They took his gold, and they dragged the lovers from their wedding chamber.

"They hung Korjonos between two trees. Valdese they threw to the ground.

" 'He'll not curse us,' said one, and they cut out his tongue.

" 'He'll not cast spells against us,' said another; and they cut off his hands.

" 'Nor seek to follow after us,' and they cut off his feet.

"Then they cut away his manhood and told her, 'He's not fit to lie with.'

"And they cut away his face and told her, 'He's not fit to look at.'

"But they spared him his eyes so that he might watch what they did to her, and they spared him his ears so he might listen to her screams.

"When they were finished . . . she died. Korjonos they left hanging. Then they divided the gold and fled, each choosing a separate path to follow. And while the infamy of their deed shamed the land, not one of them was ever punished."

"Korjonos?" asked the priest.

"Did not die. He was sworn to the Grey Lord for seven times seven years, and death could not claim him. His familiar demon cut him down and carried him away. And the rage of the sorcerer waited years upon painful years for fitting vengeance to transpire."

A chair crashed as Claesna leaped to his feet. "Gods! Don't you see? It's been near fifty years, and our faces and names were otherwise! But I thought several of your faces seemed familiar to me! Don't deny it! It's no coincidence that all six of us have returned to this inn tonight! Sorcery has drawn us here! But who . . . ?"

The innkeeper smiled in secret mirth as their startled

voices shouted in protest. He crossed over to in front of the fire. Still smiling, he peeled off the black gloves.

And they saw what manner of hands were grafted to his wrists.

With these hands he dug at the flesh of his face.

The smiling lips peeled away with the rest, and they saw the noseless horror that had been a face, saw the black reptilian tongue that lashed between broken teeth.

They sat frozen in shock. The dwarf entered unnoticed, a tiny corpse in his hairy hands.

"Stillborn, master," he snickered, holding by its heels the blue-skinned infant. "Strangled by her cord, and the mother died giving forth." He stepped into the center of their circle.

Then the chill of the autumn night bore down upon them, a chill greater than that of any natural darkness.

"Seven years time seven," hissed Korjonos. "So long have I plotted for this. I've shaped your lives from the day of your crime, let you fatten like cattle, let you live for the day when you would pay as no man has ever paid!

"Callistratis," he called aside, "this isn't for you! I don't know how you came here, but go now if you still can."

Faces set in fear, they stared at the wizard. Invisible bonds held them in their places about the circle.

Korjonos chanted and gestured. "Holy man, evil man. Wise man, fool. Brave man, coward. Six corners of the heptagon, and I, a dead man who lives, make the seventh. Contradicting opposites that invoke the chaos lords—and the final paradox is the focus of the spell: an innocent soul who has never lived, a damned soul who can never die!

"Seven times seven years have passed, and when the Grey Lord comes for me, you six shall follow into his realm!"

Suddenly Ranvyas sprang to life. "The dagger!"

The abbot stared dumbly, then fumbled at his cassock. He seemed to move at a dreamlike pace.

Hissing in rage, Korjonos rushed into the incantation.

Passlo clumsily extended the dagger, but the ranger was faster.

Tearing the dagger from Passlo's trembling fingers, he hurled it at the grinning dwarf.

Bodger shrieked and dropped the stillborn infant. Reeking smoke boiled from his chest where the crystal hilt protruded. He reeled, seemed to sag inward upon himself, like a collapsing coat of mail. Then there was only a charred greasy smear, a pile of filthy clothes—and a hairy spider that scurried away to vanish through a chink in the wall.

"Well done, Ranvyas!" Claesna gasped shakily. "You've slain his familiar, and the spell is shattered!"

He sneered at the wizard. "Unless, of course, you've another 'damned soul who cannot die' who can complete your incantation."

Korjonos's bowed shoulders signalled his defeat.

"Let's get out of here!" blubbered Jarcos. His brother was weeping mindlessly.

"Not until we slay the wizard," growled Ranvyas.

"And set me free," Hef advised. "I don't think you'll want me to tell them in Rader about my five old comrades."

"Thoem! It's cold!" chattered Passlo. "And what's wrong with the light in here?"

The priest broke into their circle and bent over the pile of seared clothing. They thought he meant to retrieve the enchanted dagger, but when he straightened he held the stillborn child in his left hand.

His cowl fell back. They saw his red hair.

They saw his eyes.

"Kane!" screamed Claesna.

Korjonos shouted out syllables that formed another name.

Hands went for futile swordhilts, but already the room was heavy with the sweet dust stench of ancient decay.

At the doorway behind them the bolt snapped with rust; boards rotted and sagged, crumbled into powdery dissolution. They stared in dread understanding. On the threshold stood a tall figure in a tattered cloak of grey.

Kane turned his face.

And the Grey Lord lifted his mask.

Kane shook the darkness from his mind. He started to come to his feet, then almost fell because he already stood.

He was standing in the gutted interior of a log building.

The floor overhead had collapsed, as had the roof, and he could see stars in the night sky. Small trees snagged up through the rotting debris. The inn had been abandoned for many years.

The air was musty with decay. He stumbled for the doorway, thought he heard the snap of dry bones beneath his boots. Outside he breathed raggedly and glanced again at the sky.

The mist crawled in wild patterns across the stars. And Kane saw a wraithlike figure of grey, his cloak flapping in the night winds. Behind him seemed to follow seven more wraiths, dragging their feet as if they would not follow.

Then another phantom. A girl in a long dress, racing after. She caught the seventh follower by the hand. Strained, then drew him away. The Grey Lord and those who must follow vanished into the night skies. The girl and her lover fell back in an embrace—then melted as one into the mist.

Kane's horse was waiting outside the ruined inn. Kane was not surprised, for he had recognized the girl in the mist. His heels touched the horse's flanks, and Kane vanished into the mist as well.

KARL EDWARD WAGNER

BLOODSTONE

The Mystic Swordsman becomes the living link with the awesome power of a vanished super-race.

In the dark swamp where toadman croak and cower, slumbers a secret relic of the days when creatures from the stars ruled the Earth. In the booty captured in a savage raid, Kane discovers a ring, a bloodstone, which is the key to the power that lies buried, inactive but not dead, within the forest.

Now Kane, whose bloody sword has slashed and killed for the glory of other rulers, can scheme to rule the Earth – himself!

Kane is a new super-hero – part savage, part savant – whose diamond sharp sword cuts through time and darkness to reveal a mind-bending new world.

CORONET BOOKS